LOST RIDERS

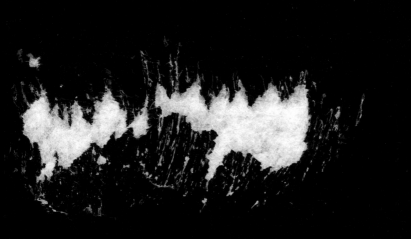

LOST RIDERS

ELIZABETH LAIRD

WOODMILL HIGH SCHOOL

MACMILLAN CHILDREN'S BOOKS

First published 2008 by Macmillan Children's Books
a division of Macmillan Publishers Limited
20 New Wharf Road, London N1 9RR
Basingstoke and Oxford
www.panmacmillan.com

Associated companies throughout the world

ISBN 978-0-230-52895-6

1 3 5 7 9 8 6 4 2

A CIP catalogue record for this book is available from
the British Library.

Typeset by Intype Libra Limited
Printed and bound in Great Britain by Mackays of Chatham plc, Kent

Preface

A city called Rahimyar Khan lies on the Indus plain in the Punjab region of Pakistan. The area is an important route for migrating birds, and a magnet for hunters. In the early 1970s, the ruling family of the United Arab Emirates – the sheikhs – built a palace at Rahimyar Khan. They have visited it for the annual hunting season ever since. Seeing how poor the area is, the sheikhs have built a big hospital, roads, housing colonies and even an airport to benefit the local people.

Back home in the Gulf, the sheikhs' most popular sport is camel racing. The fastest camels are small and light, and run best under little jockeys. In their eagerness to win the fabulous prizes on offer, camel owners began to employ smaller and smaller children as jockeys. Some were only three or four years old.

But where could such little boys be found to do this dangerous work? One obvious answer was Pakistan. Hundreds of thousands of Pakistani workers were already employed in the Gulf, and the links were strong. Unscrupulous traffickers toured the villages around Rahimyar Khan, persuading parents to send their children to the Gulf. Dazzled by the sheikhs' wealth and generosity, tricked by false promises, living in dire poverty and desperate for the wages that children could earn, many parents agreed to send their small sons. By 2005, at least three thousand boys were employed in hundreds of camel farms. They came not only from Pakistan but also from Bangladesh, India, Sudan and the Yemen.

The children were bewildered, traumatized, subject to harsh punishments, underfed and in constant danger of injury. They received no schooling and little basic care. An international outcry began to build.

I first heard about the young camel jockeys from a friend who worked for Swedish Save the Children in Pakistan.

'Come on over,' she said. 'Let me take you to meet some of the boys who've come home.'

So I went to Pakistan.

I'll never forget my first sight of young camel jockeys. They stared at me unsmilingly out of old-young eyes. One by one, as their confidence grew, they told me their stories. I went to visit their homes, bumping from village to village on the back of a little motorbike, which Mr Tayyab, my translator, expertly steered around the potholes. We sat on string beds in courtyards, under neem trees, in little shops and living rooms, and I met the boys' parents and sisters and teachers. I even met a one-time trafficker, who regretted his past involvement in the trade of children.

Later I went to Dubai and met some camel racers. They proudly showed me the robots they now use instead of live jockeys, and I watched these little machines perform at a thrilling camel race. I was assured that no children are now employed, that strict laws are being implemented and that the practice has stopped throughout the Gulf.

The Government of the UAE has made great progress in stamping out the exploitation of children, but questions remain. Of the three thousand young boys known to have been working on the camel farms in 2005, only one thousand have been returned to Pakistan. Where are the others? Did they slip home somehow, or are they still out there in those hot desert farms, no longer racing, but training the camels and doing other work? Have they been moved on to new forms of slavery? Or are they still working as jockeys in neighbouring countries where racing with small children still goes on away from prying eyes?

Lost Riders is many stories rolled into one. My characters are called Rashid, Shari, Iqbal, Amal and Puppo. But here are the names of the real heroes, the little riders I met in Rahimyar Khan, who were trafficked to the Gulf, braved terrifying dangers and have now returned home to rebuild their young lives:

Muhammad Asif, Sujjad Ali, Muhammad Imran, Bilal Ahmed, Saddam Hussain, Fiaz Ahmed, Sajid Hussain, Akhtar Ali, Muhammed Arif, Allah Ditta, Ali Raza, Yasir Ali, Shan Ali, Ahsan Ali.

This book is dedicated to them, and to the increasing numbers of children throughout the world who are being trafficked away from their homes and families to work in far countries, including the UK, in many forms of slavery.

Acknowledgements

Lost Riders owes its existence to Angela Coleridge, adviser to Save the Children Sweden in Peshawar. Without her inspiration and encouragement I would never have dared undertake this mission.

In Peshawar I was greatly assisted by Syed Mehmood Asghar (Country Manager) and Ghulam Qadri of Save the Children Sweden, who made my visit possible and gave me unstinting help.

In Rahimyar Khan I was welcomed and looked after by PRWSWO (Pakistan Rural Workers Social Welfare Organisation). Its Secretary General, Sabir Farhat, made great efforts to help me, putting his time and resources at my disposal. His advice was invaluable. Tariq Choudhry, the Project Officer, organized the details of my visit and was endlessly patient with my many demands. Muhammad Ahmad, the Social Organizer, and Muhammad Pervaiz Khan, the Job Skills Supervisor, set up my visits to the rural areas and gave me very useful information and advice.

Nothing could have been done without the help and enthusiasm of my facilitator, Muhammad Tayyab Farooq, who took me out to the villages and spent many hours in the arduous work of translation, scrupulously answering all my questions and aiding me with his deep knowledge of the boys' lives and backgrounds.

Wolfgang Friedl of Unicef helped to arrange my visit to Dubai. Once there, I was greatly assisted by Issam Jamil Azouri, spokesman of the UAE Ministry of the Interior, who drove me all the way to Abu Dhabi to attend a camel race, introduced me to the President of the Camel Racing Association and took me to a camel farm. His passionate commitment to ending the exploitation of children in the Gulf was inspirational.

In London, I was encouraged and given useful information by Catherine Turner of the Anti-Slavery Society.

I would like to thank them all.

1

Rashid was squatting under the neem tree in the dusty courtyard of his home, pushing a pebble round in a circle while his tongue explored the empty space where another milk tooth had fallen out.

'Vroom!' he said. 'Vroo – vroo – No! Not like that, Shari.'

His four-year-old brother had been trying to copy him.

'Cars don't fly,' Rashid told him severely, pressing Shari's hand with the stone inside it down on to the ground. 'You have to push it along like this.'

Their mother was sitting cross-legged on a string bed outside the little two-roomed house at the far end of the courtyard. She was turning the handle of her ancient sewing machine. Its whirring stopped and started as she fed material through it.

Another sound came from the lane that ran along the far side of the courtyard wall. It made Rashid lift his head.

'That's a motorbike,' he said, looking at Shari to make sure he was impressed by this superior knowledge.

He ran across to the door and pulled it open. It squeaked on its ancient sagging hinges. As he looked out into the lane, the putter of the motorbike engine stopped.

'Uncle Bilal!' Rashid called out, running back to his mother. 'Ma, Uncle Bilal's come. With a man!'

Amir Bibi pushed the sewing machine aside and stood up, hastily drawing her scarf up to cover her hair.

'Who is it? What man? Not the landlord?'

Zabidah, Rashid's twelve-year-old sister, came out of the house.

'Take all this inside, Zabidah,' Amir Bibi said, dumping the bundle of clothes she'd been mending into the girl's arms.

Rashid and Shari were out in the lane, bouncing up and down with excitement.

'You've got a motorbike, Uncle Bilal,' Rashid said admiringly, watching as his uncle carefully parked the shiny black bike against the wall.

'I borrowed it.' Bilal took a mobile phone out of his pocket with a flourish and checked it ostentatiously for messages.

Rashid transferred his gaze to the man who had dismounted awkwardly from the back of the bike. He was short, with powerful shoulders. He wasn't wearing the loose kameez shirt and shalwar trousers of the village men. His clothes were western: a shirt with buttons down the front, tight trousers and a belt with a shiny buckle. A big gold ring studded one thick finger and a row of pens was clipped to the inside of his shirt pocket. His hair was oiled back smartly from his forehead, and more hair sprouted from the backs of his hands.

He looked around as he stepped through the creaky old door from the lane into the courtyard, taking in the swirls of dead leaves in unswept corners, the second bed with its broken strings propped up against a wall and the chipped pots beside the outside oven.

He spoke quietly to Bilal, who nodded eagerly and ushered him across the courtyard to Amir Bibi, who was anxiously biting her lip. Few men had come to the house since her husband had died six months earlier. Rashid began to feel worried too, and moved closer to Shari, putting a protective arm round his shoulders.

The man sat down on the unbroken string bed beside the sewing machine, which Amir Bibi hadn't had time to move. He looked awkward, as if he was used to a proper chair. Amir Bibi sent Zabidah running inside for a glass of water, and the man drank it down in a single gulp. Then he lifted one foot and laid it across the other knee. Taking out of his pocket a string of beads, he began to play them through his fingers, as if he had nothing to do and had all the time in the world.

Bilal took the glass from the man's hand and sent Zabidah scurrying for another. He was smiling uncertainly.

'Mr Gaman Khan has come all the way out of town to see you, sister-ji,' nodding at Amir Bibi. 'He wants to help you. He knows how hard life has been for you since you lost your husband.'

Amir Bibi lifted both hands in a gesture of despair and broke out into a bitter speech. The death of her husband, the greed of the landlord, the price of food, the poor wages in the cotton fields, clothes for the boys, a dowry for Zabidah, no money for this, no money for that, no money at all for anything – the litany went on and on.

'And what is a poor widow with three children to do?' she finished, her voice rising high and cracking with misery. 'Where will it all end? In the brick factories. Think of it! Little children in the brick factories! What kind of a life is that?'

Rashid and Shari had long since stopped listening. They had heard their mother recite her woes many times before. They squatted together against the door of the house, with Zabidah standing beside them. But at the mention of the brick factories, Rashid felt a shiver raise the hairs on his arms. He'd seen the brick factories from a distance but had never been close to them. Thin, ragged people, men, women and children, their faces and clothes filthy with dust and soot, slaved over the piles of bricks, feeding them into the blackened mouths of the kilns in which, Rashid was sure, lived demons with eyes of fire.

But Gaman Khan was laughing.

'Oh, there's no fear of the brick factories.' His voice had a curiously harsh sound to it, as if he'd swallowed gravel. The crow on the wall took fright, and flapped off with a loud caw.

Gaman Khan didn't notice the crow. He had turned to look at Rashid and Shari, who had squashed themselves close together and were staring at him with their mouths open like a couple of hungry chicks.

'What fine boys!' he said, his restless beads still clicking through his fingers. 'Rashid and Rasoul. Aren't those your names?'

'I'm not Rasoul. I'm Shari,' Shari said indignantly. Rashid gave him a sharp nudge, afraid that he was being cheeky.

Amir Bibi laughed.

'Shari's his pet name. His real name's Rasoul.'

Gaman Khan's free hand was feeling in his pocket. He extracted a couple of sweets wrapped in bright cellophane and held them out to the boys, who stared at them, not knowing what they were.

Bilal took the sweets from Gaman Khan's hand and squatted down in front of the boys. He unwrapped them and popped them into their opened mouths.

5

Grins of delight spread over their faces as the shock of sweetness hit their tongues.

Gaman Khan's eyes were fixed on Shari.

'How would you like to eat sweets every day,' he said, 'and live in a beautiful big house like the landlord's, and ride on a bicycle, and play with toys?'

Shari giggled and squirmed. He wasn't used to being addressed by strangers. He didn't know what to say. Rashid frowned and nudged him again.

'He means it,' Bilal said earnestly to Amir Bibi. 'He can fix it up. You'd be paid well too, if you let him take Shari.'

'Let him take Shari? Take him where?' Amir Bibi looked bewildered. 'What does he want with Shari? He's only a baby.'

'Dubai, sister-ji!' Bilal said reverently. 'He'll take Shari to Dubai! To the Gulf!'

'Dubai?' Amir Bibi repeated. 'But what . . .'

Gaman Khan held up a hand to silence Bilal.

'I'm sure there's no need to tell a knowledgeable person like yourself that fortunes are made every day in Dubai,' he said, smiling courteously at Amir Bibi.

Rashid glanced at his mother. Her eyes had opened wide and there was a dreamy look in them, as if she had glimpsed Paradise far away.

'What's Dubai?' he whispered to Uncle Bilal.

'It's where the sheikhs come from,' his uncle whispered back, his nineteen-year-old face glowing at the thought. 'It's where you go to get rich.'

Gaman Khan was watching Amir Bibi as the wistful look on her face was replaced by puzzlement.

'But what's Dubai got to do with Shari?' she asked, looking doubtfully at her little son, who was sticking his tongue out as far as it would go, cross-eyed in the attempt to lick up a dribble of melted toffee that was running down his chin.

'Those rich families over there,' Gaman Khan said, 'they've got everything. Houses like palaces, air con, big cars. You wouldn't believe it.'

He stopped, as if silenced by wonders.

The family waited, entranced by the images he had conjured up. Only Shari wasn't listening.

'The kids, of course, have got the best of everything,' he went on. 'Clothes, toys, good education – you name it.' The beads were falling ever faster through his fingers. 'But the one thing they don't have is playmates. Rich children in the Gulf don't run wild and play out in the open like kids do here. They're protected all the time. Cared for in their homes. But you know what children are. Never happier than playing games with each other. So these rich Arabs, they bring little friends for them into their families. Treat them like their own. Give them bicycles and toy cars and all the food they can eat. They pay very well for them too.'

The words 'toy cars' made Rashid shiver again, not with horror this time, but with desire. On a rare trip into town before his father had died, he had seen toy cars in the bazaar. He had longed for one ever since, with his whole being.

Amir Bibi was listening to Gaman Khan's gravelly voice with painful concentration.

'Money means nothing to those people,' he was saying. 'Thousands of rupees every month flow into the pockets of families who send their sons, and the little chaps are cared for like princes. It's Pakistani children they want, of course, because they're so sturdy and intelligent and well brought up. They . . .'

'I couldn't,' Amir Bibi interrupted loudly, coming out of her dream with a jolt and throwing the end of her scarf over her shoulder as if she was throwing Gaman Khan's words away. 'It's bad enough losing my husband. Do you want to take my baby away as well?'

Gaman Khan lifted his hands, jokingly defending himself.

'Lose? Of course you won't lose him! You'll lend him for a while, that's all. A year – two years at the most, and you'd have enough money coming in to keep the family and put something aside for your daughter's dowry as well. But I quite understand your feelings, Amir Bibi. They do you credit.' He looked at his watch, and the sun, low in the horizon now, glinted so brightly off the gold strap that it made Rashid blink. 'Bilal, it's time we went.'

Amir Bibi watched him walk across the courtyard, biting her lower lip. Bilal turned at the door and shook his head at her as if he couldn't believe how stupid she'd been. But Rashid, dazzled by the picture in his head of a toy car, a red one, with wheels that turned and little doors that opened, ran across to where the two men were disappearing out into the lane and caught hold of Gaman Khan's sleeve.

'I'll go, Gaman-ji,' he said. 'Why don't you take me?'

Gaman Khan looked down at him, his eyes narrowed, as if he was weighing him up and measuring him.

'Why not?' he said. 'We'll talk about it next time I come. Two for the price of one, eh?'

2

Gaman Khan came twice more to the village house with the dusty courtyard, and twice Amir Bibi sent him away. But she was noticeably more bad tempered after the second visit, and the children kept out of her way.

When he came the third time, Bilal had a new proposal.

'I'm going to Dubai myself,' he announced, his eyes shining with excitement. 'Gaman Sahib has found me a good job over there, on a building site. I'll earn six times what I could ever get here. Let me take the boys, sister-ji. Only one or two years away, and all our problems will be over. Yours and mine. I'll be able to keep an eye on them. Visit them regularly. It's easy to call from Dubai. I'll give you my mobile and get a new one there. You'll hear from us every week.'

He laid the mobile in his sister's lap with the air of one conferring a great honour. Rashid, whose fingers itched to touch the phone, watched her pick it up gingerly, as if she was afraid that the grey plastic would burn her.

'You do it like this, Ma,' Zabidah said, taking it out of her hands. She punched a button and showed Amir Bibi the light coming on.

'What do you know about it?' Amir Bibi said, shocked.

'Uncle Bilal showed me last time he came,' Zabidah said, and looked anxious, afraid she'd done something wrong.

Amir Bibi shook her head, defeated.

'I don't understand anything any more,' she said.

Rashid and Shari left home very early in the morning when the sun had just risen and the shadows were long. The sweet-smelling cottonwood smoke still drifted up from the fire on which Amir Bibi had boiled water for tea. The breeze ruffled the leaves of the neem tree and there was a dark patch of spilled water on the ground where she had washed her sons' faces, scrubbing them hard until they had protested. Then she had turned on Zabidah, whose hair was still uncombed and whose eyes were puffy with sleep.

'Look at you! Do you want your uncle to see you like that?' she scolded, her own eyes bright with unshed tears.

Rashid was the first to hear the put-put of the rickshaw in the lane.

'He's here, Ma,' he called out. 'Uncle Bilal's here!'

11

He was rigid with excitement, dancing from foot to foot, unable to keep still. He would be riding in a bus, and at the end of it would be a palace like a sheikh's. A wonderful boy would be there to welcome him, and together they would play all day long with real toy cars.

His mother swooped on him and picked him up. He struggled out of her arms. He couldn't understand why she was crying. He dashed out of the door into the lane and scrambled into the brightly painted rickshaw, anxious to grab the front seat before Shari could take it.

But Shari hadn't run after him. He had felt Ma's arms tremble as she picked him up, and the wetness of her tears on his cheeks. He began to cry too and clung to her with all his strength, struggling and lashing out at Bilal with his small fists. When at last Bilal had peeled him away and carried him outside, he kicked and screamed, his face red with fury and distress.

It was a long time before Shari subsided into resentful hiccups, and it was only as the rickshaw left the rough country roads behind and entered the town that he fell silent and began to look around. Like Rashid he was awestruck by the trucks, the buses with their blaring horns and the shiny cars bowling along the broad tarmac roads.

The rickshaw pulled up in a back street where Gaman Khan was waiting near an open door.

'You're here at last,' he said, leading the way into a small dark room.

A woman was sitting on the only chair, studying her varnished nails. She barely looked up as the others entered.

'Have you straightened the kids out? Told them what to do?' Gaman Khan said to Bilal.

Bilal bit his lip.

'I-I'm sorry. I haven't had the chance. Shari was too upset.'

'Upset!' scoffed Gaman Khan. 'Don't you realize how much hangs on it? Get on with it. We haven't got all day. The bus goes in half an hour.'

Rashid, watching closely, saw that the friendly stranger who had come to the house had turned into someone else, someone stern, with a frightening inner power.

Bilal crouched down, gathering the boys into his arms.

'Listen,' he said. 'Rashid and Shari. You see that lady? You have to call her Ma.'

They looked across at the young woman. She glanced up at them, gave them a quick smile, then went back to studying her nails.

Bilal gave the boys a little shake, to bring back their attention.

'And,' he went on, 'you've got to remember something else. If someone asks you your name, Rashid, you have to say that it's Yasser, OK? Shari, your name is Farid.'

'That's silly,' said Shari, pushing out his lower lip. 'I'm not Farid.'

'And I'm not Yasser,' Rashid said, not wanting to be outdone.

Gaman Khan pushed Bilal aside, nearly toppling him over.

'I thought you said you could manage them,' he growled. 'Don't you realize how important this is?'

'Yes, but they've only just . . .' began Bilal.

'I see I'll have to handle them myself,' Gaman Khan said impatiently. He bent down, thrusting his face right into Shari's, so that his bushy black eyebrows nearly touched the little boy's forehead. 'Farid, Farid, Farid. Now tell me. What's your name?'

'Sha . . . I don't know,' whimpered Shari, backing away from him.

Gaman Khan's hand came down hard, smacking him across the head. Shari was so shocked that he didn't cry but just sat down on the floor and stared up at Gaman Khan with his mouth open.

'Your name! What's your name?' Gaman Khan hissed at him again.

'It's Farid. Farid!' Rashid said quickly, wanting to show that he at least had learned this strange lesson, and afraid that Shari would start to scream and that Gaman Khan would hit him again.

Gaman Khan swung round towards him.

14

'Who are you?' he said.

For a moment Rashid hesitated, then he whispered, 'Yasser.'

Bilal was picking Shari up off the floor.

'Don't worry, Gaman Sahib,' he said nervously. 'I'll make sure they remember.'

Gaman Khan ignored him.

'And who's that?' he barked at Rashid, pointing to the woman, who had taken out her mobile phone and was staring at the little screen.

Rashid bit his lip, unable to speak.

'She's your mother. Ma. Call her Ma,' Gaman Khan said, and raised his hand threateningly.

Rashid looked down. Something was wrong. Something awful was happening, but he didn't know what it was.

'Ma,' he whispered unwillingly, and as he said the word his chin started to wobble. 'I want to go home!' he cried out suddenly. 'I don't want to go to Dubai. I want my ma!'

Gaman Khan's hand came cracking down on his head and he was sent flying across the room. Not daring to make another sound, he gulped back his tears and held on to Shari, who had crept across to the corner where he was huddled, and had buried his head in Rashid's lap.

There was a long journey after that. Days in a hot, stuffy bus. Nights in strange rooms. Long waits beside mountain roads where men in uniform talked to Gaman Khan, and money changed hands, and people asked Rashid and Shari to tell them their false names.

Yasser, Farid . . . Yasser, Farid . . .

It wasn't long before home, and Ma, and Zabidah and the village became blurred in Rashid's mind, though he thought of them all the time. A girl on a bus might have a dress in the same pattern as one of Zabidah's, or a glimpse inside a whitewashed mosque courtyard as the bus flashed past might remind him of the mosque in the village at home. Once he thought he saw his mother in a crowd at a bus station, and started to run towards her. He was jerked back with a wrench from Gaman Khan's muscular arm.

He didn't dare say anything to Shari, for fear of starting a burst of shouting and tears. But as the days had passed, the little boy had become unnaturally quiet and still. He had almost stopped speaking altogether, except in a frightened whisper. Even when Bilal spoke to him he'd stiffen up and stare, then press himself against Rashid, trying to hide his face.

Bilal would crouch down whenever they changed buses, or saw officials approaching. He would take Shari gently by the arms and whisper, 'Tell them who you are, Farid. Tell them your name. Say you're Farid, nice and loud, so they're sure to hear you. Call that lady "Ma".'

And he'd point to the woman, who would be

16

tapping her manicured fingers on the strap of her bag, looking bored.

Rashid never knew who she was, or learned her name. She took no notice of the children on those long hot thirsty bus rides, except to tell Shari to stop pulling at his hair, as he'd started doing all the time, and scolding Rashid when he accidentally spilled some water down her sleeve.

But when she thought that someone was looking, or there was a man in uniform around, she would catch hold of Shari and try to make him sit on her knee. Shari wouldn't let her at first. But after she'd given him a couple of painful pinches he soon learned what he had to do. He would sit as stiff as a lump of wood, holding himself as far away from her as he could.

Bilal, who looked increasingly anxious, kept trying to explain things to Rashid.

'This is the worst part,' he'd said, 'but we've made it out of Pakistan already. That's great. You're doing well. Once we're through Iran it'll be easier. We're going on a plane from Tehran to Dubai. You'll love it.' He sounded as if he was trying to convince himself. 'This name business, it's just because of our papers. An official thing. We have to pretend that we're a family. Gaman Khan is being your pio, that lady's your ma, and I'm your uncle.'

'I don't mind you being my uncle,' Rashid said, 'because you really are.'

17

'It's not for long.' He put his arm round Rashid's shoulders. 'Just till we get to Dubai. It's like a game. If we can fool them, we'll get through safely and we'll all have everything we want. But if they realize that we're not a family, they'll arrest us. They might even send us all to prison. So you'll do your best for me, eh?'

Rashid nodded solemnly. He would do his best for Uncle Bilal. And he would go on pretending because he was afraid of the police and being in prison. He told anyone who asked that his name was Mohammed Yasser, that Gaman Khan was his father, and the woman was his mother, and he told Shari that his name was now Farid. And all the time something inside him was saying, No, no, this isn't right. I don't want to be here. I wish I'd never come. I want to go home.

It was the arguments between Bilal and Gaman Khan that frightened Rashid most of all. Uncle Bilal had always seemed so carefree, so confident in the big world outside the village, with his mobile phone and his borrowed motorbike. But when he was with Gaman Khan he seemed smaller and strangely powerless.

On the first long day's ride, which ended in the town of Quetta, still in Pakistan, Bilal had been as excited and happy as a schoolboy. He had shown off his knowledge of the different makes of car they passed on the road, and had pointed out the sights:

18

water towers, and mosques, and once or twice a distant plane in the sky.

He grew quieter after the border into Iran had been crossed, and went more regularly to the prayer rooms when the bus stopped to let the passengers out to pray.

It was at one of these wayside stops, somewhere in Iran, that Rashid overheard Bilal talking to Gaman Khan. Rashid sidled closer to listen, disturbed by the distress in his uncle's voice.

'I've paid you everything I've got,' Bilal was saying. 'We agreed the price. I can't possibly give you another fifteen thousand rupees. I haven't got it. I haven't got any more money.'

'It's not for me. It's for your visa,' Gaman Khan said, sounding indifferent. 'If you want to get into Dubai, you have to pay up. It's up to you.'

'But you said that everything was included. You said I wouldn't have to give you any more.'

'Grow up, country boy!' Gaman Khan was beginning to sound irritated. 'Unforeseen expenses. That's life. If you haven't got the money, you'll have to owe it to me. Couple of months wages, that's all it'll be. You'll pay it off in no time. I'll only expect interest on the loan at first.'

'Interest! You'll charge me interest?' Bilal's voice was rising.

Gaman Khan pushed a meaty hand against his chest, looked around and scowled in warning.

19

'Find your own way to Dubai if you don't like it. But I've got the passports. I've got all the contacts. And I'm taking the kids. If you cut loose from me, it'll be your responsibility if you end up in a police cell.'

Bilal began to cry silently, and the sight of tears rolling down his uncle's cheeks sent shivers running down Rashid's back. He turned away, not wanting to look, but couldn't stop listening.

Gaman Khan began to speak again, and his tone was softer.

'Listen, Bilal. Don't think I don't understand. But you've got to see it from my point of view. You're young. What are you? Eighteen? Nineteen? You've never been out of Pakistan. You don't know what it's like in the big bad world.'

Rashid dared to look up, and he saw to his surprise that the hot, forceful, angry look had died out of Gaman Khan's face. He was looking almost sympathetic.

'It's not just me that's in this,' Gaman Khan went on. 'If it was, you wouldn't have to pay one more rupee. But there's a bunch of others on my back. Men you wouldn't want to know. If I don't turn in a profit on this journey, they'll kill me. I mean, *kill me*. And, anyway, who's taking all the risks? I am. If I'm caught, there's a long whack in prison for me.'

There was a short silence. Rashid, daring another glance, saw that his uncle was tightly squeezing together his fingers behind his back.

'What about the boys?' Bilal lowered his voice, so that Rashid had to strain even harder to hear. 'I heard people talking in the bus. They're not really going to stay in rich families, are they? What are you going to do with them?'

Gaman Khan patted him on the shoulder.

'You know what, old son? You worry too much. The boys'll be fine. I admit, it's not exactly like I told their mother. They'll be working. But they'll be looked after. It'll be fun for them. Little monkeys, I bet they'll enjoy it.'

'What work? Working at what? Not carpet weaving? Not the brick factories?'

Gaman Khan laughed.

'Now would I? I've got kids of my own! Working with animals, that's what they'll be doing. A healthy life, out in the desert on the camel farms. Look, I know I've had to come down heavy on them, but they've got to learn how to behave. We couldn't have them kicking up a fuss all the way along the road, now could we? We'd have been caught out in no time.'

Camels? thought Rashid. What does he mean?

But at that moment the bus driver had sounded his horn and Rashid's arms were grabbed by the woman, who almost dragged him out to the bus. Bilal jumped on at the last moment, and sank down into the seat beside Rashid.

'When am I going to get my toy car?' Rashid asked

21

experimentally, testing his uncle to see if what he'd overheard was right.

'Soon, soon,' Bilal said distractedly. 'Give me a break, Rashid, OK?'

The little group arrived at last in a village near Tehran, far from the Pakistani border in the north of Iran.

'Is this it? Are we there now?' Rashid said to Bilal, swallowing his disappointment at the sight of a village house with boarded up windows.

Bilal summoned up a smile for him.

'No, of course not. I told you. We're going to Dubai on a plane. We're only here until Gaman Sahib sorts things out.'

There were other men staying in the cramped rooms of the little house. All of them were from Pakistan, all hoping for work in Dubai. They had anxious faces and argued ceaselessly about money with the men who had brought them there.

Shari, who had said barely a word for days, became a little livelier. Some of the men had left boys of their own at home, and they were kind and gentle with him, coaxing him out of his silence with games and rhymes. Shari was almost like his old self sometimes, tumbling about and talking, but as soon as he was noisy a look from Gaman Khan, and a shake of the man's raised fist, would send him scuttling back

22

to the corner that Rashid had made his own special place, his face closed and still again.

The men tried to befriend Rashid too, but he held back. How could he tell what they were really like? How did he know that they wouldn't turn nasty on him, as Gaman Khan had done? How could he be sure of anything any more?

3

The plane journey was nothing like Rashid had expected. He had played aeroplanes sometimes at home, stretching out his arms and zooming around the courtyard, tilting and wheeling and making engine noises, imagining the excitement of flying through the air. But there was nothing exciting about the real plane. There was only a seat with a strap tied over him and not even a window nearby to look out of. He played for a while with the little button inside his armrest, turning the overhead light on and off, until Bilal told him to stop.

They had had to get up in the middle of the night and had driven a long way in the dark to the airport. Shari fell asleep as soon as the plane took off and after a little while Rashid dozed off too.

Bilal shook him awake.

'We're in Dubai!' he said, tense with excitement. 'We've made it, Rashid! We're here!'

'His name's Yasser,' Gaman Khan growled at him,

his voice more gravelly than ever. 'You're not through immigration yet. Do you want to ruin everything?'

Rashid had been so sleepy that he had barely noticed the airport in Tehran, but here in Dubai everything dazzled and astonished him. There were corridors where the floor moved under his feet, carrying him along, and moving staircases too, where he held tightly to the handrail, afraid of falling. He could look through huge glass windows down and down to a kind of indoor street full of shops below. There were lifts where doors closed with a soft sigh, and little roofless cars, which beeped loudly to warn people that they were coming. And everywhere was light: brilliant, sparkling, blinding light.

Several times Bilal had to grasp his hand and haul him along. Shari, who had refused to wake up, was actually being carried by Gaman Khan, his head lolling sideways off the man's heavy shoulder.

Rashid sensed an increase in tension in their little group as they inched forward towards a desk at the far end of a long room. The man behind it was wearing a white robe, and there was a white cloth on his head, kept in place by two circular black ropes. He looked briefly at the sleeping Shari, and a little longer at Rashid, whose hand had suddenly been grasped by the woman. Then he raised his stamp, brought it down on the passports that Gaman Khan had handed him, and waved them all through.

A few minutes later they were standing by a

carousel in the huge baggage hall waiting for the woman's big suitcase to come through. The boys had no bags of their own. Bilal had been carrying a change of clothing and a sweater for each of them in his shoulder bag, along with his own few possessions.

Rashid and Shari watched mesmerized as the suitcases went round and round, but after a while Shari turned away, bored. He tugged at Rashid's sleeve.

'Look!'

There was an empty trolley nearby. Shari put out a cautious hand to touch it, glancing sideways at Gaman Khan, but Gaman Khan was scanning the hall with darting eyes, and Bilal, who was biting his lower lip, also seemed preoccupied.

Shari clutched the trolley with both hands and smiled beseechingly at Rashid. Rashid looked at Gaman Khan, but he was still watching the carousel. Daringly, Rashid sidled over to the trolley.

'Get on it,' he whispered to Shari.

His face alight with joy, Shari climbed on to the trolley and sat triumphantly, gripping the sides. Rashid gave it a shove. It went faster than he had expected and he had to haul it back before it crashed into a pile of suitcases. Shari had his hand over his mouth, trying to stop himself squealing with excitement. Rashid, laughing, gave the trolley another push, and saw too late that it was heading for Gaman Khan. Frantically he tried to wrench it round, but couldn't stop it in time. It hit Gaman Khan's leg, making him buckle at the knee.

Icy fingers of horror ran down Rashid's back. He squeezed his eyes shut, not daring to look, bracing himself for a blow. Nothing happened. He opened one eye and then the other. Amazingly, Gaman Khan seemed to have barely noticed. He was in urgent conversation with Bilal.

Something was changing again. There were new uncertainties now. Even Gaman Khan's anger couldn't be relied on.

Rashid moved up behind Bilal, trying to hear what the men were saying.

Gaman Khan had put a mobile phone into Bilal's hand.

'Take this,' he was telling him. 'There's a number on it that you'll need. The man's name is Ahmed. You can keep this thing.'

Bilal looked surprised and tried to thank Gaman Khan, but he had turned away. The woman's suitcase had at last appeared.

'Thank God,' Gaman Khan muttered. 'Come on.'

He led the way quickly towards the green exit channel. Shari scrambled off the trolley and the boys ran after him.

A big crowd was waiting outside. Men were holding up cards with writing on them. Gaman Khan slowed down. He was looking around for someone.

A man stepped out from behind a cluster of noisy

tourists. He put his hand on his chest in a swift gesture of greeting, and said something quietly. Gaman Khan turned and pointed to the woman who was hurrying up behind him, dragging her heavy case. She smiled at the stranger and lowered her eyelids. He looked her up and down, nodded briefly, then spoke to Gaman Khan again.

Gaman Khan started and half turned to look round.

'No!' the man said urgently. 'They'll see you. This way.'

He walked off fast towards the exit, the woman running to keep up with him. Bilal and the boys began to follow.

Gaman Khan pushed his hand into Bilal's chest. Rashid saw to his amazement that he was shaking.

'Not you,' he said. 'Stay here.'

'What?' Bilal said, bewildered. 'What do you mean?'

'Just wait here,' said Gaman Khan, and a second later he had disappeared into the crowd surging out through the doors to the road outside. Through the huge plate-glass windows, Rashid saw him push the woman into a car and get into it himself. He watched it drive away.

'They got into a car, Uncle Bilal,' he said. 'They went off in it.'

Bilal grabbed the boys painfully by their upper arms.

'Quick! Come on!'

They ran to the exit. Taxis and buses were waiting outside and people with trolleys full of luggage were piling into them. Men in uniform were hurrying the drivers along.

Bilal darted out into the roadway, looking desperately along the crowded pavement. A car, coming fast, had to swerve to miss him and the driver pounded on his horn. Pale and shaken, Bilal leaped back on to the pavement, then raised his arms in a despairing gesture and dropped them to his side.

'He's gone! He's just gone and left us here!'

Rashid felt a strange feeling in his stomach, as if it was churning around. The three of them stood there in silence.

'I'm hungry, Uncle Bilal,' Shari said at last.

'Me too,' said Rashid.

'Hungry? *Hungry?*' almost shouted Bilal. 'What do you expect me to do? Take you to a restaurant? I haven't got a single dirrham! I've got nothing at all!'

'You have got something,' objected Rashid. 'You've got your mobile phone.'

Bilal stared at him.

'My mobile ph—' He laughed jerkily. 'Rashid, you're a genius.'

He took Gaman Khan's mobile from his pocket and, fumbling, switched it on.

'What was the name?' he said under his breath. 'Ahmed. Here it is.'

He held the phone to his ear and stood waiting, tense with anxiety.

'I'm hungry,' Shari said again, the corners of his mouth turning down ominously.

Bilal frowned at him with unusual severity and walked away. Turning his back on the boys, he began to talk into the phone, gesticulating with his free hand.

A few minutes later he returned to them.

'Someone's coming for us. It's going to be all right,' he said, wiping beads of sweat from his forehead with the sleeve of his kameez. 'We have to wait inside. By the door to the prayer room.'

They squatted down in a row against a bare wall. 'I'm—' Shari began again.

Bilal smacked his forehead.

'Of course!'

He unzipped his bag and took out a couple of thick white-bread sandwiches, unwrapped their cellophane covers and offered them to the boys, pleased with his own cleverness.

'I saved them for you on the plane,' he said. 'You were asleep when they brought them round.'

The boys looked doubtfully at the sandwiches. They'd never eaten that kind of bread before.

'I want a chapatti,' said Shari, pushing the sandwich away.

A thunderous frown settled on Bilal's forehead.

'Don't. Don't start that, Shari. You can't have a

chapatti. This is all there is. If you don't want it, I'll give it to Rashid. Or eat it myself.'

Rashid had been about to refuse his sandwich too, but now he held out his hand for Shari's. Before he could take it, Shari snatched the sandwich back and nibbled at a corner. Rashid, keen to seem grown up, took a proper bite and chewed it bravely.

'There's something inside it,' he said.

'Egg. It's egg. Eat it,' said Bilal.

He fished inside his bag again and pulled out two boxes of juice.

'I like these ones,' said Shari, brightening. 'We had them before, on the bus.'

They had barely finished eating when they became aware of two men standing in front of them. One was wearing a long white robe. The other man was dressed like a Pakistani in a pale-brown shalwar kameez.

'Are you Bilal?' the Pakistani said in Urdu.

Bilal scrambled to his feet.

'Yes, sir.'

'These kids, what are their names?'

'Ra— Yasser and Farid.'

His mouth wavered in a nervous smile.

The two men spoke to each other in a language Rashid couldn't understand.

Arabic, he thought.

The man in the white robe pulled a wad of notes from a wallet and counted some out to the Pakistani, who thumbed through them again, grunted with approval and pocketed them.

'Go with Syed Ali,' he said to Bilal, indicating the other man, and walked away.

Syed Ali nodded at Bilal and led the way to the exit. A car was waiting outside, with a driver at the wheel. Syed Ali settled himself in the front seat, while Bilal and the boys climbed into the back.

Rashid sank back against the soft leather seat, sniffing wonderingly at the car's luxurious smell. He looked sideways at Bilal, who was examining the magnificence of the car, running his fingers over the smooth metal of the door and the stitching of the leather. He caught Rashid's eyes and winked at him.

The awfulness of the journey from home, the fear of Gaman Khan and the tension of the last few hours rolled away from Rashid and the past swallowed them up. He had quite forgotten Gaman Khan's strange, unsettling talk of camels.

Soon, he told himself. Soon I'll get my toy car.

Shari, bored almost at once, had wriggled off the back seat and was sitting on the floor of the car, poking his fingers into the driver's seatbelt mechanism. He was talking to himself in the sing-song voice he used when he was playing an imaginary game.

Rashid took Shari's place by the window and gazed out at the strangeness of it all. Buildings towered up to incredible heights above the hard clean pavements.

They offered blank facades of glass and concrete and steel. Where were the horse-drawn cabs and hand-pushed barrows, the shops with goods spilling out on to the pavement, the noise and bustle and people of Pakistan?

They passed a bus stop. A group of men was standing at it, waiting for a bus. A couple of women stood to one side, dressed like Pakistanis. They were drooping with tiredness.

Rashid thought of Ma. He needed suddenly to feel the softness of her arms under the smooth cotton of her kameez. He wanted to play with the fringe of her shawl. For the first time for years, he felt the urge to suck his thumb. Shame at looking babyish stopped him. Instead, he leaned his head against Bilal's arm.

Syed Ali turned and said something to Bilal in Arabic. Bilal leaned forward, dislodging Rashid who had to sit upright again. Bilal didn't understand Syed Ali. He smiled nervously and spread out his hands. Syed Ali shrugged and said something to the driver. They sped on along a huge wide highway. The forest of tall buildings, their glass and steel walls flashing in the hard sunlight, stretched away into the distance.

Rashid was tired of them already. He looked down. Shari had found the plastic top of a water bottle and had worked it into his game. Rashid felt like getting down beside him and joining in, but Bilal was nudging him again.

33

'Look over there,' he said. 'Look.'

The car had turned off the highway and was speeding down a narrower road. The high-rise blocks were behind them now. Here there were only a few low buildings, hugging the ground behind white-painted walls. Between them were longer and longer stretches of flat empty desert. Swirls of sand were blowing across the tarmac.

Rashid looked without interest at the few scratchy thorn bushes. The pale sand of the desert disappeared into a haze of heat and dust and merged with the bleached whiteness of the sky.

'I can't see anything,' he said.

'There. Camels,' said Bilal, pointing to the far side of the road.

Rashid had seen camels before at home. Pakistani camels were big, heavy, muscular beasts, with rough patches of fur on their humps and worn, scarred hides. They walked slowly along the roads, pulling laden wagons, their heads held high, their expressions superior.

The camels here had no loads to pull. They were smaller than the ones at home, and lighter in weight and colour. A group of a dozen or more was walking alongside the tarmac road on a sandy track. Bright cloths were tied to their backs. A man with a red checked head-covering was at the head of them, leading the front one by a rope.

The car was speeding past them, raising a cloud of

dust that quickly hid the camels from view, but before they disappeared Rashid had seen that behind the hump of every second camel, their heels tucked up beneath them, their hands clinging to the saddle cloth, was a little boy.

'Must be fun riding a camel like that, don't you think, Rashid?' Bilal said.

Something in his voice, a tone that was almost pleading, made Rashid look up at him suspiciously.

'I don't think I like camels,' he said.

Bilal put an arm round Rashid's shoulders.

'It'll be all right,' he said. 'Gaman Sahib promised me.'

But Rashid could hear uncertainty in his voice. The odd feeling in his stomach, as if a spoon was stirring his insides, came back again.

'What's the boy called?' he said.

'What boy?'

'The one we're going to play with.'

He knew the answer already.

'Listen, Rashid,' Bilal said. 'I wanted to tell you before, but I didn't know how. It's not the way we thought it was. You're not going to be staying in a family and just play all the time.'

'Why not? Why did Gaman Sahib say it then?'

'I don't know. Well – I do. He said it so that your ma would let you go.'

'So where are we going?'

Bilal shook his head. He had picked up the strap of his bag and was tapping it against his knee.

'I'm not sure. It's not . . . nothing's turning out like I thought. It's not going to be so easy.'

'I wanted to play with toy cars. He promised.'

'I know. Look, I'm sorry. It's not my fault. What can I do about it? It'll be all right. You'll see.'

Rashid suddenly saw that Bilal was smaller and younger than he had thought.

'Have I got to ride camels then, like those boys?' he said. 'What about Shari? He's too little.'

'I don't know. Leave it, Rashid, will you? I don't know any more than you do. We'll find out soon, anyway.'

The car swerved off the road and began to bump down an unmade sandy track. Shari, shaken about, was jerked out of his game and scrambled back up on to the seat.

'I want the toilet,' he said.

'Shut up, Shari,' said Bilal with a groan. 'In a minute.'

The car swerved again, this time through a rough fence made of palm fronds that were tied to a metal frame. It came to a halt. Syed Ali got out and opened the back door. He touched Rashid on the shoulder and beckoned to him. Rashid jumped out obediently and stood looking around, but before he could take anything in he heard the car door slam behind him, and the engine rev up. He spun round. Syed Ali had jumped back into the car, which was already driving back out through the gap in the fence.

In a moment they had gone, leaving him there alone.

4

It seemed to Rashid that he had been standing for hours, crying, lost and alone, on the empty stretch of sand inside the gate. His eyes were so tightly shut that he didn't sense anyone approach, and when a hand tugged at his arm he twisted violently away. Then he opened his eyes and looked round to see who had touched him.

There was a boy beside him, taller than himself. He looked about eight years old. His features were sharp in his thin face and the fingers that had touched Rashid were as skinny as twigs.

'Why are you crying like that? What are you doing here?'

He spoke Punjabi, but in an odd way.

Rashid tried to control his tears. His sobs turned to violent hiccups.

'Don't know,' he managed to say at last. 'They left me here. Uncle Bilal and Shari.'

'Who's Shari?'

'My little brother.'

'I'm Iqbal,' the boy said. 'Are you a camel jockey?'

'I don't know,' Rashid said again. 'No.'

'You are, I bet. You're instead of Mujib. He fell off in a race last week. What's your name?'

'Rashid,' Rashid said automatically. He hesitated, and said, 'No, Yasser.'

'Is that the name they gave you? The one on your passport?' Iqbal said shrewdly. 'You'd better be Yasser then. Can you play football? Have you got any marbles?'

Rashid stared at him, but before he could answer a bellow came from behind.

'Iqbal! Where are you, you lazy little tyke? Why aren't you cleaning up this uzba like I told you?'

Both boys swung round. A big man was coming out of a small white building, which was half hidden behind a rough wooden shed. His blue kameez was tight over his large belly. In his hand he carried a short length of plastic hose. He saw Rashid and strode down the sloping ground towards him.

'It's Haji Faroukh. He's the masoul. The supervisor. Watch out for him. You've got to do everything he tells you,' Iqbal had time to say quickly.

'Who's this?' Haji Faroukh said, coming to a halt in front of the boys.

'He's Yasser,' Iqbal said helpfully. 'He's the new camel jockey. Instead of Mujib.'

Haji Faroukh raised the hose and swiped out at

Iqbal, who ducked and ran away. Then he put his hands on his hips and stared down at Rashid.

'So you're Yasser, are you?'

Rashid didn't dare look up.

'Yes, sahib,' he whispered.

'Haji. Call me Haji. They said you were coming today. I thought I heard the car. Why didn't the driver wait?'

Rashid twisted his fingers together and said nothing.

'How old are you?'

'Eight,' guessed Rashid. He didn't know for sure. There had never been talk of ages or birthdays at home.

'You ever ridden a camel before?'

Rashid shook his head.

'When did you arrive in Dubai?'

'Today.'

'From Pakistan, eh? Punjab?'

Rashid nodded.

Haji Faroukh said nothing. Rashid dared to look up at him. The man's red face and staring eyes seemed far away above his mountainous bulk.

The masoul patted Rashid on the shoulder with one pudgy hand.

'You look like a good boy, Yasser. A nice boy. You do what I tell you and you'll be all right. You have to work hard. Keep yourself clean. Look after the camels properly. You let a camel eat a poisonous plant, or

40

scratch itself on a thorn bush, or come to any harm at all, you'll know all about it. Got that?'

He swung the hose end again. Rashid flinched. Tears welled up again. He felt them running down his cheeks.

Haji Faroukh tutted.

'No need for that. No point in snivelling. You're a big boy now. Where's your bag?'

Rashid controlled his tears with a gigantic effort and scrubbed his nose and cheeks with his sleeve.

'I haven't got one.' His voice was still no more than a whisper. 'Uncle Bilal's got my sweater and my other shalwar. He went off in the car with my brother.'

'Uncle Bilal, eh? Is that your real uncle?'

'Yes. He's Ma's brother.'

The mention of Ma threatened to bring his tears on again.

'Never mind.' Haji Faroukh sounded almost sympathetic. 'We've got some extra clothes here. You'll need a blanket in the night as well. It gets cold here in the desert.' He raised his head. 'Salman! Where is that dratted boy? Never around when he's wanted. Salman!'

A tall, gangling boy came running at an uneven trot. Rashid stared at him. He had never seen anyone with such tight curly hair, or such dark skin.

'This is Yasser,' Haji Faroukh said to boy. 'Fetch Mujib's blanket and give it to him. His other clothes too. Take him up with you. Show him where he'll sleep.'

A chiming noise came from his pocket. He pulled out his mobile and held it to his ear.

Rashid heard the words *Syed Ali*, then understood no more of Haji Faroukh's rapid Arabic.

Salman smiled down at Rashid but Rashid backed away from him, frightened. One of the boy's eyes was a normal clear brown, lit with a friendly intelligence. But the other was blank, the whole surface of it obscured by a blue-white film.

Salman understood his reaction, pointed to his blind eye and said something in Arabic. Rashid, not understanding, gaped at him.

'You no speak Arabic?'

Rashid shook his head.

'Punjabi.'

'OK, I tell you,' Salman said in halting Punjabi. 'This eye no good. Camel tail go like this.' He swung his arm forward and up towards his face. 'Hit eye. Big infection. No see now.'

He stopped talking and examined Rashid, taking in his straight black hair and pale coffee skin.

'You not Sudanese, like me. Punjab Indian boy? Or Punjab Pakistan?'

'Pakistan.'

'Mujib was Bangladeshi. Never laugh. Always cry, cry, want ma, want go home. Never watch out for

42

trouble. He fall down from camel. Camel kick him head. Now he dead. You be careful, huh?'

Rashid barely took in what Salman was saying. The other boy had begun walking up the short slope towards the cluster of sheds. Rashid trotted to keep up with him.

To their left was another palm-frond fence, like the one that surrounded the whole camel farm, and through a gap in it Rashid caught a glimpse of a dozen or more camels. They were kneeling on the sand, chewing.

Salman was hurrying on. They were in front of the first shed now.

'Food store for camel,' Salman said, laying his hand flat against the stained plywood wall as if he was its owner. 'Kitchen,' he went on, moving to the next one. 'Masoul and me only in here. You go in kitchen you get beat. Understand?'

Rashid nodded.

'That one house there.' Salman was pointing beyond the kitchen to the only concrete building on the uzba. It was single storeyed, painted white and fronted by a shady veranda. Inside it, Rashid could see red rugs covering the floor and cushions for leaning on laid around the walls. 'Guest room, for bedu.'

'What?' Rashid didn't understand.

'Bedu. Arab. Syed Ali, he is bedu. This uzba belong to Syed Ali.'

'What's uzba?'

'This place. Camel farm. Uzba mean camel farm. You listening, or what? Only bedu and friend go into guest room. You in there, you get—'

'Beat,' whispered Rashid.

Salman grinned.

'You clever boy. Not like Mujib.'

He led the way into a shady shelter, roofed with yet more palm branches that were laid over metal frames. Alongside this was another windowless shed.

'Camel jockey sleep in here,' said Salman, indicating the door.

Rashid peered into the dark little room. The light outside was so brilliant that he could barely make out the couple of mattresses laid on a mat, and the tangle of blankets and clothes lying in a corner. He stepped back out into the shelter. He hadn't yet understood that this dark little room was his new home.

Outside he heard a car engine approach, then it cut out and doors slammed.

Uncle Bilal! he thought. He's come back with Shari!

He ran back into the open. Syed Ali and the driver had both got out of the car and were walking up to the guest house, but there was no sign of anyone else with them. Rashid ran down towards them.

'No! Come back!' Salman called after him.

Rashid darted in front of Syed Ali so that the man had to stop.

44

'Where are they? Where's my uncle and Shari?' he asked desperately.

Syed Ali frowned and said something in Arabic. Salman had run up. He listened to Syed Ali for a moment, then said to Rashid, 'He say no be cheeky. You respect. You be a good boy, no have any trouble.'

'Where's my brother?' Rashid asked again.

Salman interpreted unwillingly. Syed Ali's frown cleared and he nodded, looking kindly.

'Not to worry,' Salman translated. 'Your brother near. In a very good uzba. He happy there. You see him on racing day. Your uncle go to Abu Dhabi. Got good job. Make plenty money. Some time soon he come and see you.'

Syed Ali spoke again.

'He say you a nice boy. He like you. Tomorrow you start train for camel racing. You like it very much.'

Syed Ali was already moving on, walking up towards the guest house. Haji Faroukh had seen him and was coming forward as fast as his portly figure would allow, an ingratiating smile creasing his cheeks.

'*Ya* Syed Ali!' he called out. 'You have come! Salman, bring tea. Coffee. Hurry.'

Together, the two men disappeared into the guest house with the driver following at a polite distance. Salman touched Rashid's arm, and looking up Rashid saw a friendly smile light up the older boy's one good eye.

'They busy now. I get them coffee, then we play football. You like?'

Rashid's heart, which had been heavy with sorrow, as if a stone had been pressing down on it, suddenly felt lighter.

'I think I like it. I never tried much. I never had a ball.'

Iqbal appeared from behind the guest house.

'No more work today,' he said joyfully. 'Haji Faroukh won't notice us now that Syed Ali's here. Where's the ball, Salman?'

Salman was already hurrying to the kitchen.

'You think I know? It is where you leave it last time.'

Iqbal disappeared into the dark little sleeping shed and came out a few moments later with a plastic football twirling triumphantly on one finger.

'Come on, Yasser!'

Iqbal led the way further up the slope. Behind the camel pen was an open stretch of sand, bordered on two sides by the outer perimeter of the uzba. Iqbal put the ball down, posed for a moment with it balanced under his foot, then kicked it towards Rashid, who launched himself forward in an effort to stop it, but missed, and skidded to a fall in the sand.

'Me! I want to play!'

A little boy, no bigger than Shari, was trotting up towards them. The clothes he wore hung loosely on his skinny body and his eyes were huge in his thin face.

'In a minute, Puppo,' Iqbal shouted. 'I'm having a go first with Yasser. Just me and Yasser.'

Puppo plumped down on the ground, picked up a handful of sand and threw it crossly towards Iqbal.

'Don't sit there,' Iqbal said impatiently. 'You're in the way.'

Rashid, seeing Puppo's chin begin to tremble, thought of Shari. He went over to Puppo and knelt beside him.

'Don't cry, Puppo,' he said. 'I'm going to play with you – a special game – in a minute. All right?'

Puppo stared up at him for a long moment, as if he was trying to make out if he could trust this new person. At last he smiled.

'I like you,' he said.

Rashid gave him a pat, then jumped up and fetched the ball. He swiped at it wildly with his foot, sending it dangerously high so that for a heart-stopping moment he was afraid it would soar over into the camel pen. It arced down just in time and bounced against the fence. Iqbal laughed and sent it spinning expertly back to him.

He was good. Rashid could tell. He took a deep breath. He'd learn to do clever stuff like that and play as well as Iqbal. He wanted more than anything else, now, to please this wonderful boy, and make him his friend.

5

Although it was now late afternoon, the heat was still intense. Rashid was used to the blistering summers of Pakistan, but it was even hotter here. He had kicked off his sandals in order to chase the ball more freely, but the sand burned his feet when he stood still for more than a moment.

He was glad when Iqbal flopped down at last against the fence of the cattle pen, where a little shade was slowly stretching out across the sand. He put his sandals on again and played with Puppo, kicking the ball lethargically towards him, and letting the little boy do all the running.

Salman came at last. Iqbal jumped up, eager to play with him, but Salman ignored him. He looked at Rashid and jerked his head towards the cluster of buildings.

'Haji Faroukh call you,' he said.

'Why? What does he want with him?' said Iqbal

resentfully. 'It's more fun when there are more of us playing.'

Salman frowned, suddenly on his dignity.

'You think I know what masoul want? You go quick, Yasser. You do like I tell you; hurry up, no bother.'

Rashid ran towards the buildings. Syed Ali's car was driving out through the entrance to the uzba and Haji Faroukh was watching it go, bending at the waist as he waved and smiled.

The smile dropped from his face as he heard Rashid approach.

'Come,' he said, and strode off towards the camel pen.

Some of the camels were still kneeling, but several had risen and moved over to the feeding racks that edged the pen. They were lipping over the green fodder laid out for them. Haji Faroukh looked around, as if making a choice, then walked up to one of the kneeling camels. From the far side of the fence came the scuffling sound of the other boys' feet in the sand, and the hollow thump of the ball being kicked.

'Iqbal!' shouted Haji Faroukh suddenly, making Rashid jump. 'Fetch a muzzle!'

'Yes, Haji,' Iqbal's voice floated back from the far side of the fence.

A few moments later he appeared holding a looped rope in one hand, and a heavy cotton bag with dangling strings in the other. Haji Faroukh took them without a word, passed the looped rope over the camel's head, then fitted the bag over its mouth, tying the strips behind its ears. Rashid looked on apprehensively, wondering what he was supposed to do.

'Don't just stand there,' Haji Faroukh said crossly. 'A saddle!'

Rashid looked around, trying to see if there was something he ought to be picking up.

'Not you! Iqbal!'

Iqbal darted off and returned with a pad of bright cloth and some straps. Haji Faroukh jerked on the rope. The camel shook its head irritably, then slowly, grunting as if in protest, it rose to its feet. Haji Faroukh took the pad from Iqbal and threw it up on the camel's back, settling it into position behind the hump. Iqbal needed no more instructions. Deftly, he helped to tie it in place with the straps, passing them under the camel's belly, then pulled them tight and fastened the buckles.

Rashid suddenly realized what was going to happen, and the thought of it was so frightening that he wanted to run away and hide. Iqbal, stepping back from the camel, caught the look on his face and nodded at him, as if he understood. He waggled his head and made a funny face, as if to tell Rashid not to worry. Rashid smiled feebly, clasping his hands together.

The masoul had bent over to inspect the tightness of the girth, so that his large behind was up in the air.

Iqbal winked at Rashid, then lifted his foot and kicked out, stopping just in time before it made contact with Haji Faroukh's bottom.

Rashid, stunned by his daring, forgot his fear and allowed a giggle to escape him. Then, horrified at the noise he'd made, he bit his lip and waited in agony for Haji Faroukh to turn round.

He was saved by the camel. Irritated at having its usual routine disturbed, it trampled backwards and lashed out with one hind leg, almost landing a violent blow on the side of Iqbal's head with its heavy clawed foot. Just in time, Iqbal jumped out of the way, the cheeky grin wiped from his face.

'Get out,' Haji Faroukh snapped at him, as if sensing that mischief had been going on behind his back.

'Yes, sir,' said Iqbal respectfully. He looked pale and shaken as he ran out of the pen, aware that he'd had a narrow escape.

Before Rashid knew what was happening, he felt himself lifted in the air and a moment later was perched aloft on the pad-like saddle, breathless with fright, gripping the front edge with all his strength. The camel turned its long neck and stared at him resentfully, its throat rippling in its effort to grunt against the constraining muzzle.

'Don't bend over like that,' said Haji Faroukh. 'Sit up straight. Knees forward. Tuck your feet up behind you. Like this.' He caught hold of one of Rashid's feet and forced it up and backwards. 'Don't hang on like that. You're not a monkey. Find your balance. It's easy.'

Rashid was panting as if he'd run a race. He could feel the camel shift beneath him as it moved from one foot to another. At any moment he expected it to bolt and send him flying. He would crash to the ground, miles below. He would be trampled by those great feet, and torn by the sharp nails. Was that what had happened to Mujib, the boy who had died, the boy whose clothes and blanket would now be his?

Haji Faroukh was by the camel's head now, pulling on the rope. The camel lurched and moved forward.

'I'm falling off! I'm going to fall!' Rashid shouted shrilly, unable to contain his fear any longer.

'Be quiet. You're not falling. Do you want to scare him?' the masoul said, leading the camel on.

'I can't! I don't like it! I want to get down!' Rashid cried desperately.

Haji Faroukh jerked the camel to a halt and came back to stand by Rashid's knee.

'You give me any more of that, you make a stupid fuss, you pretend you're scared, and startle the camel, and take a fall, and you'll get a beating like you've never had before in the whole of your life. You hear me?'

Rashid stared down, terrified, into the man's hot red eyes. He nodded dumbly. However frightening it was to be balanced on top of this big unpredictable beast, the promise of violent anger in Haji Faroukh's face was worse. He gave a shuddering sigh, and when Haji Faroukh led the camel off again, he clung on, concentrating furiously, his breathing slowly steadying.

He found, after a short while, that it was becoming a little easier. The camel's jolting, swinging gait, so disconcerting at first, had fallen into a rhythm. He could even begin to predict how the animal would move, and let his body move with it. But he was stiff with tension when Haji Faroukh finally brought the camel to a halt and lifted him down. His fingers were cramped so hard round the edge of the saddle pad that he could barely let it go.

Haji Faroukh seemed pleased with him.

'You see? It's not difficult. You're going to like it. No more fuss, eh?'

Rashid looked down and shuffled his feet.

Haji Faroukh seemed to hesitate.

'You know how much depends on you kids?'

'No, Haji.'

'Everything! If you ride a camel to victory, Syed Ali will be very happy. I'll be very happy. You'll be rewarded. But if you're lazy and don't ride well, if you don't try your best, there'll be trouble. Do you understand, Yasser?'

'Yes, Haji,' said Rashid, but Haji Faroukh's words made little sense to him.

What does victory mean? he wondered. How can I try my best?

He squinted up at the masoul, the light from the setting sun in his eyes, trying to read the man's expression. The important thing from now on, Rashid could tell, was pleasing Haji Faroukh, and keeping the anger away. He would have to learn how to do it.

Haji Faroukh was unbuckling the saddle straps.

'Take off the muzzle,' he told Rashid.

Rashid went round to the front of the camel. Its head was high above him, far out of reach.

'Pull the rope down,' Haji Faroukh said, releasing the last strap and lifting the saddle clear. 'Not like that. Jerk it. Pull harder.'

Rashid tugged at the bridle rope as hard as he could. The camel lowered its head and then, to Rashid's astonishment, sank to its knees and settled itself to the ground, its expression lofty, as if it was doing Rashid a favour. Its large brown eye, lavishly fringed with thick black lashes, was now level with Rashid's face.

'The muzzle,' Haji Faroukh said. 'Take it off.'

Nervously, Rashid reached for the loops that held the muzzle in place and pulled them forward over the camel's ears. They caught on the bridle rope. He tried to unscramble them, and was suddenly cuffed aside by Haji Faroukh. He landed on his back in the sand.

The camel, irritated by his fumbling, had curled back his upper lip to show its long, strong teeth. It was snapping at Haji Faroukh's arm. Haji Faroukh controlled it with a curse and another jerk on the bridle rope, and in one quick movement lifted the muzzle clear.

'A lesson for you,' he said, as Rashid scrambled back up to his feet. 'See those teeth? They could take your arm off. When a camel bites, he means it. Stay away from his head till you know what to do. And from his back legs as well. A kick from the rear end could kill you. Now take all this stuff back to the store. Salman will show you where to put it.'

He piled the saddle pad, muzzle and ropes into Rashid's arms, and, heavily laden, Rashid staggered out of the pen towards the cluster of buildings.

The other boys had finished their game of football and were in the shady shelter. Puppo was leaning against the wall of the sleeping shed. His thumb was in his mouth and his eyelids were drooping. Iqbal was lying on his tummy, making patterns in the sand with a stick. He sat up when he saw Rashid.

'Did you think you were going to fall off?' he said. 'I did, the first time. But if you think that's bad, wait till you're in a race.'

'What race?' asked Rashid.

'Don't you know? When the racing season starts we're doing it all the time. We have to make the camels go really fast and whip them. If we don't win, Haji Faroukh gets very angry and beats us.'

Puppo had put his hands over his ears and was singing tunelessly.

'He's scared of racing,' Iqbal said, shrugging. 'He

cries and screams when they put him on the camel, even though he always gets beaten for it.'

'Are you scared?' Rashid said.

'Me? Course not!' said Iqbal, but Rashid saw a flicker in his eyes and knew that he was lying. 'Amal is, all the time.'

'Who's Amal?'

'He's the other camel jockey. He's not here today. He fell off his camel in the dark when we were exercising. Broke his arm. They took him to hospital. He's coming back tomorrow.'

'In the dark?' Rashid was bewildered. 'Why was he riding in the dark?'

'We have to do it every night. We take the camels out. It's too hot for them in the day. It's horrible. You feel really tired and it's cold. You'll see.' He yawned. 'Where's Salman? I want my supper.'

Rashid suddenly realized that he was ravenously hungry. The sandwich Uncle Bilal had given him that morning belonged to another world.

'Me too,' he said. 'And I want a drink.'

'Don't go to the kitchen till they call you,' Iqbal warned. 'Haji shouts at you if you do. There's a hose for the camel troughs. You can drink there. I'll show you.'

He led the way towards the far side of the uzba. A long hose snaked across the sand, the end of it lying by a trough.

'No one's looking,' Iqbal said. 'I'll turn it on. Drink from the end.'

A minute later, water gushed out of the hose. It was warm, but at least it was wet. Rashid held it close to his mouth and drank greedily.

Salman came out of the kitchen with a tray in his hand. Iqbal turned the tap off and ran towards him. Salman put the tray down on the kitchen step.

'Puppo!' he called. 'Yasser!'

Rashid dropped the end of the hose and ran to the step. There were three bowls on the tray. Iqbal was already squatting down with one of them in his hand. Puppo had come running too. Rashid picked up the third bowl eagerly. There was very little food in it, even less than the smallest meals that Ma had produced in the worst of times. A handful of cooked rice barely covered the bottom of the bowl, and a small splash of lentils covered the top. He ate quickly, then waited for Salman to come out of the kitchen so that he could ask for more.

'Salman, I'm still hungry,' he said daringly, after a while.

Salman came to the kitchen door.

'No more food,' he said. 'You eat too much, you get heavy. Camel jockey only good when he small.'

'But I'm hungry,' Rashid said again.

Looking up at Salman, he saw a conflict in the older boy's face. Pity and friendliness vied with a need to assert his authority. Pity won. Salman disappeared for a moment into the kitchen and came back with a large chapatti. He broke it into three and gave one piece to each boy.

'No tell masoul,' he said, nervously looking around. 'Only bread this time because Yasser new boy. First day special treatment, all right?'

Iqbal and Puppo nodded gratefully. They tore pieces off the chapatti and ran them round the bowl to scoop up every lingering smear of lentils. Rashid copied them. He couldn't make Salman out. Was he a boy, like the others, a camel jockey, or was he a grown-up, like the masoul?

'Are you scared of riding camels, Salman?' he asked, handing back his bowl regretfully.

'Me? I no ride camel any more,' Salman said, leaning against the door post. 'I too big. Too heavy. I was camel jockey like you. Five, six years. Long time. Win a lot of races.'

Rashid wanted him to say more, but he didn't know what questions to ask.

'You're not Pakistani, are you?' he said at last.

'No. Sudan. Very big country.'

'Aren't you going home?' asked Rashid. 'What about your ma and pio?'

A peculiar look crossed Salman's face.

'I no remember ma and pio. When I come this uzba, only a little boy. Two, three years old. Smaller than Puppo. No one come for me. No one look for me. How I can go home? Where is home? You shut up, Yasser, OK? Too big mouth. I give you more bread, you only give me cheeky.'

Iqbal had been sucking the last rice grain from his teeth.

'I'm going to be a soldier when I grow up,' he said, holding his hand out with two fingers straight to make a gun. 'I'm going to be an army officer in Pakistan. With a uniform.' He squinted along his gun barrel at Salman. 'You're going to be a masoul, aren't you, Salman?' He was trying to cheer Salman up, Rashid could tell.

'Yes,' said Salman, calming down. 'Very good masoul one day. Good job. Make plenty money like Haji. You be clever, Yasser, one day you be like me. No more camel jockey. Train to be masoul.'

Rashid wanted to say, No, never. I'm going home. Uncle Bilal will come for me. He'll find Shari and take us both home. Ma won't let me stay when she knows where I am. I won't be like you. I won't forget my ma. I'll never be like you.

But he said nothing, and when Iqbal and Puppo got up to return to the shelter, he followed them in silence.

6

'Up, up! Get up!'

Urgent voices broke into Rashid's dream. He had been at home, curled up on the string bed with Zabidah beside him, only Zabidah had stopped being herself and had become a proud lady with long finger-nails, who was threatening to bite off his arm. A small hand was tugging at his shoulder.

'Yasser! Get up!'

He half woke, and sat up. He was in a small place, a dark place, with no light except for a beam from the moon lying in a white stripe outside the door. A sharp rap on the thin boards of the shed brought him fully awake and suddenly he knew where he was.

'Are you going to sleep all day? Get on out of there!' came Haji Faroukh's voice.

Rashid stumbled out of the shed. The air was cold and the sand, which had burned his feet yesterday, chilled them now. Iqbal and Puppo were already up, running after Haji Faroukh towards the camel pen. Haji Faroukh looked over his shoulder.

'Put on your sweater,' he barked at Rashid. 'Do you expect me to nurse you if you get sick?'

Rashid had slept in his clothes. It had still been hot last night, when he'd lain down beside Iqbal and Puppo and closed his eyes, and his exhausted sleep had been so deep that he hadn't felt the cold seep into the shed. Now it shocked him. He fumbled among the tangle of blankets and clothes at the far end of the mattress until he found the sweater Salman had given him last night. Mujib's sweater. The dead boy must have been the last one to wear it.

There was no time to think of that now. The moon-light was so bright that it was easy to see the others. They were at the store, loading up with saddles and bridle ropes. He joined them, and stood shivering and yawning, not knowing what to do.

Salman was there, his curly hair tousled into thick knots.

'Here, you take this,' he said to Rashid, his voice dazed with sleep.

Rashid was about to step forward to take the bundle, but just in time saw the moonlight glint on something small and shiny moving near his bare foot. Salman saw it too.

'Stop!' he shouted. 'Don't move!'

He jumped forward and stamped on the thing with his sandalled foot, punching it into the ground.

'What is it?' said Rashid.

'Scorpion. You know what is scorpion?'

Rashid shuddered. He knew about scorpions. He had seen a few at home. A boy in the next house had trodden on one in the middle of the night last winter, and his screams had woken the whole village.

Iqbal and Puppo were already carrying their gear to the camel pen.

'Stop dawdling there, Yasser,' Haji Faroukh called out. 'Hurry up!'

Rashid wanted to run back to the shed and find his sandals but he didn't dare make Haji Faroukh wait. His toes curled nervously as he trotted to the camel pen.

Iqbal was already saddling a camel. Rashid could see how expert he was, pulling the straps tight and testing them with a tug of his forefinger. Even Puppo was helping, picking up the ends of the straps and handing them to Salman, who was working on the second camel.

'Watch out for Nanga,' Haji Faroukh was saying to Salman. 'Her right forehock looked weak yesterday. Bring her back if she seems to go lame.'

Salman rubbed his head, as if he was trying to make himself wake up.

'Five times round the circuit for each camel and no running today. You can ride Khamri first, then Hamlul. Got that?'

'Yes, Haji.'

'Watch Yasser. If he gets cramps, he can walk for a bit.'

Iqbal had made one of the camels kneel and had already mounted it. Even Puppo had forced the second one down, with an imperious tug on its rope, and was scrambling unaided into its saddle. Haji Faroukh lifted Rashid on to the camel Salman had saddled, and waited while he attended to the fourth one.

'Off you go,' he said at last. 'Take care. Don't make a mistake, Salman. Abu Nazir will be back tomorrow, with Amal. This is your chance. I'm giving you responsibility. I'm relying on you.'

'Yes, Haji.'

Even in the dim light, Rashid could see the seriousness in Salman's face as he spoke.

Haji Faroukh slapped Salman's camel on the rump and it lurched off, grunting noisily. The others fell in behind it. Rashid waited nervously for his own camel to move. The cold was penetrating, in spite of the sweater, making him shiver, and he was afraid of losing control, losing his balance, toppling sideways and crashing to the ground, ending up helpless under the camel's heavy feet.

Rashid heard the slap of Haji Faroukh's palm on his camel's side and gasped as it jolted into motion. He swayed alarmingly, clutching at the saddle's edge with all his strength, shuddering with fear now as much as with cold.

Then he heard a thin, high, babyish voice ahead chanting a meaningless string of words. Puppo was singing to comfort himself.

If he can do this, so can I, Rashid told himself, concentrating on finding the camel's rhythm and moving with it.

They were already outside the uzba and were following car tracks across the desert sand. In the moonlight, Rashid could vaguely see ghostly shapes moving ahead. He peered into the darkness and made out another string of camels, with the hunched shapes of little boys perched on top of them. They were coming from what seemed to be another uzba several hundred metres from his own.

Maybe Shari's there, he thought, his interest sharpening. I bet he can't ride a camel like me. I bet he screamed his head off if they tried to make him.

He liked the idea of Shari making a fuss. He'd be proud if he could see it.

Rashid could see yet another line of camels now, coming from a different direction. They were all moving towards the same point – a gap in a palm-frond fence, like the one that encircled his own uzba. Rashid half hoped that Salman would make the camels hurry so that they could catch up with the others, but Salman, nervous with responsibility, was moving carefully and slowly, turning all the time to check on the three children following him.

Inside the fence, Rashid could make out a wide

bare stretch of sand. There was a kind of soft track with metal rails on each side running into the distance. The other two strings of camels were on it too, far ahead now, walking silently into the dimness.

Rashid's camel suddenly stumbled and for a sickening moment he was afraid he was falling. Salman had seen.

'What you are doing, Yasser?' he shouted back nervously.

'Nothing. He tripped,' Rashid called in reply.

'Watch it,' Salman said, trying to sound threatening. 'You let camel fall, you get . . .'

'Beat, I know,' Rashid muttered under his breath, before Salman had finished speaking.

More than two hours passed before the first faint promise of dawn appeared in the east. The flush spread slowly across the great dome of the sky, putting out the stars and turning the desert first pearly grey, then pink, until the fiery rim of the sun glared out like an angry eye.

Rashid had sunk into a wretched, dreaming state, his mind rocking emptily with the movement of the camel. He was so tired that he might almost have fallen asleep if the cold and the fear of falling hadn't kept him awake.

As the sun lifted clear of the horizon, the call to prayer sounded faintly from a mosque some way away, just as it had in Pakistan. With it came such a powerful sense of home that he almost gasped, seeing in his mind's eye the courtyard, and the rough boards of the door leading into the lane, and the white puff-balls of cotton lying out to dry in the sun. But before he could catch hold of it firmly, the vision died away as the cry from the distant mosque fell silent.

The first rays of the sun hit him and he shuddered in gratitude. The warmth pulled him properly awake. He could see now that five or six small strings of camels were walking round a fenced track that formed an enormous circle across the desert, the far side of which was so distant that it almost disap-peared from view. The other groups of camels were too far away for him to make out if Shari was there. He screwed his eyes up and looked as hard as he could, but he couldn't see anything clearly.

They had been round the course several times and were nearly at the end again. Salman was leading them away from it, back across the open ground towards the uzba.

Rashid brightened. Perhaps there'd be breakfast now. Perhaps they'd be able to play football again. But Haji Faroukh was waiting for them at the camel pen. He lifted Puppo down to the ground, while Iqbal and Salman slid effortlessly off their saddles without needing any help. Rashid tried to copy them, swing-ing both legs over to one side and dropping to the ground, but instead of landing lightly on his feet, his legs gave way under him and he fell heavily. Pain shot through his thighs and shins.

'It hurts!' he blurted out. 'I can't stand up!'

He was afraid in case he'd be punished for complaining, but Haji Faroukh didn't look angry. He crouched down beside Rashid and began to massage his calves.

'Cramp,' he said. 'It'll go off in a minute. It's because you're not used to riding yet.'

His sympathy made Rashid want to cry, but he gulped back the tears.

'Good boy,' said Haji Faroukh, noticing. 'No more riding today. You can walk the next round. Try standing up. That's it. Now get off to the store and fetch a muzzle.'

Rashid took a tentative step. All his muscles protested, but he found he could just about walk after all. He hobbled to the store and came back with the muzzle in his hand.

The four camels the boys had been exercising had been unsaddled, but Rashid saw with a sinking heart that four others were being prepared. Three were already saddled, and Haji Faroukh was fitting the muzzle on to the fourth. Surely they weren't going to take another lot out on the tracks again?

But the other three boys were already mounting. Looking up at Iqbal, Rashid saw nothing but weariness and boredom in his face. It was as if he had pulled away into some hidden place inside himself.

Puppo, too, was quiet now. He was sitting on his camel with one arm raised, rubbing the soft sleeve of his sweater against his cheek.

Haji Faroukh put the end of the muzzled camel's bridle rope into Rashid's hands.

'Walk behind the others,' he said. 'Keep her on a short rein. Don't let her stray, whatever you do. She'll try to wander off before you get to the race track. Don't let her, or she'll scratch herself on the scrub and spoil her hide. Just keep up with the others and do what Salman tells you.'

Rashid stared up at him, unable to believe that the miles and miles of weary, silent plodding were about to start again. His insides ached with hunger. His heart smarted with the injustice of it all.

'Please, Haji,' he said. 'Can I fetch my shoes?'

But Haji Faroukh hadn't heard. He was saying something to Salman, pointing to the hind legs of Iqbal's camel. Salman was nodding gravely, taking in the masoul's warnings and instructions.

'Giddup! Go on!' Haji Faroukh called out at last, slapping Salman's camel on the rump, and the little cavalcade set off, with Rashid walking miserably in the rear, his camel's head, high above his own, nodding as it walked.

The first half mile was agony. The cramps in Rashid's legs came and went, and even when they'd eased, every muscle protested with stiffness. The pain went off at last, and he could walk more easily.

Luckily, the camel seemed to have no wish to stray. It trod quietly along behind Puppo's, lifting its great padded feet and setting them down again rhythmically in the soft sand.

An hour passed. Rashid had fallen back into a weary daze, mesmerized by the swaying rump of Puppo's camel in front of his eyes as the four of them inched slowly round the vast race track.

The sun, which had come as a friend at first, defeating the chill of the night, was still bearably low in the sky. The air was fresh, and the sand cool under his bare feet.

But perhaps we'll be doing this all day long, Rashid thought. We'll be out here when it gets really hot, and I haven't got my sandals on and my feet will burn.

He felt overwhelmed. He wanted to throw himself down, beat his fists on the sand and scream and yell like Shari used to do when he was upset. He could feel his temper rising. Rebellion stirred in him.

'Salman!' he yelled.

The three other boys had been riding on and on in a stupefied silence, but their heads whipped round.

'What?' Salman twisted round in his saddle. 'What happen?'

Rashid didn't know what to say.

'I want my sandals,' he brought out at last.

Salman's jaw dropped.

'You are crazy boy, Yasser, or what? How you can get your sandals? You see where we are?'

He flung out his arm to indicate the empty land-scape, the vast race course and the huddle of uzbas in the distance.

'My feet'll start burning,' Rashid said sulkily, afraid of looking stupid.

Salman frowned at him for a long moment, then he nodded, seeming to understand.

'You feeling bad, Yasser, first time out. But we go back now. Look. Halfway round track already. One hour, two hour more, then home. Nice breakfast, all right? Sand not getting hot yet. You doing OK.'

But Puppo was laughing.

'Yasser wants his sandals,' he was saying. 'He's a crazy boy!'

Rashid flushed angrily. He hated being laughed at.

'I'm not Yasser, anyway,' he yelled back. 'I'm Rashid, all right? Rashid!'

Puppo was still crowing, but to Rashid's relief, Iqbal was nodding.

'You're Rashid like I'm Javid,' he said. 'But you have to be Yasser here. Yasser, Iqbal, they're our silly names. But we know our real ones.'

'I haven't got a silly name,' said Puppo. 'I'm Puppo.'

It was Iqbal's turn to laugh.

'Puppo's a baby name. You've got a real name too. Don't you know your own name?'

'It's Puppo!' Puppo said, suddenly anxious. 'I haven't got a silly name. I'm Puppo!'

70

'You're just a stupid baby,' Iqbal began scornfully, but Salman had turned again in his saddle.

'Stop all that!' he roared, trying to sound fierce. 'This name, that name, not important. We are not here to enjoy. We are exercising camel. Big job. You start talk, play, you get accident.'

Silence fell on the little convoy again, but Rashid was beginning to feel more cheerful. Slowly, metre by metre, the length of track in front of him was dwindling, and the buildings of the clutch of uzbas were growing bigger as they approached. There would be something to eat soon, Salman had promised. And he would be able to stop this endless walking and rest.

Best of all, he had made a stand. He had said his real name. And Iqbal had understood.

7

It was after nine in the morning when at last the boys returned to the uzba. They were dazed with exhaustion. Salman was the only one with any life left in him.

Haji Faroukh was waiting for them at the entrance.

'No problems?' he asked Salman.

'No, Haji.'

Salman, looking pleased and important, began to talk in Arabic as the masoul inspected each camel in turn, firing questions at the boy as he did so.

Rashid followed Iqbal and Puppo back to the shelter. He was so tired that he could hardly stand. His feet hurt and his legs ached and his stomach yawned with hunger.

'I'm not going to do that again,' he said, to no one in particular.

'Do what?' asked Iqbal, without interest.

'Go out in the middle of the night.'

Iqbal stared at him, then laughed in derision.

'You will. Every night. Every single night. Every every every every—'

'Stop saying that!' said Rashid. 'It's not true.'

Puppo had started clapping his hands, sensing a game.

'Every every every every . . .' he chanted.

Rashid put his hands over his ears.

I can't, he thought. I can't. I won't. I don't care if Haji Faroukh beats me. Even if he kills me, I won't go out in the night again.

The others were too tired to go on teasing him. They lay listlessly, picking up handfuls of sand and letting it dribble through their fingers.

At last, Salman called from the kitchen door. They stood up, enlivened by the thought of food.

Flaps of bread, a bowl of thick yoghurt and a little cold rice lay waiting for them on the step. There were also three long glasses of cold water, and three smaller ones of sweetened tea.

Rashid, watching the others, ate more slowly this time, making the little bit of food last longer, relishing each small morsel. He felt better when he'd had his share, though he could have eaten twice as much.

He had just swallowed his last mouthful when the sound of a car engine made him look up. A big white Land Cruiser was pulling into the uzba. His heart leaped.

Uncle Bilal! He's come back for me! He's going to take me away!

He was about to run down towards it when the doors of the Land Cruiser swung open and a boy jumped out, followed by a tall thin Arab man.

'Amal! Hey, Amal, you're back!' Puppo called out.

'Yes, but watch out,' muttered Iqbal. 'That's Abu Nazir with him.'

Disappointed, Rashid sank back down on to his heels. There was no one else in the car. Uncle Bilal hadn't come. And there was no sign of Shari either.

'Who's Abu Nazir?' he asked Iqbal.

'Syed Ali's cousin. He's horrible. Really strict. He trains the camels.'

Salman had appeared at the door of the kitchen, a tea towel in his hand.

'And he train the camel jockey too,' he said, 'so you taking care, Yasser.'

He bent down, picked up the dirty dishes from the step and took them back into the kitchen.

Amal walked over to them but there was no spring in his step, and his smile was half-hearted. His left arm was in a plaster cast and there was a patch of dark bruising down the side of his face. His dark hair had been cropped close to his skull, showing a line of stitches and the scab that had formed on a long wound.

Amal stared at Rashid.

'Who are you?' he said.

'He's Yasser,' Puppo explained, before Rashid

could answer. 'He's instead of Mujib. He played foot-ball with us yesterday.'

Amal looked older than the other boys, and yet there was something about his long, sad face – a far-away look – that made him seem younger.

'The hospital was nice,' he said.

Rashid waited for him to say more, but he had fallen silent again.

'Did they give you sweets?' Iqbal asked.

'No, but the food was lovely.' A brief smile lit Amal's face. 'There was lots of it. Chicken, and milk, and bananas.'

Puppo frowned, looking jealous.

'I want to go to hospital,' he said.

They were walking away from the kitchen door now, back towards the shelter. Rashid trailed a little behind the others.

'No you don't, Puppo,' Amal was saying. 'It hurts when they stick needles into you. And my head feels funny now, all the time.'

'You were lucky.' Iqbal had draped an affectionate arm round Amal's shoulders, and Rashid bit his lip, feeling left out. 'When you fell and got kicked like that I thought you were dead.'

'Yes, like Mujib,' Puppo joined in earnestly. 'I thought they were going to take you away, Amal, like they took Mujib. Where did Mujib go, Iqbal?'

I wish they'd stop going on and on about Mujib, thought Rashid.

They'd reached the shelter, and the four of them settled down on the sand, under the palm-frond shade. The intense sunlight was draining the colour from the sky, and the heat was making the tin roof of the sleeping shed creak and crack as it expanded.

'Go on about the hospital, Amal,' said Iqbal.

Amal frowned, as if he was thinking.

'There are nurses to look after you,' he said at last. 'They're really kind. I had to pee in a bottle.'

'Wah!' Puppo laughed delightedly. 'What about your poo?'

'Don't be disgusting, Puppo,' snapped Iqbal.

'Abu Nazir made me say I'd fallen off my bicycle,' Amal went on.

Puppo looked puzzled.

'What? Why did they give you a bicycle?'

'They didn't, silly. I just had to say it. You're not supposed to tell about camel racing accidents in the hospital. Abu Nazir said.'

'What about this then?' Iqbal tapped the cast on Amal's arm with one skinny forefinger. 'Does it hurt?'

'Not much. It did at first. It makes my arm feel hot and itchy, that's all. It wasn't hot in the hospital. They've got air con.'

'What's air con?' asked Puppo.

The others ignored him.

'I've got to go back there in two weeks, just to see the doctor, not to stay,' Amal said. 'They'll take the stuff off my arm and it'll be better. I'm not supposed to work till then. I've got to rest, because I banged my head. They said.'

'What's in your bag?' Puppo asked, after a pause. 'Did you bring us any sweets?'

Amal pulled his little bag towards him and fished inside it.

'No, but a man gave me something to play with. Look.'

He brought out a small cardboard box. Opening the flap, he tipped out on to the sand a pack of scuffed, battered playing cards.

'What are they?' Iqbal asked curiously, turning them over. 'Look, there's pictures on some of them.'

Amal didn't seem interested.

'I don't know. You play games with them. The man made a sort of tower out of them. He said you can make up sets with the numbers and patterns. He was nice. He was from India. He came round every morning and cleaned the floor with a mop. He said his son was a camel jockey, but he got him out and sent him home.'

'What games? What do you mean, sets?' Iqbal asked curiously.

Before Amal could answer, Haji Faroukh appeared at the entrance to the shelter. The boys jumped respectfully to their feet, scattering the cards.

'So, Amal, you're back again. All well now, I suppose,' Haji Faroukh said jovially. 'You see how we care for you? First-class medical treatment, eh?'

Amal looked down at his feet.

'Yes, Haji.'

Haji Faroukh bent down to examine the wound running down Amal's scalp.

'Nice neat stitches,' he said approvingly. 'Once your hair grows back there won't even be a scar. Now, boys, work time! Camels won't water themselves. Iqbal, you'll show Yasser what to do.' He turned away, then came back. He cupped a hand under Amal's chin and lifted it, scrutinizing his face. 'Not you, Amal. Better rest today. A head injury needs time.'

He smiled as if pleased with himself, and walked off back to the guest house.

Rashid frowned at Haji Faroukh's departing back. He couldn't work him out. He'd been calm and almost kind when Rashid had first arrived, and he was being kind to Amal now. But yesterday, when Rashid had been frightened on the camel, he'd seen a whirlpool of rage and violence in the masoul's eyes.

'Do you like Haji?' he asked Iqbal, as they walked across to the water troughs.

Iqbal shrugged.

'I don't know. He's nice sometimes. At Eid he gave us new clothes, and the football. And we had a big dinner too.'

'But he gets angry, doesn't he?'

'Yes, if you don't try to ride properly, and let the camels get hurt. Especially if you don't win races.

That's all anyone cares about here. Him and Syed Ali and Abu Nazir. Just winning races.'

'Haji gave me my sweater,' Puppo chimed in. 'It's got a picture of a bear on the front. I like it.'

'Doesn't he beat you sometimes?'

Iqbal nodded.

'Yes, when he's got one of his tempers on. Then he goes really, really mad. But he doesn't mean to hurt you badly. Not like Abu Nazir. He's the worst.'

Rashid thought about this, and said nothing.

'Abu Nazir only comes here sometimes,' Iqbal went on, picking up the end of the hose and dropping it into the first trough.

'He's the trainer,' Puppo said eagerly, proud of himself for being able to explain. 'He hurts you with his stick. It's got electricity in it.'

'But he's a good trainer,' Iqbal said, as if he wanted to sound fair, like a grown-up. 'This is the best uzba around here. We win a lot of races. I won a big one last season. Syed Ali was really pleased with me.'

'What stick?' Rashid asked. 'What do you mean, electricity?'

'It's a prod,' explained Iqbal. 'Abu Nazir gives the camels shocks with it to make them run, and if we don't move fast enough he does it on us.'

He spoke carelessly, but Rashid could see that he was blinking rapidly.

'It's so horrible. It gives you a big, big pain,' said Puppo.

'He only uses it sometimes.' Iqbal was talking like a grown-up again. 'There's other uzbas where they hold you down and put electricity on you, from a wire, and you can't stop screaming. A boy told me, last race day. He said it hurts so much, you can't imagine. They do it to punish you.'

'No they don't, Iqbal,' Puppo contradicted him. 'It's to stop you growing. So you can go on riding camels. Salman told me.'

Iqbal turned away, went across to the tap to which the far end of the hose was attached and turned it on.

'Look what I can do, Yasser,' Puppo said. He picked the hose up and held a finger half over the end of it. 'It makes the water go all squirty when you do it like this.'

Iqbal ran back from the tap. Puppo giggled and turned the hose on to him, making the water shoot up in a glistening arc, hitting Iqbal's chest and drenching him down the front.

Iqbal lunged forward and wrenched the hose away from him.

'Not today, you little idiot. Are you crazy? Abu Nazir's here. He'll go mad if he sees us mucking about.'

Puppo looked uneasily towards the guest house. Salman was just going into it, carrying a tray in his hands with a coffee pot and some little cups.

Iqbal grinned at Rashid.

'We'll have a water fight when Abu Nazir's gone,

if Haji goes too. We do it when no one's here. Salman lets us. It's great. Specially when it's really hot.'

Rashid grinned back at him. He was glad Amal wasn't allowed to help today. He had Iqbal to himself.

Except for Puppo, he thought, and he doesn't count. He's only a baby.

Salman came out of the guest house.

'What you standing there for?' he shouted importantly. 'You make camel drink quick, then clean up dung. No lazy boys, or I give you beat.'

Iqbal winked at Rashid.

'Salman always shouts at us when Abu Nazir's here. He doesn't mean it.'

'Salman's nice,' Rashid said, testing Iqbal. He was still trying to make sense of the people in this new, frightening world, to work out who he could trust and who he must fear.

Iqbal picked the hose up out of the first trough and laid it in the second.

'Yeah, Salman's OK,' he said.

8

There was tension in the stables all afternoon. Cooled by a whirring fan, Abu Nazir stayed inside the whitewashed guest house with Haji Faroukh, relaxing against the cushions. Though he was out of sight, his presence unsettled the boys, turning Salman from an easy-going friend into a nervous task master. He was gaunt with tiredness, but he chivvied the exhausted children from one task to another, making them run back and forth in the blistering heat from the store to the camel's feeding racks with buckets full of fodder, and when that job was done, sending them to the camel pen with sacks to pick up the dung.

At last, even he could bear it no longer, and he gave the weary boys long drinks of water and sent them off to the shelter. Amal was lying asleep, the hollows of his eyes dark in his pale face. Rashid, Iqbal and Puppo collapsed beside him, and they were all asleep a few minutes later.

The sound of car doors banging startled Rashid

awake several hours later. He had been dreaming. He woke with a sob in his throat, but whatever it was that had made him cry fled away as he opened his eyes. He lay for a minute with his cheek pressed into the sand, trying to work out where he was, then he heard Iqbal yawn and Puppo whimper, and the present rushed back upon him.

The sun was mercifully lower and the heat was a little less crushing. Salman appeared at the entrance to the shelter.

'Abu Nazir gone,' he said. 'He and Haji eat a big dinner. Chicken. I keep some for you.'

He looked apologetic, as if wanting to make up for being strict earlier.

Puppo was the first to jump up. He put up his hand to hold Salman's, and trotted beside him towards the kitchen. Iqbal and Rashid followed, stretching to chase the last cramps of sleep from their arms and legs.

'Aren't you coming, Amal?' Iqbal said over his shoulder.

'Yes,' said Amal, following slowly. 'Yes.'

There wasn't much of the adults' lavish dinner left, but Salman had ladled what remained over the boys' usual ration of rice. They relished every scrap, savouring the drops of rich gravy and the succulent vegetables in silence, their faces rapt.

The food fuelled them with new energy.

'Come on,' said Iqbal, handing his empty bowl back to Salman. 'Let's play with the water.'

Salman shook his head.

'Sorry, Iqbal. Water cut. Come back this evening.'

'Football then,' said Iqbal.

Rashid would never have believed, half an hour ago, that he would feel like running about, but he wanted to now. Puppo, looking pleased, was bouncing up and down on the spot. Only Amal hadn't moved. He was still squatting by the kitchen step, staring into his empty bowl.

'Aren't you coming, Amal?' Iqbal said, surprised.

Amal didn't move.

'Got a headache.'

'You go rest,' said Salman. 'Be all right tomorrow. Find the ball, Iqbal. I coming to play with you.'

By the end of the fifth day, Rashid felt as if he'd been at the stables forever. The first day had laid down the pattern for all the rest. The night-time was still the worst part. Wrenched from sleep long before dawn, shivering in the desert chill, riding on and on round the same dreary track, the six hours of exercise were times of such misery that he imagined, often, how he would run away. He would slip down off his camel and disappear into the night, go anywhere, endure anything, till he could find his way home.

But if I run away from here, Uncle Bilal will never find me, he told himself. I won't have a chance of finding Shari either. I'll be lost forever.

At least he had learned to ride. His body now

responded automatically to the camel's odd, loping stride. He no longer needed to clutch the edge of the saddle, and was less afraid of falling. He was learning, like Iqbal and Puppo, to let his mind drift during the long lonely hours.

Salman, now routinely in charge of the night exercise, was growing in confidence.

'You lucky boys,' he told them earnestly. 'I too kind to you. Soon Abu Nazir begin camel training. Then you see.'

Amal was still allowed to rest.

'Don't get lazy,' Haji Faroukh kept saying to him severely, as if he was afraid of his own indulgence. 'When that plaster's off your arm, I'll expect some work out of you. Don't think you'll be spoiled forever.'

'Yes, Haji,' Amal would reply listlessly.

Rashid had lost count of the days of the week, and he was surprised, on his sixth morning at the stables, when the routine was interrupted. He found Iqbal, who had washed out his best Eid shalwar kameez the night before, changing into it in the sleeping shed. Amal, too, was wearing clean clothes.

'Are you going somewhere?' Rashid asked.

'Yes and you are too,' answered Iqbal. 'Friday prayers, at the mosque. We're supposed to look nice, Haji Faroukh says, or people won't think he looks after us properly.'

Rashid looked down at himself. His clothes were

smeared with dirt. He hadn't thought of washing them. He didn't know how to.

'Didn't Haji Faroukh give you Mujib's stuff?' Iqbal said. 'Put on the green things. They were new at Eid.'

Mujib's bag was in the corner of the sleeping shed. Reluctantly, Rashid groped inside it and pulled out a pale green shalwar and matching kameez. Slowly, he took off his own clothes and dressed himself in the others, shuddering in spite of the heat. He didn't like the thought of the dead boy's arms and legs moving inside the same clothes.

'It's too big, but it doesn't matter,' Iqbal said indifferently when he emerged. 'Come on.'

It felt strange to be walking out of the stable. Rashid looked over his shoulder, worried in case they were doing something wrong, but Haji Faroukh, who was inspecting a camel's nostrils, saw them pass and did nothing to stop them, and Salman came running to join them as they headed up towards the road. He was carrying a bundle of little white skull caps. He handed one to each boy, and positioned the largest carefully on his own curly hair.

Rashid looked around curiously. Since he'd arrived at the stables he had only left them for the night exercises, following the same long track straight ahead to the race course. He hadn't realized that the road on the far side of the palm fence led to a village. His eyes lit up with interest as the cluster of buildings approached. He could see a little row of shops, and the arches and minaret of a small mosque behind them. This place looked as if normal people lived here, like in the village in Pakistan.

It took only a few minutes for the children to reach the first shop. Outside it, Salman told the three younger boys to wait, then went up the two or three steps into the shady interior and started talking to the man behind the counter. The four others stood silently outside, staring at the boxes of fruit displayed on the step, and peering in at the shelves inside, which were stacked with packets of biscuits, brightly labelled cans and boxes of sugar.

A woman came out. She was dressed in black from head to toe and wore a black scarf on her head. When she saw the row of children, their eyes wide with longing, she smiled, then bent down and began to collect some beans that had fallen on to the step.

Rashid couldn't take his eyes off her. She was the first woman he'd seen since the lady had disappeared with Gaman Khan at Dubai airport. The sight of her made him feel happy and sad at the same time. He thought of Ma, and Zabidah, and home, and food, and comfort, and love.

Unable to stop himself, Rashid ran forward.

'Please!' he burst out. 'I'm looking for my Uncle Bilal and my little brother, Shari. Do you know them? Do you know where they are? No, I mean, it's not Shari. They call him Farid here, but he thinks he's called Shari.'

She shook her head. She didn't understand.

'Please,' Rashid began again.

Salman came out of the shop.

'What you doing, Yasser?' he said, frowning.

'I'm not doing anything bad,' Rashid said guiltily. 'I'm only asking if she's seen my uncle and my little brother. Uncle Bilal, and Farid.'

Salman rolled his eyes.

'You silly. What she know?'

'Ask her, Salman, please,' begged Rashid. 'Bilal and Farid. A little boy. Like Puppo. Just ask her, please.'

Salman shrugged and said something in rapid Arabic. The woman, surprised, stepped backwards, then she seemed to realise how young Salman was, and what he was saying. She shook her head.

'*La*,' she said. 'No.'

But her eyes, resting on Rashid, were full of sympathy. She took an orange from one of the display boxes and put it into his hands.

The shopkeeper appeared. He saw Rashid holding the orange and said something angry to the woman. She went hastily back inside. Salman spread out his hands apologetically and Rashid could see that he was trying to explain. To his relief, the man's face softened, as the woman's had done.

'Bilal *na* Farid?' he said, as if searching his memory. '*La*.'

He clapped his hand on Rashid's shoulder in a sympathetic gesture, and spoke again. Rashid understood only the last word.

'*Inshallah*,' the man had said. 'God willing.'

Salman said nothing as they walked on towards the mosque. There was no need. Rashid had understood that there was nothing to say.

Puppo ran up beside Salman.

'What did you buy? Was it sweets? Did you get some for me?'

Salman pulled something out of his pocket and showed it to Puppo, whose face fell.

'What's that? You can't eat that.'

'Batteries, for Haji Faroukh,' said Salman impatiently. 'You think I have money for sweets?'

The mosque was set back from the road down a short sandy track. On the corner was an auto-repair shop. A pick-up truck was in the forecourt, its engine hood propped open. A man was leaning over it, wiping something with an oily rag. As Rashid watched, he threw the rag down, let the hood fall with a clang and patted it with obvious satisfaction. Then he jumped into the driving seat and a moment later the engine roared into life.

Rashid blinked at him admiringly, and made an instant decision.

'That's going to be me,' he said to Iqbal. 'I'm going to do that when I grow up.'

Iqbal glanced indifferently at the truck.

'A soldier's better.'

A few minutes later, they were already kicking off their shoes at the wide, white-pillared entrance to the mosque.

Once or twice, Rashid's father had taken him to the village mosque at home, but no one had bothered after pio had died. Rashid had forgotten what he was supposed to do. He hung back, watching the others, then joined the bustle near the taps, copying Salman, who was vigorously washing his arms, feet and face, and rinsing out his mouth. Then he followed them into the prayer hall, which ran along one side of the small paved courtyard.

It was lovely here. Fans on long stems hung from the ceiling, stirring the heavy air with their powerful blades. The rug covering the prayer hall's floor was soft and smooth to the touch. The men and boys sitting down in rows greeted each other quietly, or didn't speak at all. No one was angry here. There was nothing to fear.

A faint smell made him lift his head and sniff the air. Someone was wearing hair oil like the kind his father had sometimes used.

Pio, he thought, trying to capture and hold a sudden memory of his father's large hand holding his small one.

He looked behind him, almost expecting his father to be there. Instead he saw a group of five or six boys enter from outside and go over to the taps to wash.

After them came another group of four more. Iqbal had recognized one of them and was waving at him.

'They're all camel jockeys like us,' he whispered to Rashid, leaning across in front of Salman.

Rashid's heart skipped. Perhaps Shari would come. Perhaps he only had to wait and even Uncle Bilal would be here. He stared at the entrance, willing them to appear, but the trickle of worshippers had slowed now, and there was only one last old man hobbling up the step.

Salman nudged him to make him turn round. The imam, his head covered with a white shawl, had taken his place on the little platform at the front of the prayer hall ready to lead the prayers. He wore round glasses with lenses as thick as pebbles, and his beard was streaked with white.

The prayers began. Rashid knelt, rose and bowed with the others, then settled down for the sermon. The imam cleared his throat and began to speak in heavily accented Punjabi.

After the first minute or two, Rashid stopped trying to follow his high-pitched, quavering voice. A jumble of pictures bubbled in his mind. Pio. The lady at the shop picking up beans. Camels jostling in the pen. Pio. A bus station somewhere in Iran. Pio and Ma. Shari chasing a goat. The man at the auto-repair shop flinging his rag down with a flourish. The shadowy, frightening figure of Abu Nazir. Uncle Bilal showing off his mobile phone. Gaman Khan walking off at Dubai airport. Pio. Ma. Ma.

I want to go home, he told himself.

The thought turned into a prayer.

God, help me. Take me away from here. Look after Shari. Please, God, help me to go home.

As soon as prayers were over, Iqbal jumped up and ran to talk to the other boys. Rashid followed. He felt shy, but he was desperate to ask if any of them had seen Shari.

He hovered at the edge of the group, listening. Only some of them were speaking Punjabi. Three or four, who looked African like Salman, were speaking Arabic. They were already drifting out of the mosque and searching for their sandals in the pile by the door.

Rashid found his own quickly, and followed them out into the lane. He tugged at Iqbal's sleeve.

'Ask them about Bilal and Sh— Farid,' he whispered.

Iqbal nodded and said loudly, 'Hey, any of you know a kid called Farid?' He pointed to Puppo. 'He's little, like him. He's Yasser's brother. This is Yasser.'

The boys looked at each other and shrugged.

'And Bilal,' Rashid insisted. 'Ask them about him.'

'Our masoul's called Bilal,' one of the older boys said, frowning. 'He's really strict. He's not your uncle, is he?'

'Uncle Bilal's here? You know him?' cried Rashid, shocked with joy.

Salman had come up and had overheard.

'That Bilal, he not your uncle, Yasser,' he said. 'I know that masoul. Old man. Long time here in Dubai.'

'Oh.'

Disappointment made Rashid angry. He kicked out at a stone, and missed. It flopped over and buried itself in the sand.

I'm useless, he thought miserably. I'll never find them. I can't even kick a stone.

They had already reached the auto-repair shop. Rashid didn't even turn his head to look at it.

'Not to give up hoping for your little brother,' Salman said kindly, coming up beside him and putting a friendly arm round his shoulders. 'Plenty other uzba around here. Only some masoul let camel jockey go to Friday prayer. Your brother in another one, maybe.'

Rashid looked up and nodded at Salman gratefully. Perhaps he was right. Shari might still be nearby. He only had to go on looking.

'Race day you find him,' Salman said. 'Sure and certain.'

'Yeah,' Iqbal chipped in. 'You see everyone on race day.'

Amal made a face.

'What are you grinning like that for? Anyone would think you were looking forward to it.'

It was the longest speech Rashid had heard him make.

'Don't you like race day then, Amal?' he asked curiously.

Amal shook his head, then winced at the pain the movement caused him.

'I hate it. I hate it. It's the worst. It's horrible. You'll see.'

Iqbal was teasing Puppo, bouncing a fist lightly and playfully on the little boy's head.

'Go on then, tell us what the sermon was all about.'

'What?' said Puppo, puzzled.

'I'm asking you. You ought to know. You were staring at the imam with your mouth wide open all the way through. I thought you were trying to catch a fly.'

'Puppo good boy,' Salman said approvingly. 'Listen to imam, learn to be a good Muslim.'

'I wasn't listening,' Puppo said indignantly, as if he'd been accused of doing something wrong. 'I was watching his glasses. Didn't you see? They were falling down his nose. I was just waiting for them to drop right off.'

9

As time passed, Rashid's hold on the memories of his old life at home became weak. They were unreal, as if they were part of a story that someone had told him a long, long time ago. It seemed as if he was being slowly cut adrift, floating into a new life, becoming someone else, the boy Yasser, and leaving the real Rashid far behind.

At first he had looked up with excitement every time a car pulled into the uzba, hoping to see Uncle Bilal jump out of it. At the mosque, too, he would continue to watch the door in case Shari should appear with another group of boys.

Slowly, though, he gave up expecting to see either of them. Constant disappointment began to snuff out his hope, until only a flicker of it remained.

On the morning when Uncle Bilal finally came, Rashid was at work as usual, staggering under a heavy sack of fodder as he carried it from the store to the food trays in the camel pen. It was a Friday, and it would soon be time to set off for the mosque. Rashid didn't notice his young uncle standing shyly by the fence, looking around, but when Bilal called, 'Rashid, is that you?' he felt a thrill run through him that raised the hairs on his arms and legs.

'Uncle Bilal,' he whispered.

The words sounded strange and almost foreign. He didn't dare turn round, certain of another disappointment.

But Uncle Bilal was saying, 'Rashid! Don't you know me any more? It's me!' and now he was right behind him, and kneeling down, and catching him in a squeezing hug.

Rashid stood frozen in his uncle's arms.

'Can we go home now?' he said at last. 'Can Iqbal come too?'

Uncle Bilal didn't seem to hear. He had released Rashid and was holding him at arm's length, looking at him and frowning.

'You're so thin,' he said. 'Have you been sick, or what?'

Rashid shook his head. He felt strange and was afraid he was going to cry.

Uncle Bilal shook him gently.

'Are you all right, Rashid? I wanted to come months ago, but I couldn't find my way back here again. You're miles out in the desert. Anyway, I hardly ever get the day off. In all this time, just think of it, only two lousy days off. And all the money I still owe Gaman Khan . . .'

He had seemed unable to stop talking as his shocked eyes took in Rashid's gaunt face and stick-like arms, but at last he broke off, lifted his hands, and shook them in the air.

'Don't they feed you?' he burst out. 'You're all bones!'

Rashid felt a dreadful wave rise up inside him, growing and growing, till it spilled out in a wild wail.

'Take me home, Uncle Bilal! I want to go home!'

Bilal reached out for him again, but Rashid pushed him away.

'Listen, I'm sorry, all right?' Bilal said, rocking back on his heels. 'I didn't know it was going to be like this. I really, really didn't. I'd never have brought you if I had. I wanted to take you away at once when I saw where they'd brought you, but they wouldn't let me. I can't take you home, Rashid. You've got to understand. Because of the money. We have to pay Gaman Khan for the fares and visas and everything. Anyway, he's got a contract with your boss. He told me. He came to find me, after I started work. He comes all the time to get my money. I begged him to let you go, but he wouldn't. What can I do, Rashid?'

The sobs that Rashid was fighting down made him gulp and heave.

'Tell Ma,' he gasped at last. 'She won't make me stay. She wouldn't like me being here.'

'I called her,' Bilal said, dashing his last hope. 'She was so shocked when she realized where you were. She wishes and wishes she'd never let you go. But what can she do? She can't come here. Where would she get the money? She just told me to find you both and try to look after you. I will, I promise you. I'll come whenever I can, now that I've found you again.'

'Where's Shari?' Rashid managed to ask.

Bilal looked surprised.

'You mean you don't know? He's quite near here, in another uzba. You want to see him? I'll take you if you like.'

Rashid stared at him, silenced by this astonishing news. How could Shari have been close by all this time, without him knowing?

'Hey! You!' a loud, angry voice shouted. Haji Faroukh had seen Bilal and was coming towards them.

Bilal hurriedly stood up, dusting the sand off his knees. Rashid felt him tense, as if he was preparing for trouble.

'I'm this boy's uncle,' he said. 'I came to visit him.'

Rashid waited hopefully, expecting Uncle Bilal to make a fuss, to stand up to Haji Faroukh and tell him – tell him – he didn't quite know what. But he saw at once that Uncle Bilal was no match for the masoul. Haji Faroukh towered over him. He was frowning, his eyes narrowed, sizing the younger man up for signs of defiance. Bilal's mouth softened into a placating smile.

'Please, Haji,' Rashid said daringly, desperation making him cunning. 'My uncle came to take me to Friday prayers.' He saw the masoul hesitate. 'It's Friday,' he added unnecessarily.

Haji Faroukh, making one of his disconcerting transformations from frightening master to kindly friend, suddenly smiled and put out his hand to shake Bilal's.

'Good. Good. Tell Salman, Yasser, that your uncle's going with you.' As Rashid ran off to find Salman, he heard Haji Faroukh say, 'You bring him straight back here after the mosque, eh? No funny ideas.' And with dismay he caught the timid note in Uncle Bilal's voice as he answered, 'Yes, sahib. It's just a visit. Just to see how he's getting on. He's a good boy, isn't he? You are satisfied with him, I'm sure.'

The other boys stared curiously at Bilal as they made their way down the familiar track towards the village and the mosque. He had smiled at them briefly and repeated their names, but it was Salman he looked at longest, and as they walked along the outer fence of the uzba, up towards the road that led to the village, he was glancing sideways at him, as if he was sizing the boy up.

When the little group turned on to the road and began heading towards the village, Bilal stopped and put a hand on Rashid's shoulder, drawing him close.

'You go on,' he said to the others. 'Yasser and me, we have to go somewhere.'

Salman had been walking ahead but he stopped, his eyes widening with alarm.

'No, ji. We go to mosque together. Haji no like you going another place.'

Bilal frowned. The masoul had humiliated him back in the uzba. Now he wanted to seize his chance to win back some authority.

'Don't argue with me,' he said sternly. 'Rashid is my responsibility.'

'Who's Rashid?' Puppo asked, bewildered.

'I'm Yasser here, Uncle Bilal,' Rashid said, embarrassed. He could see that Salman was offended and wanted to make a fuss. 'It's all right, Salman. Uncle Bilal's found Shari. We're going to see him. Please, Salman. I've got to see my brother. I've got to.'

'Wow! You found Shari!' Iqbal was staring at Bilal, impressed. 'Yasser, he's been on about Shari all the time. We kept asking everyone about him, didn't we, Yasser? No one knew where he was.'

Salman was biting his lip, anxious and uncertain.

'No permission from Haji. Very angry if you come late back.'

Bilal cleared his throat as if he was about to make another speech.

'But we won't be late, Salman. I promise. I *promise*,' Rashid said quickly. 'Let me go. Please. Please.'

'You've got to let him, Salman,' Iqbal urged. 'We'll never hear the end of it.'

Even Amal was nodding. Puppo, seeing him, began nodding violently too.

'We meet you here then after mosque,' Salman said at last. 'After one hour. You have watch, Mr Bilal?'

'Of course.' Bilal grandly shot out his arm to show it. 'An hour is fine. Come on, Rashid. We've wasted enough time already.'

He strode off, heading along the road in the opposite direction, away from the village, with Rashid at his heels.

'Say hi to Shari for us!' Iqbal called after them.

In all his months at the uzba, Rashid had only ever gone in one of two directions outside: either towards the race track during the exercise hours, or to the mosque in the village for Friday prayers. It was the first time he had turned off the smaller track on to the main tarmac road, which was raised above the surrounding desert. From there he could look out over miles of flat desert and the sprawl of uzbas, each within their palm-frond fences.

For the first time he realized how many there were. Ten, fifteen, twenty even. He was cross with himself. Why hadn't he slipped away and explored along here before? He might have found Shari ages ago, all by himself.

But the idea of wandering about on his own made him shiver, in spite of the noonday heat. Iqbal had run out of the uzba once, clutching a few coins he had found in the sand outside the guest house, determined to get to the shop in the village and buy something to eat. But by bad luck Abu Nazir had been bumping down towards the uzba in his Land Cruiser, and he'd spotted Iqbal before he'd had time to hide. Haji Faroukh had flown into one of his unpredictable rages, and had beaten Iqbal so severely with the piece of plastic hose that Iqbal had limped for days afterwards, and had pulled away to some place inside himself where Rashid couldn't follow. Even though Haji Faroukh had seemed sorry afterwards, and had been nice to Iqbal to make up for it, the thought of bringing down such fury on his head made Rashid feel sick. He took hold of Bilal's hand and held it tightly.

'It's not far is it, Uncle Bilal? Only I mustn't be back late. Haji will kill me if he finds out.'

'No. It's over there.'

Bilal was pointing to the last uzba that stood alone, a little apart from the others, across a small stretch of rubble-strewn desert. Even from this distance, the place looked poor and run down, the palm-frond fence dry and brittle with age.

Now that he could see where Shari was, Rashid

was burning with impatience. He tugged at Bilal's hand to make him go faster.

'Listen, Rashid,' Bilal began hesitantly. 'Don't be – I mean, I only saw Shari for a few minutes, but he . . .'

'What?'

'He doesn't look – just don't be surprised, that's all.'

Rashid tried to summon up an image of his little brother, but found that he could hardly remember his face. The anxiety in Bilal's voice was catching. He freed his hand and began to run.

'Be careful!' Bilal called after him. 'You can't just go in there.' Rashid stopped, and Bilal hurried to catch up with him. 'Shari's masoul, he's not reasonable like yours. He wouldn't let me talk to Shari. He – he shouted at me. Told me not to come back. We'll have to go round by the side. One of the older boys was nice. He said there's a gap in the fence at the back. He said we might be able to see Shari from there.'

They were already almost in front of the run-down uzba.

'What gap? Where is it?' Rashid said, filled with dread.

Bilal led him away from the entrance, along a tyre-rutted track. Anyone catching sight of them would think they were making for a broken-down shack a little way away. Once out of sight of the uzba's entrance, though, he turned sharp right, and a few minutes later Rashid was following him along the side fence, their feet making no sound in the soft sand.

'There. This must be it. Look through here,' Bilal said quietly.

The brittle palm fronds were bent and broken here. Rashid parted them easily and looked through.

It was odd seeing another uzba, so similar and yet so different from his own. This part of it seemed to be an old camel pen, though there were no camels in it now. The fodder racks tilted drunkenly and sand drifts had blown up against them. Beyond the pen he could see a white-painted brick building, like Syed Ali's guest house, and behind it a tent. Through its open flaps he could make out a tangle of bedding.

'Move over, Rashid,' Bilal said, pushing him aside and putting his own face to the gap, then he puckered his mouth and whistled three rising notes between his teeth.

In spite of the tension churning inside him, Rashid couldn't help smiling. Whistling like a bird was one of Uncle Bilal's tricks. He'd often done it at home.

A moment later, Bilal stepped back.

'He heard me. He's coming. Look, Rashid, but be careful. Don't let anyone else see you.'

Rashid was back at the gap now, staring at the little boy who was walking fearfully towards him, looking over his shoulder as he came.

That can't be Shari, he thought.

The child was limp and listless and was trailing a

cloth behind him in the sand. It was impossible to recognize, in this thin, pathetic creature, the brother who had endlessly maddened and provoked him, whom he had played with and quarrelled with and loved and loathed ever since he could remember.

Behind Rashid, Bilal was whistling again to guide Shari to the right place. He was inches away now.

'Shari,' hissed Rashid. 'It's me. Rashid.'

Shari turned huge, startled eyes towards the fence. Rashid pulled the fronds further apart. He could see more clearly now how changed Shari was, how thin and scared, with blank eyes and a body drooping with exhaustion.

'Shari! Don't you know me? I'm Rashid!'

He'd expected Shari to brighten and turn at once into his old self, to raise his voice in his high, gleeful laugh. Instead, he saw the corners of Shari's mouth turn down, and his chin tremble, and tears well up out of his eyes.

'Don't start, Shari! You know me. It's Rashid. Can't you even say hello?'

Rashid dared to push his hand through the fence and catch hold of Shari's shoulder. His fingers felt nothing but bird-light bones. His touch seemed to upset Shari even more, who opened his mouth and let out a long despairing cry, rocking his head from side to side.

'Shut up, Shari!' Bilal said. 'They'll hear you. Tell him to be quiet, Rashid.'

It was too late. A man was hurrying across the sand towards them, his big belly covered by a dirty white vest. Bilal pushed Rashid aside.

'Say you saw a scorpion, Shari. Say it made you cry. Don't tell him we were here.'

The man was upon Shari already. Rashid had let the fronds fall back into place, but not before he had seen the man's hand lift and come down in a vicious smack on Shari's head.

'Sc— scor—' Shari was trying to say.

The man grabbed him by the upper arm and was half dragging, half carrying him away. As they went, Rashid saw a dark patch of wetness spreading down the legs of Shari's trousers.

Bilal and Rashid walked silently back to the road. Rashid was biting his lip so hard that it hurt.

'Shari's going to be all right though, isn't he, Uncle Bilal?' he said anxiously.

Bilal hunched his shoulders helplessly, and let them fall again.

'I don't know! You saw him. Yes, of course he's going to be all right. Anyway, it's not my fault, OK? I told you. I didn't know what it was going to be like.'

Rashid was following his own line of thought.

'That man, is he Shari's masoul?'

'How should I know? I suppose so.'

'He looks horrible.'

'Yes, and you know what, Rashid? I think you're lucky. Your haji, he's not that bad. And that boy,

Salman, he's been reasonable. They even let you go to Friday prayers.'

Rashid said nothing. How could he tell Uncle Bilal what it was really like? He had no words to describe the desolation of the night-time, and the weariness of the day, the hunger and fear, and the pain at being cast off from home. But Uncle Bilal was right, he knew. He was lucky. As he had peered through the fence into Shari's uzba, he had sensed a horror far worse than anything in his own. He didn't want to think about it.

Shari'll be all right. He'll be all right, he chanted to himself.

They walked on in silence.

'I'd better give you my mobile number,' said Bilal.

Rashid looked up at him. Worry had gouged a deep groove between his uncle's brows. The sight of it made Rashid even more anxious.

'What for, Uncle Bilal? I can't call you. Nobody's got a mobile here, and anyway I don't know how to use one.'

'Just in case.'

Bilal recited the string of numbers and made Rashid repeat them until he was sure they were fixed in his head.

Rashid liked learning the numbers. It was like knowing a secret. Something magic. Something powerful.

Salman and the others met them at the place where

they had first parted. Salman beamed with relief at the sight of them.

'Did you find him? Did you see Shari?' asked Iqbal.

'Yes.'

Iqbal waited, but Rashid didn't go on.

'Where is he? Is he all right?'

'He's right over there.' Rashid pointed with his chin. 'It's the last uzba, the old one. There's only desert on the other side.'

Salman sucked his breath in through his teeth.

'I know that one. Very bad masoul. Name is Boota. Very strict. Punish boy with electric shock. Two camel jockey dead last year in Boota uzba.'

Rashid turned on him.

'Shut up! Shut up! Don't talk about it! I don't want to talk about it!'

He felt his face go red with anger. He wanted to hit Salman. He wanted to hit out at everyone, to punch and kick the whole world.

10

Although he never had enough to eat, Rashid was growing. He noticed this when his sandals became too tight, and one day he threw them aside, unable to force them on to his feet. In any case, he didn't need them so much now. The soles of his feet were hardening and they could bear the heat more easily.

Weeks had passed since Bilal had taken him to see Shari. For nights afterwards Rashid had had confused, frightening dreams, waking to the sound of his own crying, but as the days went by he settled back into the routine of the uzba and forgot the terrible sight of Shari's despairing eyes and the sound of his agonized wailing. He didn't, however, forget Bilal's mobile number. He hugged it to himself, repeating it under his breath, and when he needed comfort he chanted its magic rhythm like a prayer.

There was more activity at the uzba as the race season approached. Syed Ali and Abu Nazir came almost every day. They spent long hours examining each camel, with Haji Faroukh and Salman in respectful attendance. The camels were groomed and washed constantly. Salve was rubbed into every little cut or bruise, and they were covered at night with sheets and blankets. Experts and vets came and went.

'Goat's milk mixed with honey for this one,' Rashid heard one of them say, as he peeled back Khamri's leathery upper lip to inspect her long yellow teeth. 'Increase the vitamin supplements. Dates, I think also, mixed in with her barley.'

'What's vitamins?' Rashid asked Iqbal, who was listening too.

'Don't know,' said Iqbal, 'but I wish I was a camel. I wish I could have milk with honey. And dates.'

The night-exercise time was changing too. As the weather cooled, they set off later, only an hour before dawn. Abu Nazir came with the sun, his Land Cruiser sparkling white in the morning light. There was no quiet plodding round the race track once he arrived. The boys had to make the camels run.

Rashid had become so used to walking the camels that he had felt no fear for a long time as he mounted and set off into the dark each night, but it was a different matter when the running began. Amal, Iqbal and even Puppo had all been through at least one racing season. Even so, they were tense as they saddled up for the first morning's running training.

'Don't fall off, Yasser, that's all,' Iqbal said earnestly, seeing how nervous Rashid was, fumbling with his camel's girth. 'And if you do, roll off the track as quick as you can so you don't get trodden on.'

'Get on with it! Stop chattering!' Abu Nazir barked at them, handing out long black whips to each boy.

Puppo was already perched on the smallest, youngest camel. He was sitting on his heels, rocking back and forth unhappily. Amal, mounted on an older, darker one, had sucked in his cheeks and was fiddling with his whip. Rashid saw that he was blinking nervously.

Rashid was to ride Hamlul. He mounted, and Hamlul rose protestingly to his feet. Rashid looked at Iqbal, trying to see how to hold the whip, but before he was properly settled, he saw Abu Nazir flick a switch on the prod he was holding, and touch the rump of Iqbal's camel. Galvanized by the electric shock, the camel let out a shrill whistle of protest and bounded forward. Amal's mount took off after it, and then Puppo's.

'Use your whip! Keep up with the others!' Abu Nazir called up to Rashid, and brandished the electric prod again. Rashid's breath was knocked out of him as Hamlul shot forward. He slipped back on the saddle and had to lean over to clutch at the front edge of it.

His stomach boiling with fright, his eyes wide, every hair on his body standing on end, he clung on, his feet tensed beneath him, willing himself not to fall.

He was aware suddenly of the rumble of a car engine beside him and out of the corner of his eye saw that Abu Nazir's white Land Cruiser was driving alongside the race track. Abu Nazir was leaning out of the driver's window, yelling at him.

'Whip! Whip him, you little fool!'

Rashid forced himself to relax his right hand's grip on the saddle and tried to raise the whip, but the action made him lose his precarious balance and he swayed, almost falling. The whip slid out of his hand, and he clutched at the saddle's edge again with desperate fingers.

'What are you doing? Stupid idiot!' yelled Abu Nazir, then he pulled his head back in and accelerated on towards the other running camels, who were already far ahead.

To Rashid's intense relief, Hamlul began to slow down, dropping from a fast run to his usual leisurely walk. Rashid looked over his shoulder. Where was his whip? Should he try to go back for it? What if Hamlul ran off while he had dismounted?

'Yasser! Not to worry! Whip is here!'

Salman was running up behind him, the whip in his hand. He passed it up to Rashid, then laid a friendly hand on his knee.

'First time running on camel very difficult. You do good already, Yasser. Easy to fall off.'

Rashid barely heard him. He was twisting the whip anxiously between his fingers.

'Abu Nazir's really angry. He's going to beat me, I know he is.'

Salman clicked his tongue.

'You no think about Abu Nazir. Learn to ride camel when he go fast, Abu Nazir very happy with you. Listen. I tell you what to do.' His one good eye was blinking earnestly. He shook Rashid's knee gently, forcing him to look down.

'You just sit easy, all right, Yasser? No all tighten up like that. Think like camel. Think how he run, how he use his leg. Go with him. Whole body. Now start again. Ready? I give Hamlul smack, make him go, then you use whip.'

Rashid took a deep breath. His insides were churning again, but he would do it. He must do it. He would show Abu Nazir that he wasn't an idiot, and that he was as good as the others. He would make Hamlul run and run. He'd stay on and whip as hard as he could, and catch the others up.

He felt a little sprout of confidence.

'All right, Salman,' he said. 'I'm ready.'

He was prepared for it this time when Hamlul bolted off and he didn't panic.

Think like the camel, Salman had said.

He hadn't understood what Salman had meant, but he found that he did now. He could tell what Hamlul was going to do. He could make his own body go with him, in the same rhythm. It wasn't so different from walking, after all.

113

I can do this! he told himself.

Hamlul's speed was slackening now. Rashid bit his lip. He had to use the whip.

He was scared again. It had been all right as long as he could concentrate on simply riding, on not falling off, but raising his whip arm and bringing it down with force on the camel's rump threatened to unbalance him again. He tried once, rocking dangerously in the saddle as he did so. Hamlul was ignoring him, slowing almost contemptuously to a walk. Rashid, feeling more confident at this sedate pace, managed to lift the whip and whacked it down as hard as he could.

The effect was immediate. Hamlul, with a grunt of surprise, raced off, gusts of sand spinning out from beneath his feet. Rashid raised the whip higher this time. It was easier than he'd thought. He brought it down with another satisfying crack.

Hamlul seemed to be flying now, his neck stretched out, his rhythm steady. Rashid was concentrating so hard that he didn't notice the SUV, driving alongside him.

'Make him go faster! Catch the others up! Are you deaf, or what?'

Abu Nazir's voice was rough with anger. It startled Rashid. He lost the rhythm of Hamlul's stride and began to jolt about awkwardly in the saddle. He wanted to fling the whip away again, and clutch with both hands at the saddle's edge.

Then he heard Salman's voice inside his head.

Go with the camel. Think how he runs.

He steadied down. His knees, which had tensed to the point of cramp, began to relax a little. His back was moving better than ever with Hamlul's long stride. He was all right now. He lifted the whip and at the feel of it Hamlul's pace quickened.

The SUV accelerated on towards Iqbal and the others, far on down the track.

After that first time, it was never as hard again. Rashid fell off once, taken by surprise when Hamlul skittered nervously away from the bigger camel that Amal was riding, but he landed in soft sand, and as no others were running behind him he was in no danger of being trampled. He even felt better for his fall. The thing he'd dreaded had happened, and he'd survived it. He wouldn't be so scared again.

The training intensified. Haji Faroukh often came out now to watch the camels run. The boys were given helmets to wear, and little radio receivers that fitted into pouches on their chests. Abu Nazir no longer had to shout at them through the open windows of the SUV as he drove along the race track beside them. His urgings and curses were transmitted straight to each boy's radio.

The loud voice from the transmitter had startled and confused Rashid the first time he'd heard it.

'You get used to it,' Iqbal said.

To his surprise Rashid found that he was good at running camels. He'd learned fast to find his balance and use the whip. He'd thought at first that he would only be able to manage Hamlul, but he wasn't so different from the other camels, after all. Only Khamri, the biggest and strongest camel of the uzba, was hard to ride. She was bad-tempered and wilful, prone to lash out with a hind leg in a kick, or snap viciously with her powerful teeth. All the boys were afraid of riding her.

As Rashid became more expert, he noticed how the other boys rode. Puppo was so small that he could do little more than cling to the back of his camel like a monkey. He always rode the smallest camels, who would be slowed by a heavier jockey. Amal was frightened all the time. He was the worst rider, always tense, unable to catch the camel's rhythm. He jolted along in a miserable huddle, only daring to use his whip when Abu Nazir yelled at him through his headset.

Rashid had expected Iqbal to be the champion of them all, to ride with grace and confidence, coming first every time, and he was surprised when, after only a few training sessions, he left Iqbal trailing at least a length behind. He felt triumphant and beamed at his hero, expecting praise, but Iqbal turned his face away, his mouth set in a tight line, and Rashid, without quite understanding why, almost wished he hadn't won.

There was still a little edge of fear every time the camel he was riding shot forward into a fast run, and sometimes, if things went badly, or if he was riding Khamri, the fear lasted till the end of the ride and he felt shaky and sick as he dismounted. But often there was a thrill of excitement too, moments of sheer exhilaration, when he felt as if he was flying like a bird.

Two weeks before the first big race day of the season, Khamri went off her feed and began to cough. She was separated from the other camels in a small pen on her own and the vet came out from Dubai to look at her. Abu Nazir stood leaning on the iron rail, watching the vet inspect Khamri's watering eyes, while Haji Faroukh and Syed Ali walked across to join him.

'What's the problem?' Syed Ali called out anxiously. 'Is it serious?'

Rashid was busy nearby collecting up dung and putting it into a sack. He heard the vet say, 'Can't be sure till I've given her a proper examination. Wait till I get my bag from the car,' and understood the words 'examination', 'bag' and 'car'.

'Khamri's always been a tricky one,' Syed Ali said. 'I've never had a camel that's given me more trouble.'

'Yes, but she's a potential winner,' said Abu Nazir. 'She's got the aggression. She could win you the golden sword this season, if she's on form.'

'How is she performing in training?' asked Syed Ali. 'Which boy's riding her? Can they manage her?'

Rashid began to pay more attention, trying to understand, edging closer to the huddle of men as he looked for droppings in the sand.

'I've tried them all out on her,' Abu Nazir said. 'It ought to be Amal. He's the heaviest. But that child's a wash-out. Needs a good thrashing if you ask me.'

Haji Faroukh had been standing back respectfully, but now he cleared his throat.

'Since he had the accident—' he began.

'Accident!' scoffed Abu Nazir. 'We organized proper treatment for him and the hospital's signed him off. Cost us a fortune! He's a skiver, that one. He's putting on weight too. I'm sure that crafty Sudanese boy slips them too much food.'

'No, sir, he can't. I keep a firm hand on all that side of things,' Haji Faroukh said earnestly. 'We can't cut their diet back any further. They're growing boys, after all.'

'Growing, that's the problem,' grumbled Abu Nazir. 'Still, I have heard – in other uzbas – there are ways of dealing with it. Electricity treatment for one.'

Rashid shivered. He knew what electricity meant.

'What do you mean?' Syed Ali turned a troubled face to him.

'Shocks. It stops the growth rate. Keeps them obedient too. Quite a useful deterrent to lazy, cheeky boys.'

'So painful though, sir, wouldn't it be?' Haji Faroukh said, shaking his head.

Abu Nazir shrugged.

'Kids of their kind don't feel pain. Anyway, they soon forget it.'

'No.' Syed Ali was shaking his head. 'I won't permit that sort of thing. Not on my uzba.'

'Look, cousin, you want to win the golden sword or not?' Abu Nazir said impatiently. 'There'll be no chance at all with overweight jockeys.'

'There must be other ways of keeping their weight down. Use your judgment, my dear fellow, but no cruelty, please.'

'It'll have to be laxatives then,' Abu Nazir said discontentedly. 'Only two weeks to go. And we'll have to sweat the weight off them. Get them running laps, Haji. You'll have to see to it.'

'How's Yasser doing? Shaping up all right?' Syed Ali asked, after a pause.

'Very well, sir.' Haji Faroukh seemed relieved to change the subject.

'Yes, he's got quite a flair for it,' agreed Abu Nazir. 'He's our best hope for a good win. If we can get Khamri fit in time, I'll team her up with Yasser. They might even pull off the big one.'

Rashid, hearing the name Yasser, was listening even more intently.

The vet had finished his work. He let himself out of the pen.

119

'Nothing serious,' he said, closing his bag. 'She's got a cold, that's all. Blanket her up at night, keep her nostrils clear, feed her well and let her rest for a day or two. Should be fine next week.'

The men began to walk back slowly towards the guest house.

'Interesting rumours about these new changes to the law,' remarked the vet, handing his bag to Haji Faroukh to carry.

'Changes? Affecting racing?' Syed Ali asked, surprised.

'Haven't you heard . . .'

They had reached the guest house and Syed Ali was politely ushering the vet inside. They would be settled in there for hours now, Rashid knew. He couldn't hear their conversation any more. In any case, he was no longer interested.

They think I'm good, he told himself with pride. But a second thought made him shiver. I've got to ride Khamri in the big race.

11

As the first big race day of the season approached, Rashid could almost feel the tension crackling in the air of the uzba. Under Abu Nazir's eagle eyes the boys' diet had been cut back even further, and they had been sent out on long runs, forced to go on when they flagged with agonizing touches of the electric prod. Weakened by exhaustion, as well as the laxatives that had sent them running to the toilet, they had no energy for football, but flopped down wearily in their shelter whenever they had the chance.

The day before the race, the camels were as restless and irritable as the men and boys. Their stomachs had been purged, they had been given no food and were hungry and hard to handle. Irritated by her muzzle, Lashmi had lashed out at Salman with a blow that would have broken his leg if it had hit its mark. Salman had jumped aside, but a little too slowly, and Lashmi had caught him in the back, sending him spinning into a fall. Salman had been hobbling about all day, angry with himself and everyone else.

Evening came at last. The boys flopped down wearily in their shelter, too tired to play. Puppo was holding something in his hand, rubbing it on his cheek and crooning a meaningless string of words.

'Shut that noise up!' Iqbal burst out suddenly. 'You're driving me crazy!'

Puppo stared back at him and sang louder than ever.

Iqbal lurched forward and grabbed Puppo's hand, prising his fingers open.

'What have you got? What are you doing?'

A shiny metal buckle fell out of Puppo's hand on to the sand.

'That's mine!' Iqbal said indignantly. 'You nicked it off my bag.'

Both boys lunged for it. Iqbal got there first and snatched it away.

'It's not! It's mine! I want it!' yelled Puppo.

'Little thief, little thief, little thief,' chanted Iqbal, waving the buckle high up, out of Puppo's reach.

Puppo's face was red with rage and he flailed his arms, hitting out wildly at Iqbal.

'I'm not a thief! I hate you!'

'You are a thief, Puppo,' Rashid said, looking sideways at Iqbal. 'It's Iqbal's buckle.'

Iqbal was holding Puppo away from himself by the arms. Puppo was trying to kick him. He lost his balance and fell in a heap on the ground. He gave up trying to fight and filled his lungs with shuddering breaths, preparing to bellow.

'Puppo's a thief! Puppo's a thief!' chanted Iqbal nastily.

Rashid began to feel uncomfortable. He looked at Amal, but Amal seemed unaware that anything was happening. He was sitting on his heels, his hands clasped between his knees, his shoulders hunched, rocking. Rashid wished Iqbal would stop baiting Puppo.

'You can have my sandals if you like, Puppo,' he said. 'They're too small for me now.'

Puppo was getting his breath back for a second roar, but he stopped to think about this offer. He rolled over, picked up a playing card that had become separated from the pack and flung it at Iqbal. Iqbal ignored him. He had turned on Rashid, his eyes sparkling with aggression.

'Think you're so clever,' he said, in the same hateful, teasing voice. 'Mister Clever Clever. Think you can win all the races.'

Rashid's heart began to hammer.

'I don't! I never did!'

Puppo, distracted by this new quarrel, had fallen silent and was watching the other two, a slick of snot sliding down from his nose to his mouth.

'Mister Know-it-all,' spat Iqbal, his face screwed

up tightly. 'Me and Amal, we're better than you. Won loads of races, haven't we, Amal?'

All three boys looked at Amal, who went on rocking, taking no notice of them.

'I know you have,' Rashid said, bewildered. 'I'll never be as good as you, Iqbal. Not ever. I know I won't.'

'You don't know anything.' Iqbal looked away from him and bit his lip.

Rashid saw that for some reason the tide of anger was draining out of him.

'I do know you're better than me,' he said humbly.

'Yeah, but you're going to win, aren't you? Everyone knows that. You're going to ride Khamri. I heard Haji Faroukh say,' said Iqbal.

Rashid shut his eyes and shuddered. He didn't want to think about it.

'I don't want to ride Khamri. I hate Khamri. She's scary. You can ride her, Iqbal. I'll ask Haji.'

'Ask Haji?' scoffed Iqbal. 'Are you crazy?'

He had been staring angrily out of the shelter but now he glanced quickly at Rashid's unhappy face. For a moment their eyes met. Iqbal looked away first.

'Khamri's not so bad if you get off to a good start,' he said reluctantly. Rashid held his breath. He could see that Iqbal's mood was changing. 'You have to be careful at the beginning, that's all. You've got to watch out for the barrier.' He frowned importantly, resuming his role of guide and mentor. 'It goes up

124

when the race starts. You've got to watch out and duck underneath it. Don't let it catch you or it'll knock you off the camel. Might even knock you out. Might even kill you, if it hits you in the neck. That's the worst bit. The start. Getting out under the barrier.'

Rashid let out a sigh of relief. He had hardly heard what Iqbal was saying. He only knew that the quarrel was over, and that Iqbal was his old self again, taking the lead, telling him what to do.

The buckle had slipped out of Iqbal's grasp and was lying in the sand. Puppo's hand was creeping towards it. Iqbal noticed, snatched it up and dropped it on Puppo's head.

'Take it, you silly baby,' he said. 'Who wants a stupid old buckle anyway?'

Puppo pulled the buckle out of his hair and held it in a tight fist, staring at Iqbal, not sure whether to thank him or to object to being called a baby.

They were distracted by Amal, who was creeping into the sleeping hut. He lay down in a corner and turned his face to the wall.

Rashid slept deeply that night, in spite of his anxiety. He was woken by a shake from Salman.

'Here, put this on.' Salman was holding out an armful of thin, brightly coloured clothes.

Sleepily, Rashid struggled into a tight fitting silky top and a pair of light cotton trousers. The others were silently dressing too. They staggered out into the dawn light, and Iqbal led the way to the kitchen.

'Is that all?' Rashid said, looking down at the half piece of bread that Salman had given him before running off to join Haji Faroukh in the camel pen.

'Yes, and you don't get anything else all day when you're racing,' Iqbal said.

He spoke in his old superior way, and Rashid nodded, relieved that last night's quarrel seemed to have been forgotten. He couldn't bear the thought that Iqbal might turn on him again.

'Muzzles! Harnesses! Saddles! Helmets! Get on with it, you lazy kids!' Haji Faroukh yelled across at them.

With automatic obedience, the four children trotted to the store and emerged a moment later, their helmets on their heads, their arms laden with ropes and cloths.

'What's that stuff?' Rashid said, nodding at the pile of thick webbed harnesses that Iqbal was carrying.

'You have to wear one,' Amal answered unexpectedly. 'They put a rope through it up your back and tie you on to the camel.'

'Oh.' Rashid's face brightened. 'So you can't fall off so easily?'

'Supposed to be. But when you do fall off you get dragged along the ground and can't roll clear,' Amal went on bitterly. 'And all the other camels coming along behind stamp all over you.'

126

He looked as if he wanted to be sick.

'Get on with it! Hurry up!' Haji Faroukh called out. 'Late already! Abu Nazir will be at the race course by now.'

Iqbal and Amal were putting their harnesses on, folding the velcro shoulder straps in place. Puppo was standing with his arms raised, waiting for someone to do it for him.

'Do it yourself, Puppo,' snapped Salman. 'You not a baby now.'

Rashid put on his own harness, copying the others, then he bent down to help Puppo, who was struggling with his straps. Puppo pushed him away.

'I do it. Not a baby any more.'

Haji Faroukh had forced Hamlul, Lashmi, Duda and Soudani to kneel. Amal, Puppo and Iqbal mounted, and their camels rose with protesting groans.

Rashid hopped on to Hamlul, relieved that at least he could ride his favourite camel as far as the race track. The harness felt strange and itchy, but he hardly noticed it. His stomach was fluttering uncomfortably and his mouth was dry. Salman was attaching another camel to Hamlul's bridle. He would ride Khamri in the rear.

It was a relief to be outside the uzba on the familiar path to the race track. The camels were settling down. It was still early, and a cool breeze was blowing eddies of sand and thorn twigs across the ground between the palm-frond fences.

They rode out into the open ground, and Rashid could see, streaming in from all directions across the desert, strings of camels, their saddle cloths fluttering, their tiny riders' bright plastic helmets glinting in the sun. Far away, on the flat horizon, the skyscrapers of Dubai shimmered in the haze.

Rashid had ridden round the race track so often during the night exercises that he had thought every metre of it was familiar, but the place looked different today. Dozens of white four-by-four vehicles were parked near the start of the track. The camel owners, each man dressed in a white dishdash and black-roped headdress, were standing together in knots, touching their chests in courteous gestures as they greeted new arrivals, while their masouls and trainers led the camels into the starting pen.

Rashid picked out Syed Ali and Abu Nazir, but he wasn't interested in the camel owners. He was scrutinizing the other small boys riding in on their camels, recognizing a few that he'd met at Friday prayers. Guiltily, he realized that he was half hoping that Shari wouldn't be there. His last sight of Shari, through the gap in the palm-frond fence, had upset him so much that he almost dreaded the thought of seeing him again.

There was much more noise today than usual. A generator was clanking, and car engines, reversing into the parking places, added to the mechanical roar. Camels were groaning in throaty resignation. Flocks of pigeons fluttered, pecking at dung.

Haji Faroukh led his string of camels to an unoccupied corner of the holding pen and jerked on one bridle after another to make the camels kneel. He and Salman set about muzzling them, and, their mouths covered, their backs swathed with blankets, the camels sat quietly, subdued.

All around the holding pen, masouls from the different uzbas were eyeing each other and their camels with wary friendliness. Some, like Haji Faroukh, were wearing the shalwar kameez of Pakistan, but there were Africans here, and Indians as well.

Iqbal had been watching Haji Faroukh walk across to talk to someone he knew, and he took the chance to slip off to the side of the holding pen where a knot of boys had gathered. Puppo followed on his heels. Salman had been watching Khamri. The big camel was more jittery than the others, twisting her head from side to side. Salman took hold of her bridle and squatted down on the sand beside her to keep her calm. Amal sat on his own some way off, pouring rivulets of sand rhythmically through his fingers on to his big toe.

Rashid wasn't sure what to do. He felt shy of the other camel jockeys. He'd only ever tagged along behind Iqbal at the mosque, and had hardly spoken to any of them on his own. Since Iqbal had turned on him last night, he was scared of offending him again. He was worried though, in case he looked silly, standing in the middle of the holding pen all by himself. There was no point in trying to talk to Amal.

He took a deep breath and walked across to join the gang of jockeys.

There were dozens of boys here that he hadn't met before. More were coming up all the time. Some seemed to know each other well. Others hung back shyly, as he was doing. Puppo was already playing with two four- or five-year-olds. They were whacking their whips down on the sand. Iqbal had his arm round another eight-year-old's shoulders. They were whispering to each other and giggling.

A stab of jealousy shot through Rashid. Were they talking about him? Were they laughing at him?

An older boy came up to him.

'You're that boy Yasser, aren't you? Did you ever find your brother, the one you were looking for? What was his name?'

'Farid,' Rashid said unwillingly. 'Yes.'

He didn't want to talk about Shari.

'He's OK then?'

Rashid shrugged.

'I don't know.'

The boy waited a moment longer, but when Rashid said nothing more, he walked off.

Suddenly, from all over the holding pen, masouls

130

were returning to their camels, and blankets and muzzles were being removed. The little jockeys didn't need to be summoned. They were already pattering in their bare feet back across the sand towards their masters. Rashid returned to Haji Faroukh alongside Iqbal.

'Who was that boy?' he couldn't help asking. 'Is he your friend?'

Iqbal's face was tight.

'Yes, and he doesn't ask stupid questions all the time.'

Rashid's heart plummeted. He couldn't bear it if Iqbal was horrible to him again, now, before the start of the race, when he was suddenly feeling more scared than he had ever been in the whole of his life.

To his relief, Iqbal relented, and put an arm round Rashid's shoulders.

'You're my friend too, silly. Listen, like I said, you've got to be careful at the beginning, when the barrier goes up. Look out for it and duck down if you have to.'

Abu Nazir had come into the holding pen and was standing beside Haji Faroukh, slapping an irritable palm against his thigh.

'The handicaps have been sorted out,' he was saying to the masoul. 'Get on with it, can't you? Get the boys mounted.'

Iqbal was first up, on Soudani. Rashid watched while Salman fed the rope through the back of his harness and tied it under Soudani's belly. Iqbal had tucked his whip under his arm and was fiddling with the straps of his helmet.

'Stop doing that,' barked Abu Nazir. 'Stop fussing.'

Amal was on Duda. He sat twitching his whip back and forth, blinking hard, while Salman worked on the straps. Haji Faroukh had lifted Puppo up on to Lashmi, who was already standing. The little boy's short legs kicked in the air and he landed awkwardly on the saddle, nearly tumbling down the far side. Rashid's heart was thudding. Would he have to ride Khamri already, in the very first race of the day?

But it was Hamlul's muzzle that Salman was removing. He nodded at Rashid, who shut his eyes tight for a moment, then climbed on to Hamlul's back. The camel rose with his usual lurch and groan. Salman was fiddling now with the rope, threading it through the harness and tying it under Hamlul's belly. Rashid wriggled his shoulders. It felt awkward and uncomfortable.

The radio in his harness pouch crackled.

'Show Abu Nazir if you can hear!' came Syed Ali's voice. 'Raise your hands!'

One after another, the four boys raised their hands.

Abu Nazir was frowning up at them.

'You know what you have to do. Listen for the instructions and follow them exactly. Any silliness, any mistakes, you know what you'll get. Playtime's over. You've got a job to do.'

He turned and almost ran out of the holding pen. The other trainers and camel owners were running off too, scrambling to get into their cars before the race began.

Two men swung open the big gates at the far end of the pen. There was a barrier just beyond it, a pair of horizontal metal bars at about the height of the camels' chests. Little strips of cloth hung from it all along its length.

I'll never get under that, Rashid thought, feeling panicky.

But it was too late now to think of anything. Salman was holding Lashmi's and Duda's bridles, running forward with them towards the open gates. Haji Faroukh was holding Soudani's and Hamlul's. The camels were nervous, shaking their upper lips and grunting, dodging skittishly away from each other.

Alongside the race track, the owners were ready in their vehicles, poised to drive alongside the metal barriers and keep pace with their camels. A cameraman with a big TV camera sat on one car, his red keffiyeh tucked round his nose and mouth to protect him from flying sand.

Fifteen or twenty camels were through the gates now, cavorting and side-stepping. There was a sudden loud report and the metal barrier began to rise. Rashid ducked his head. He was under the barrier and through. He felt Hamlul spurt into a run.

'Whip him on the rump, you little fool! Start him properly!' came Abu Nazir's furious voice through his radio.

I'm racing, thought Rashid, his heart hammering with fright. This is it. I'm racing.

12

Riding a racing camel was not at all like the riding exercises that Abu Nazir had put the boys through in preparation for the big day. There was a terrible muddle and confusion. The camels were crowded and nervy, jammed together, their tiny frightened jockeys flailing their whips wildly. Rashid was horribly confused by the noise. Above the roar of the camel owners' powerful vehicles, careering along beside the running camels, was the crackle and spit of the radio on his chest. He could barely take in Abu Nazir's screaming instructions at first, and was only aware of a stream of curses.

It took a few terrifying moments to settle into the rhythm of the run.

'Whip him, you little idiot! On the neck! The neck!' came Abu Nazir's voice from his chest.

He leaned forward, trying to obey. The camel on his right veered suddenly towards him, almost colliding with Hamlul. Rashid's whip, raised to obey Abu

Nazir, flicked the other jockey's knee. The boy turned a shocked face to him and swayed alarmingly on his saddle, but there was no time to look at him again. Hamlul had swerved away. He was slowing down, losing pace. Rashid could feel it.

'I'll kill you! Kill you! On the rump! Whip him!'

Rashid took a deep breath and lifted the whip again. He managed this time to bring it down with a good crack. Hamlul shot forward.

The camels had spread out. Three or four were already well ahead, running smoothly and fast down the straight, their necks stretched out, flecks of foam flying from their rubbery lips. Several no-hopers had dropped behind. Hamlul was in the middle bunch.

The first long stretch of the course was behind them already, and they were near the curve at the far end. Rashid's panic had begun to subside. He was starting to feel in control, to sense what Hamlul was feeling.

He wants to stay running in the middle of this lot. He wants to be one of the gang. He doesn't want to get ahead, he thought.

'On the neck! The neck!' shrieked his earpiece.

He's wrong. That won't work, Rashid thought. It'll make him swerve again.

He gave the camel's neck a small swipe to show that he'd heard, then shifted his weight, rising up and leaning forward, and whacked at Hamlul's rump.

It was as if the camel had read his mind too. He

quickened his pace, accepting that he had to run ahead of the pack.

They were round the curve now and the straight run back to the finish was ahead. Hamlul was out on his own, away from the middle bunch. He was still far behind the leaders but was slowly gaining on them, closing the gap, and Rashid, sensing him run with new enthusiasm, felt an uprush of excitement, a sense of power he'd never known before.

I'm flying, he thought. I can fly!

The gap was too great to close altogether. The winner had passed the finishing line. The race was over, and Hamlul had only come fourth. Rashid let him slow to a canter as they approached the end, and looked to see if one of his own uzba's jockeys was in the first three. Only Lashmi, ridden by Puppo, was ahead of him, but he had come second. He was already being led back to the holding pen by Salman.

Rashid's knees buckled under him as he slid to the ground beside Puppo. He felt shaky, as if his body was only just catching up with the fear and excitement of the race. Iqbal and Amal straggled in and dismounted in dejected silence.

Salman and Haji Faroukh started working at once on the camels, rubbing them down, blanketing them and clearing the foam from their nostrils. Rashid suddenly felt desperately thirsty.

'Salman, have you got some water? I need a drink.'
Salman shook his head.

'No water on race day.'

'Please, Salman.'

Salman looked away from him.

'I tell you, Yasser. No drink. Water make you heavy. No bother me now.'

Syed Ali and Abu Nazir came hurrying into the pen.

'What happened to Lashmi?' Syed Ali asked Haji Faroukh. 'He was ahead in that race. Should have kept the lead in the final straight.'

'He would have done if this stupid kid hadn't messed up,' Abu Nazir said through tight lips, hauling Puppo up by his arm and hitting him hard across the back with his other hand.

He dropped Puppo, who crawled quickly away, out of reach.

'And you,' Abu Nazir went on, shooting out a finger to point at Rashid, who was mercifully out of reach. 'What was all that mess about at the start? Hamlul should have been out ahead of the pack before the first curve.'

'It's Yasser's first ever race,' Haji Faroukh said quietly.

'Yes, and he did quite well.' To Rashid's relief, Syed Ali was smiling at him, and even patting him on the shoulder. 'A promising start. We'll see how you shape up in the next race. Half an hour, boys. Rest now.'

Iqbal, relieved to have escaped without being noticed, slipped off at once towards the side of the pen where the other jockeys were already congregating. Amal walked slowly behind him. Rashid set off after them. Puppo ran up alongside and tried to put his hand into Rashid's but Rashid shook him off so that he could undo the strap of his helmet. He was tired already, hungry and very thirsty, and it was only the start of the day.

He was looking around for Iqbal when he felt someone rush at him from behind. Two skinny little arms were flung round his waist. They were squeezing him with desperate strength.

'Shari!' he gasped. 'You're pushing me over!'

But Shari's grip tightened. He was trembling convulsively.

Rashid put his own arms round Shari's shoulders. The warmth of his brother's body, the familiar feel and smell of it, seemed to penetrate right through him. He walked the two of them stumblingly over to a bare bit of fence and sat down against it, with Shari still clinging to him.

'There wasn't a scorpion,' Shari said at last. 'You didn't come back, you and Uncle Bilal. I went to the hole in the fence every day. I kept waiting for you.'

The unfairness of this stung Rashid.

'How could I come back? It was really hard coming that day. Uncle Bilal hasn't been back to see me either. I wanted to come, Shari. I tried, lots of times. I kept asking but they wouldn't let me.'

He was lying, but it was worth it. Shari's grip loosened a little.

'I'm hungry, Rashid,' he said.

The sound of his own name, his real name, pierced Rashid with a painful sweetness.

'Me too.'

'Give me something to eat.'

'Don't be an idiot, Shari. I haven't got anything.'

'I want a drink.'

'Yeah, and so do I. We've got to wait, that's all.'

Shari let go of him and sat back far enough so that he could stare up into Rashid's face.

'Did you go in that race?'

'Yes. Did you? I didn't see you.'

Shari shook his head.

'What's it like, Rashid? Did you fall off?'

'Course not.' Rashid, with a rush of elder-brother superiority, felt an urge to show off, but Shari was looking so small and thin and scared that all he could feel was pity. Iqbal's advice and Salman's wisdom weighed on him like a responsibility, valuable pieces of knowledge that had to be passed on.

'Listen, Shari,' he said earnestly. 'You know about the barrier that goes up when the race begins? You've got to duck your head if it doesn't go up fast enough.'

Shari was looking at him vacantly. It was clear that he didn't understand.

'I don't want to go in the race. I don't like camels. I don't like racing.'

'Yeah, I know that, Shari, but you've got to. It's not too bad. It's sort of like flying. Didn't they teach you to ride? Haven't you ridden fast before?'

'We went out in the night all the time. It was cold. They made my camel run and I fell off. It really hurt, Rashid. Look.'

He stuck out a skinny leg and hauled up his thin cotton trousers. A bruise disfigured his whole shin from the ankle to the knee.

'But you did it more than once, didn't you? You didn't fall off every time?' Rashid wanted to give vent to his exasperation, but anxiety for Shari won. 'You won't fall off in the race if you're careful. Look, I'll tell you how you do it. You have to pretend you're the camel, see? You have to think like he does. Look ahead and guess what he's going to do.'

'I don't want to be a camel. I hate camels,' Shari said crossly.

'I know you do, but—'

'You shouldn't say I'm a camel. Camels are nasty.'

'I didn't say you were a camel! Look, drop it, OK? I'm only trying to help you. Forget about being a camel. The barrier, Shari, that's the main thing. Look out for the barrier. Don't let it catch you.'

At home in Pakistan, a long, long time ago, Shari used to shout and cry at full volume when he was upset. Rashid could see that he was upset now. He waited for a noise, but nothing came out of Shari's tightly pursed mouth except shuddering breaths from

141

suppressed sobs, while tears slid silently out of his eyes. He rubbed them away roughly with the back of his hand.

'We'll go home soon,' Rashid said, knowing it wasn't true. 'Uncle Bilal will come and take us. We'll go back to Ma and Zabidah.'

'Who's Zabidah?' asked Shari.

Rashid stared at him, shocked.

'You don't remember Zabidah? She's your sister. *Our* sister. You do remember Ma, don't you?'

'Yes,' said Shari, as if he was trying to give the right answer.

'And home. The goats. The place where we played under the tree.'

'The goats butted me with their horns. I liked it.'

'That's right. They did.' Rashid nodded, relieved. He'd been worried for a moment. His own sense of what was true and not true had wobbled. If Shari hadn't known about home, and Ma, and Zabidah, how could he be sure that they really existed at all? Perhaps they only lived in his dreams.

The jockeys were standing up already, heading back to their masouls for the next race.

'Come on, Farid,' a big boy said. He stared curiously at Rashid. 'Are you his brother? He kept on about having a brother. I didn't know if it was true or not.'

Shari put his hand into the older boy's, and for the first time Rashid saw him smile.

'He is my brother, Imran. I told you. He's Rashid.'

Imran pumped Shari's hand up and down affectionately, looking at Rashid. Rashid felt jealous. He ought to be the one to look after Shari, not this strange boy.

Iqbal walked past, glancing at them curiously.

'You'd better come, Yasser. Look, they're mounting already.'

Rashid gave Shari a playful punch.

'You'll be all right. Just don't panic when the race starts. It's easier after the first bit.'

But he was biting his lip as he watched Shari and Imran run back to their masoul. He couldn't bear the thought of Shari trying to stay on an agitated camel in the scrum of a race. He couldn't imagine what would happen if he fell and was trampled under those heavy, horned feet.

The second race was harder than the first. Rashid had thought it would be easier, as at least he knew what to expect. He was riding Shahin, too, who was one of the less excitable camels. But he was desperately anxious about Shari. He'd glimpsed him, mounted, in the crowd of jittery camels before the start of the race, as they milled about behind the barrier, then he'd lost sight of him.

Once the race had started he kept trying to look over his shoulder to see if Shari was there, but it was impossible to make out which jockey was which, under their big helmets. Twice he nearly lost his balance, and once he almost dropped his whip. His camel seemed to sense that he wasn't concentrating, and slipped back from an early lead. It took frantic efforts to drive her on up the final straight.

He nearly cried with relief when he saw Shari ride back into the holding pen. He watched his masoul untie him from his harness, and saw him, with Imran and two other jockeys from his uzba, slip back to the resting place. He ran after them, before Abu Nazir could get at him, and sank down beside Shari on the sand.

'You did all right. You didn't fall off.'

Shari blinked at him, his eyes huge in his thin face.

'I was scared. Boota sahib kept yelling at me inside my head.

'Boota sahib? He's your masoul?'

Shari didn't bother to answer.

Iqbal suddenly appeared and squatted down beside them.

'You're Shari, are you?' he said. 'Yasser went on and on about you.'

'He's not Shari. He's Farid,' Imran chipped in.

'And he's not Yasser, he's Rashid,' Shari said, pointing to Rashid.

Iqbal and Imran nodded.

'It doesn't matter, anyway,' Iqbal said.

'I – just – want – a – drink.' Rashid tapped his whip on the ground with each word, and as he spoke his voice cracked with dryness.

144

Iqbal pulled something out of his pocket and handed it to him.

'Suck this. It helps.'

Rashid took the little object eagerly, thinking it was a sweet, then stared down, disappointed, at the button lying on his palm.

'You suck it,' Iqbal said again. 'It makes your mouth feel better. You have to know tricks like that when you're in the army. Don't swallow it though.'

Rashid put the button in his mouth and sucked on it. A little saliva gushed on to his tongue. Iqbal was right. It did help a bit.

Iqbal and Imran started talking to each other. They had met during the last racing season. Iqbal began telling Imran about Mujib, and how he had died.

Not him again, thought Rashid.

Shari crawled closer to sit beside him, leaning against his shoulder.

'Let me have a go, Rashid.'

'At what.'

'The button.'

'You'll swallow it.'

'I won't.'

Reluctantly, Rashid fished the button out of his mouth, wiped it and handed it to Shari, who put it in his own mouth, his eyes big with hope.

'I thought it would taste nice,' he said, making a face. 'It's silly,' and he spat it out on to the sand.

'Don't! You'll lose it!'

Rashid scrabbled in the sand, picked the button up, rubbed it on his sleeve and put it back in his mouth. It was Iqbal's button. It had to make him feel less thirsty. He was sure it would.

There was a long interval before the next race. Rashid and Shari sat close together. Some of the other children were already lying down. Famished and exhausted, they were soon asleep. Rashid felt his own eyes closing. There were things he'd meant to say to Shari, he was sure there were. There were questions he'd meant to ask. He ought to teach him Uncle Bilal's mobile phone number, at the very least. But the heat and the weariness were weighing on him, cloying and heavy. His eyelids drifted down and he slept.

A rough shake woke him. Salman and the workers from the other uzbas were going among the sleeping boys, fetching their jockeys for the next race. Shari had gone.

'Hurry up, Yasser,' Salman was saying. 'This very big race. Important one. You ride Khamri now.'

13

Rashid had been sleeping deeply. Dragged suddenly out of the depths, he felt horrible, heavy and lifeless. The afternoon sun was blinding and very hot. His head ached, and his mouth was as dry and scratchy as the sand itself.

All around him, other boys were sitting up and yawning, reaching for their helmets and whips. A kick of fear hit Rashid as he took in what Salman had said. It was the last race of the day. The big, important one, and he was riding Khamri.

He stumbled to his feet and stood, still groggy, yawning and stretching. Then someone took hold of his raised arm and shook it.

'I'm looking for my son, Ejaz,' an anxious voice said in Punjabi. 'Do you know him? Have you seen him?'

Rashid squinted up at the man, but the sun was in his eyes. He couldn't see his face clearly.

'He's nearly five years old. Must be this big by

now.' The man put his hand out to indicate a small child's height. 'Ejaz. That's his name. Ejaz. One of you boys must know him.'

Rashid shook his head. The man gave up on him and darted off after a clutch of little jockeys who were drifting back towards their masoul.

'Ejaz!' Rashid heard him call out desperately. 'Don't any of you know him? I'm his father!'

He had been seen. Two uniformed policemen were running towards him. They grabbed his arms roughly.

'Out of here, you! This is a restricted area. Who let you in?'

The man looked thin and weedy beside them. They hustled him easily towards the entrance of the holding pen. As his eyes followed them, Rashid caught a momentary glimpse of a woman outside. She was wearing Pakistani clothes and hugging herself with anxiety. A policeman approached her and began to gesticulate. She shrank away from him, retreating.

A cough distracted Rashid. Puppo, who always took a long time to wake up, was still sitting on the sand, his helmet tilted over one ear, fiddling with his whip.

'Come on, Puppo,' Rashid said impatiently. 'The race'll start in a minute.'

Puppo took no notice.

Rashid tapped on his helmet. Puppo jumped, startled, and frowned at him, ripping his helmet off and throwing it peevishly away.

'Don't do that, Yasser. You scared me,' he said crossly.

'You've got to come,' Rashid said impatiently. 'Now.'

All over the holding pen, camels were being prepared, their blankets removed, and their jockeys strapped into their harnesses and helmets.

'Was that Shari? You didn't let me say hello,' Iqbal said, frowning at Rashid as he slotted his radio receiver into the pouch on his harness.

Rashid said nothing, afraid he'd offended him.

'So you found him at last,' Iqbal went on.

'Yes.'

'You're lucky, having a brother.'

'Haven't you got one?'

Iqbal shrugged, as if he didn't know.

Rashid thought about this. Iqbal had never said anything about his family, and Rashid had never asked him. He couldn't imagine Iqbal with a family, anyway, with a mother or a father, brothers and sisters. He would be a different kind of person, hardly Iqbal at all. Rashid didn't like the idea. Iqbal was complete in himself, strong and brave, the best person in the world.

There were questions, though, that he wanted to ask. Where had Iqbal come from before Dubai? How old had he been? Who had brought him here? But before he could make the questions sound right, and say them out loud, Abu Nazir had appeared. He was grabbing Rashid by the shoulders and shaking him.

'No more fooling around this time. No more excuses. Don't dare pretend any longer that you don't know what you're doing. You mess up this time and I'll beat you so hard you won't sit down for a week.'

Rashid nodded, his eyes obediently lowered. He'd been distracted by Iqbal, but now he had to think about the race. His heart began to hammer.

Syed Ali was talking to Haji Faroukh. Salman was standing by Khamri's head, tugging on her rope, forcing her to kneel. Rashid took a deep breath and climbed on to her back. Syed Ali turned away from Haji Faroukh and watched Khamri rise to her feet with irritable grunts. He smiled up at Rashid.

'I'm sure you'll do your best,' he said pleasantly. 'There's a lot of prize money on this race. You'll get a tip if you win.'

Salman had removed Khamri's muzzle. Rashid, settling himself in the saddle, felt her tense and her neck muscles begin to work.

'Watch out, Salman!' he called.

Salman dropped her bridle and jumped out of the way just as Khamri lunged at him with her teeth, snapping viciously at his arm.

'What do you think you're doing?' shouted Haji Faroukh. Salman had tripped over, and was trying to get up. Haji Faroukh shoved him out of the way and grabbed Khamri's bridle, jerking it to bring her under control.

Syed Ali laughed nervously.

'Full of spirit! Excellent! She can't wait to start running. I've got a good feeling about this one. *Inshallah*, we have a winner on our hands.'

There were at least twice as many camels ready and mounted for this race as there had been for the earlier ones. It was going to be a nightmare on the starting line, Rashid could tell. There would be horrible moments as the camels milled about, pushing and shoving, before they settled into the race.

Shari can't do this. He'll be hopeless at this, he thought. He'll fall off. I know he will.

Salman was leading the last four of the uzba's camels out of the holding pen now. There was a buzz of excitement outside as men closely watched their camels position themselves for the race, the drivers revved their engines, and the masouls and uzba hands struggled to control the nervous animals.

The pistol shot rang out. The barrier began to lift. The first camels were under it and through already. Then the scream of a child rang out, and behind him, out of the corner of his eye, Rashid saw a little jockey lose his balance and fall, to disappear from sight between the trampling camels.

Shari, he thought for a second, but the child's jacket had been blue, and the one Shari had been wearing was red.

There was no time to think about it any more. Khamri was sidestepping jerkily towards the barrier. Now she was under it, with the long run of the first straight ahead.

Rashid shivered with relief. The worst bit was over. He had to hang on now, and try to force Khamri through the mob of camels ahead.

He had settled down, feeling the power of Khamri's running.

'On the back leg! Whip her!'

His pulse quickened in response to the excitement in Abu Nazir's voice as it crackled through the receiver.

They were halfway down the first straight. Khamri had pulled ahead, and Rashid could see only two camels in front of him.

I can take them, I know I can, he thought. I can win this. I'm going to win!

A scream behind sent a shudder through him. He half turned to look, and saw a tiny jockey slide helplessly sideways from his saddle. Tied on by the rope, the child was soon dangling by the back legs of his camel, which was kicking out, trying to free itself. Rashid saw enough to know that it wasn't Shari or Puppo. Shaken, he turned forward again.

'You child of Satan! You dirty little animal!' came Abu Nazir's hysterical voice. 'Don't look round! Ride! Whip her!'

But Khamri's momentum had been lost. Another

camel was coming up from behind, overtaking him inch by inch. Rashid glanced sideways and saw that it was Nanga, being ridden by Iqbal, and that Iqbal's face was set in a grimace of fearful determination.

The finishing line was in view already. The two leaders were far ahead, the gap impossible to close, but Iqbal was whipping Nanga on as if he still had a chance of winning.

'You're falling behind! I'll kill you!' Abu Nazir's voice screeched up at him from the receiver on his chest.

Rashid took a deep breath and forced his mind back into the race. Yes, he had it now. The rhythm was back. He and Khamri were one creature, riding for victory, gaining on the pair ahead, going neck and neck with Nanga alongside. Then, wanting to share his elation, he looked sideways at Iqbal, and read absolute desperation on his face. He lifted the whip again, but knew with instant clarity that he had to let Iqbal win. Ignoring Abu Nazir's frantic yells, he let the whip fall harmlessly on Khamri's rump, and watched Nanga run on ahead.

Ten minutes later, back in the holding pen, Iqbal was jubilant. Rashid tried to catch his eye, wanting praise for holding Khamri back, but Iqbal wouldn't look at him.

'Third place! Nearly second! Best race that Nanga's ever run!' he was bragging to Salman, who, without replying, handed him a bottle of water. 'Haji said so. He was really pleased with me. I'm still top jockey. Didn't you hear him, Salman? That's what he actually said.' He turned at last to Rashid. 'You've got to keep them going when they're on the straight, Yasser,' he said grandly. 'You lost it then. Khamri was a better bet than Nanga too.'

That's not fair, Rashid wanted to say. I *let* you win.

He bit his lip. He'd wanted Iqbal to be grateful. Things weren't turning out the way he'd meant. And he'd be punished for it now.

But the bottle which Salman was holding out to him wiped everything else from his mind. He grabbed it and raised it to his lips. The cool feel of the water was wonderful.

The joy of it was short-lived. Abu Nazir, hurrying into the holding pen ahead of Syed Ali, had snatched the bottle away before Rashid had drained it. He struck Rashid hard across the face, felling him.

'Not here,' Rashid heard Syed Ali whisper. 'Restrain yourself.'

Rashid was hauled to his feet and told curtly to follow. He trailed miserably out of the holding pen in the wake of the two men, Abu Nazir's driver opened the back door of the Land Cruiser and he scrambled up on to the seat, with the help of a kick from Abu Nazir's sandalled foot.

*

154

Whenever Haji Faroukh punished the boys, he used the plastic hose and beat them in the heat of his anger. He was quick to calm down, and bore no grudges, but his beatings were bad enough. Abu Nazir, though, used a camel whip, with agonizing force and precision, and his anger was cold and vindictive. By the time he had finished beating Rashid, near the rubbish bins behind the guest house, Rashid was a quivering, wretched, sobbing little creature, his back, arms and legs striped scarlet with weals.

His heart, though, hurt even more than his body.

It's not fair, he shouted silently inside his head. I did it for Iqbal!

Abu Nazir finished his punishment with a final contemptuous kick.

'Don't ever – ever – throw a race away again. When you ride my camels you ride to win.'

He threw the whip aside and stalked off. A moment later, Rashid heard Abu Nazir's car engine start, and knew he had left the uzba. No one was about now. The others had not yet returned from the race track with the camels.

'Zero five zero seven seven . . .' he began to whisper hoarsely, but even Uncle Bilal's phone number had no power to comfort him.

After what seemed like a long time, he picked himself up and began to hobble across to the water tank, but before he had reached it, the camels, led by Haji Faroukh, were turning in through the entrance to the uzba. The three boys, drooping with fatigue, were riding, and Salman was bringing up the rear.

Haji Faroukh frowned and shook his head at the sight of Rashid, but there was concern, not anger, in his face. He led the camels into the pen. Amal and Iqbal slid to the ground, and reached up to lift Puppo down. Then they all started across the sand towards Rashid.

'Come back here,' Haji Faroukh called out. 'Water the camels first.'

He spoke quietly to Salman. Salman went up to Rashid and gently took his hand.

'You come kitchen with me,' he said.

He sat Rashid down on the step and brought him first a long glass of cool water. Rashid sipped gingerly. Every movement hurt.

Salman came back out of the kitchen and put a bowl into his hands, smiling with the pleasure of one offering a treat. There was rice and lentils, chicken and vegetables, with a thick flap of bread. Rashid looked down at the food, bemused. He had been half dead with hunger earlier in the day, and this was the best food he'd ever been offered, but now he didn't want to eat at all. He put the bowl down beside him on the step.

'Better you should eat, Yasser,' Salman said kindly, squatting down beside him. 'Abu Nazir very bad for beating. He beat me when I little boy, camel jockey like you. Not your fault. Haji Faroukh, he not angry with you at all.'

Rashid didn't take in his words, hearing only the gentleness in his voice. Salman delicately lifted the shirt up to look at his back. Rashid flinched, afraid of being touched.

Salman sucked in his breath.

'He beat you so bad. Just for let Khamri go a bit slow. Abu Nazir, he like to beat every boy one time. Now he finish with you. No more beat you again.'

He picked up the bowl and put it back in Rashid's hands.

'Eat, Yasser. Everything better tomorrow.'

The other boys had been released at last. They were trudging across the open ground towards the kitchen, half dead with hunger and exhaustion. They squatted silently round Rashid, waiting for Salman to give them their supper.

'Abu Nazir's horrible, like a – like a tiger,' Puppo said at last, his eyes big with sympathy. 'Or a snake.'

Salman handed round their bowls.

'Chicken!' Iqbal said, smiling with pleasure. 'And beans!'

He picked up his drumstick and ripped at the meat with this teeth. They ate on, saying nothing.

'Haji Faroukh can give you some cream for your back,' Amal said at last. 'It'll hurt really badly tomorrow, but then it'll start feeling better.'

'If Abu Nazir beats me, I'm going to bite his legs,' announced Puppo.

'You're going to do what?' scoffed Iqbal. 'You don't know what you're talking about.'

'I wanted to kill Abu Nazir when he beat me,' Amal said softly. 'If I'd had a gun, I'd have shot him dead. Through the head.' He shuffled sideways, moving closer to Rashid. 'With Haji, at least there's a reason, and he's nice to you afterwards. Abu Nazir's just a – a—'

'A tiger snake,' giggled Puppo, pleased with himself.

'I told you, Yasser, didn't I?' Amal went on. 'Race days are the worst. Your little brother, he did all right. He didn't fall or anything. I saw him go off afterwards.'

Rashid nodded gratefully. He had forgotten about Shari. Amal was trying to cheer him up, he could tell. He wished, though, that it was Iqbal who was talking to him like this.

'There was a boy who fell behind us,' he said to Iqbal, his voice husky. 'What happened to him?'

Iqbal shrugged.

'I didn't see.'

'I did.' Amal was picking the last scraps of meat off his bone. 'They put him in an ambulance and took him away.'

'Was he dead?' asked Puppo.

Amal frowned at the casualness of his tone.

158

'No. I saw his leg move.'

'I wish I could go to hospital,' sighed Puppo.

'No you don't, you little idiot,' Amal said with unusual sharpness, then lapsed back into silence.

'Syed Ali gave you something, didn't he, Iqbal?' Puppo asked, making a quick recovery.

'Yes!' Iqbal grinned and pulled a bank note from his pocket. 'Fifty dirhams!'

'But you didn't even win.' Rashid was stung by the triumph in Iqbal's face.

'No, but I made Nanga run really, really well, and third place is still good. They didn't think she'd ever beat Khamri. She's not bad, Nanga. I don't mind riding her so much. She doesn't jerk about all the time.'

He sat back on his heels, emanating satisfaction.

He doesn't care, Rashid thought sourly. I got beaten because of him and he doesn't even realize.

He stood up. His head was swimming and it took him a moment to find his balance.

He knew suddenly that he wanted nothing more than to be on his own, to lie down and rest for a long, long time. As he stumbled away, he heard Puppo say, 'What are you going to buy with your money, Iqbal?' and Iqbal answer, 'I'm going to save some, and buy a bag of marbles with the rest.'

14

Now that the racing season was in full swing, the pattern of life changed on the uzba. The boys were driven even harder during the day, and the night-time exercise was more intense. The camels were fussed over, groomed and medicated. Every change in them was monitored. If Shahin slipped on loose sand, her hip was carefully watched for signs of strain. If Duda's long-lashed eyes began to run, the vet was summoned at once, and an anxious conference took place in the pen. No one noticed how haggard the children were, how tired and thin. No doctors diagnosed their stunted growth, or complained of their poor, meagre diet.

Rashid approached each race day with a mixture of excitement and dread. He was still afraid – horribly afraid – of the crush of camels and the fearsome starting barrier, but now he wanted to pit himself against the others and win. He hadn't yet come first, though on his fifth race day he was placed second in the last big event of the afternoon, even earning a tight smile of congratulation from Abu Nazir. Luckily, he hadn't been riding against Iqbal, who had been sent off in the truck with several of the uzba's camels to another race course for the day.

Rashid had confused feelings, too, about seeing Shari. The sight and smell and feel of him gave him a painful sense of home. His memories of Pakistan were beginning to fade, like drifts of morning mist burned off to nothing by the sun. He didn't welcome them now. It was easier to forget. Part of him longed for Shari, but the sight of his little brother's wretchedness made him feel ashamed and helpless at the same time, and unfairly angry with Shari too.

The guest house was kept spruced up for the racing season. The crimson carpets were swept daily, the cushions plumped up around the walls, and supplies of sweets and biscuits kept in for visitors who might call.

Syed Ali's racing friends came often. They would arrive in a flurry of big white cars, their long robes pristine, and settle in the guest house with their host for coffee and conversation, or follow him out to the camel pens to inspect his star racers' finer points.

No one was expecting a visit from the big sheikh, and when he arrived in his convoy of royal vehicles, and strolled into the uzba, with Syed Ali beaming by his side, there was near panic. Salman rushed to sweep sand from the guest house steps. Haji Faroukh shouted orders at the two extra hands who had been hired to help out in this busy season, and the boys peeped out from behind their sleeping shed, their mouths open like baby birds' at the sight of so much splendour.

Salman saw them and beckoned urgently. Iqbal was sent to take charge of the visitors' shoes and line them neatly outside the guest-house door. Amal was dispatched to fetch water from the tank. Salman thrust a tray at Rashid, and told him to take it into the guest house.

Syed Ali took it from him with his own hands, and set it down in front of the princely visitor, who had arranged himself comfortably on the central cushions and was looking around at Syed Ali, Abu Nazir and his retinue, smiling but watchful.

'Wait outside,' Salman whispered to Rashid as he emerged. 'Be ready. Maybe they call for something.'

Rashid, his toes still remembering the unfamiliar softness of the carpet, settled himself cross-legged outside the door and waited for further orders. From inside the guest house came the rattle of cups and the splash of poured coffee as Syed Ali served the sheikh.

There was silence as everyone sipped their drinks, then the sheikh cleared his throat.

'A very good day yesterday on the course. I've never seen such fine camels. Top speed forty miles per hour! Quite remarkable. Lovely to watch. My grandfather would have been proud and amazed to see it. And our young men so involved in the sport. Excellent to keep the tradition alive. Camel racing might have died out altogether, you know, if we hadn't brought it up to date.'

There were respectful murmurs from the room full of men.

'How many camels are you racing this year, Syed Ali?' the sheikh asked.

'Ten so far, Your Excellency.'

'And have you tried water exercises? We've found it very beneficial. We've constructed a special pool and walk the camels through it. The water reaches shoulder height. Very strengthening for the leg muscles.'

Rashid stopped listening. His Arabic still wasn't good enough to pick up more than the gist, and anyway the endless talk of camels bored him.

It's all grown-ups ever talk about, he thought. Camels, camels, camels.

He became aware that Salman was signalling to him from the kitchen and ran over to him. Salman put a pot of fresh coffee into his hands.

'Carry carefully, Yasser. Don't you drop it.'

Rashid carried the pot back to the guest house. He hesitated at the door, feeling shy of the roomful of important men, but Syed Ali had seen him and he had to go inside. Syed Ali took the coffee from him and nodded to dismiss him. Rashid returned to his post outside the door.

'How many boys do you keep?' the sheikh was asking.

Boys? That means us, Rashid thought.

He started listening more carefully.

'Four, sir.'

'All from Pakistan?'

'Yes, all of them.'

The sheikh sighed.

'You should see the problems in Pakistan! The poverty!'

What problems? thought Rashid, ready to be offended. What's poverty? There's nothing wrong with Pakistan.

'We've built roads, clinics, an airport over there,' the sheikh went on. 'And given work over here to thousands. Good paid work even for our little jockeys! What they earn is sometimes their families' only income.'

Rashid frowned, trying to understand.

Are they really paying for us? he wondered. Are they paying Ma? The idea made him feel proud, but angry too.

The sheikh sighed again.

'But the system isn't working. Too many injuries to the boys. Even deaths! You, Syed Ali, obviously take excellent care of your children. No accidents have befallen them, I'm sure.'

There was a moment's awkward silence, then Abu

Nazir said jerkily, 'Thank God, all our boys are safe and well.'

'Excellent!'

Rashid, his ears acutely tuned, detected the hint of a threat in sheikh's voice.

'As you all know,' the smooth voice continued, 'it's impossible to regulate everything. We've done our best! All of us want to win trophies. Why else would we race camels? But there's carelessness. I've seen it myself. The boys in some uzbas are not treated well, and it's causing a scandal. On an international scale. Stories are appearing in the foreign press. The government is very concerned about it.'

Rashid was frowning, trying to understand. In the guest house, no one was speaking. A few awkward coughs filled the silence.

'But as Your Excellency knows,' Abu Nazir said at last, 'camels must have jockeys, and the lighter the jockey the better the chance of winning. You said yourself, these boys are escaping from terrible poverty at home. Here they're housed and fed and their parents paid . . . Anyway, it does no harm to work them hard. Little monkeys, most of them are, up to mischief all the time. They take every advantage, given the chance.'

Rashid couldn't see Abu Nazir's face, but he could picture the impatient look on it.

He's saying bad things about us, he thought.

Monkey, I know what that means. He's a monkey, not us.

'Rogue elements! The need to avoid scandal!' The sheikh had ignored Abu Nazir's interruption. 'Unscrupulous traffickers! Illegal entry to Dubai! It's going on under our very noses. It's got to the point where the publicity is proving harmful to our reputation and our tourist industry.'

'But what are we to do, sir, if we can't race with little jockeys?' asked Syed Ali, sounding genuinely puzzled.

'Heavier jockeys will kill the sport,' Abu Nazir burst in, unable to conceal his anger. 'It'll make everything impossible!'

Rashid leaned forward and gripped his knees as he struggled to understand.

What was Syed Ali saying about no little jockeys? And who did Abu Nazir want to kill?

Daringly, he craned sideways so that he could peep round the doorpost into the guest room. The men leaning on the cushions round the walls were staring in respectful consternation at the sheikh, but he was looking pleased, as if he was about to spring a surprise.

'Robots,' he said.

At that moment, Abu Nazir looked up and caught sight of Rashid's curious face. He scowled. Rashid jerked back smartly out of sight. He saw a movement out of the corner of his eye. Salman was beckoning to him again. He ran across to the kitchen.

'No more you need to stay there. I watch out for them. Others rest time. You go play now.'

'What's a robot, Salman?'

'Robot? How you think I know? No Arab word.'

Rashid ran back to join the others. They had been kicking the ball about but they had flopped down in the shelter now and were playing with Iqbal's marbles.

'Are they going soon?' asked Puppo. 'I want my supper.'

'They're talking,' said Rashid. 'About camels, as usual. But about jockeys too. And a word like "robot". I didn't understand.'

'Robots? I know about them,' Amal said surprisingly. 'They were talking about robots in the hospital. They're machines. They can do stuff people do.'

'What, you mean like eat and sleep and talk?' said Iqbal.

'And play football?' gaped Puppo.

'No, silly. Work. They do the work so people don't have to.'

'It would be great if we had robots here, to clean up after the camels,' said Iqbal.

'And take them out for exercises,' said Rashid.

'And ride them in races,' said Amal. 'Robot camel jockeys. That would be the best.'

167

A little while later they heard car engines start up and ran out to watch the guests leave.

'Look at Haji,' whispered Iqbal. 'If he bows any lower, he'll bump his nose on his knees.'

The sheikh was saying courteous farewells at the door of his car, which his driver was respectfully holding open for him. He caught sight of the row of staring boys and said something to Syed Ali, who unwillingly beckoned them over.

Too scared to move, the boys stood still, looking sideways at each other.

'Come, come!' called Haji Faroukh, his smile of beaming benevolence at odds with the anxiety in his eyes.

The boys approached the sheikh, but didn't dare raise their eyes to his face. They stood in front of him, staring down at his feet.

'Are you happy here, boys? Well treated, eh?'

They nodded dumbly.

'And I'm sure you enjoy the racing?'

Images flashed through Rashid's mind: the screams of falling children, the little boy dragged along by the rope, the ghost of Mujib, the thirst and hunger and exhaustion. They rose like monsters inside him, wanting to burst from his mouth. But Abu Nazir, Syed Ali and Haji Faroukh were ranged behind the sheikh, and their eyes were sternly on him.

'Yes, sir,' he chorused with the others.

'And you hear from your people at home? They're making good use, I'm sure, of the money you earn.'

'What's home?' said Puppo, bewildered.

Most of the adults laughed, but the sheikh was frowning as he was driven away.

15

Race days now came with horrible frequency. The boys had been living already on the edge of hunger and exhaustion before the season began, but on race days they were pushed almost beyond what they could bear.

In his heart, though, Rashid knew that he felt different from the others. His dread of racing was mixed with excitement and, increasingly, with confidence. Puppo and Amal faced each event with only one aim – to stay mounted and avoid injury. They had no expectation of winning. Iqbal, though he hid it well, was also terribly afraid, but like Rashid he longed to win. When Iqbal and Rashid were pitted against each other in the same race, they competed fiercely, sometimes one pulling ahead, and sometimes the other.

The first time Rashid won a race, he felt a surge of joy. The race was an important one, the course crowded with the cars of camel owners and their guests. There were even foreign tourists watching at the starting point. The prize – a state-of-the-art brand-new Land Cruiser – was awarded to Syed Ali. Beaming with his camel's success, he handed Rashid a tip of 300 dirhams, and even Abu Nazir congratulated him, while Haji Faroukh patted him kindly on the back, and let him off the chore of watering the camels.

Rashid was afraid that Iqbal would be upset by all the attention he was receiving, but Iqbal shrugged it off.

'Who cares about winning races anyway?' he said. 'You grow out of that sort of thing. Anyway, you only won because you're lighter than me.'

Rashid nodded, understanding that there was more than there seemed behind Iqbal's words. Another shift was occurring. They were no longer hero and follower. He was Iqbal's equal now.

Apart from Syed Ali's camel-owning friends, the only other routine visitors to the uzba were the delivery men who came with supplies, and sometimes masouls from other uzbas, paying visits to Haji Faroukh.

Uncle Bilal had visited the uzba only one more time. Unfortunately, he had come on a race day, and Rashid had been out at the course. The person around had been one of the temporary hands.

'A man came to see you,' he told Rashid when the

boys returned, silent with fatigue at the end of the day. 'Said he was your uncle.'

Rashid had felt a brief flaring of joy, snuffed out by disappointment, but he had soon forgotten. Uncle Bilal belonged to another life, another world, which was disappearing now.

Late one afternoon, a visitor stood hesitating in the entrance. His eyes darted around the open, sandy compound, then he approached Salman, spreading out his hands pleadingly.

The boys, on their way to answer a summons from Haji Faroukh, ignored him, but then came a woman's piercing cry, a sound so rare and unexpected that they stopped in their tracks to turn and stare at the dishevelled creature who was running towards them.

I've seen her before, and the man, Rashid thought. At the race track. Looking for a boy.

'Puppo!' the woman was crying. 'My little Puppo!'

Her scarf was falling back off her hair. She reached the group of boys and slid to her knees in front of Puppo, holding out her arms. The man was running towards them too.

'It is! It's Ejaz!' he was gasping, looking at Puppo. 'Ejaz, don't you know me? I'm your father! I'm your pio!'

Puppo stepped back in alarm and hid behind Rashid, grabbing his shirt and holding it bunched in his fist.

The woman lurched forward, reaching for him.

'Puppo, it's Ma! I'm your ma! We've found you at last! Come here, darling. Don't be afraid of me.'

But Puppo only edged further behind Rashid, clinging to him more tightly than ever.

Heavy footsteps approached.

'What's this?' Haji Faroukh said sternly. 'Who are you?'

The man had been circling behind Rashid, about to prise Puppo away, but he started, and as he turned to face the older, heavier man, Rashid saw that he was blinking rapidly, and was staring up at Haji Faroukh with frightened, pleading eyes.

'This is our son, sir,' he said. 'We've been hunting for him everywhere.'

The woman was trying to touch Puppo and draw him into a hug, but he turned away from her, smacking at her hand.

Haji Faroukh's eyes narrowed.

'What do you mean, he's your son? Anyone can come in here and—'

'Ejaz, his name's Ejaz,' the man interrupted eagerly. 'Mohammed Ejaz Rasoul.'

'No he isn't,' Iqbal declared. 'He's Puppo.'

'His baby name,' the man said. 'Look, his mother knows. That's what she calls him. It's what we called him at home.'

'This boy's official name is certainly not Ejaz,' Haji Faroukh said coldly. 'You're troublemakers. Get out of here before I throw you out.'

'No, no, sir, please, listen!' The man was almost weeping with distress. 'The agent gave him another name, for the passport. We only heard later. He wouldn't even tell us what it was. He cheated us! Everything he said was lies! We didn't know he was going to do this kind of work. This is our son, sir. Can't you tell? Look at him!'

'Puppo, come here,' barked Haji Faroukh.

Trained to obey that voice, Puppo edged reluctantly out from behind Rashid.

'Do you know these people?' demanded Haji Faroukh. 'Are they your mother and father?'

His tone told Puppo the answer he was supposed to give. He didn't even look up.

'No, Haji,' he whispered.

'What's your game?' Haji Faroukh snarled, turning on the couple. 'You get hold of boys, do you? Sell them on? I've heard of people like you.'

'No, no, we're not like that!' Tears were choking the woman's voice. 'We only want our son. Look at him. His eyes! The cleft in his chin – just like his father's. Lift your shirt up, Puppo. Show the gentleman the spot on your shoulder you had when you were born. And the scar above the elbow where you burned yourself on the teapot. Show him, darling, for Ma. Lift your shirt!'

Puppo gave her a fleeting glance and stubbornly shook his head.

'He was only a baby – two years old. How could

174

he remember us? We've spent everything we had, everything we were paid for him working here.' The man tried to take Haji Faroukh by the sleeve, but was roughly shaken off. 'We heard such stories, about what the boys are made to do here. We've been hunting and hunting. Think, sir, if he was your son!'

A car had arrived and Abu Nazir was getting out of it.

'Trouble, Faroukh?' he asked the masoul. 'Who are these people?'

'They're no one, sir. I can deal with it.' He turned to the man and raised a threatening hand. 'Get out of here before I have you arrested.'

Frightened, the man backed away. He hauled the woman to her feet.

'What have you done to my son?' she shouted. 'Look at him! He's a little skeleton! You've starved him!'

She was shaking with distress.

Abu Nazir took a step towards her. The man grabbed her arm and dragged her away.

'He didn't even recognize me!' she was wailing as she let herself be drawn away. 'My Puppo! He doesn't know who I am!'

The boys stood in shocked silence as the sound of her crying died away.

'You know those people?' Abu Nazir said to Haji Faroukh, frowning.

'Never seen them before, sir. They claim to be

Puppo's parents. All nonsense. Didn't even know his name.'

But Rashid saw doubt in his eyes and heard it in his voice.

I bet he is that woman's son, he thought. Ejaz, or whatever they called him. It'll be his real name, like mine's Rashid.

He became aware that Puppo was crying, not bawling, like he did when he was angry, but weeping silently, big tears rolling down his thin cheeks.

'I haven't . . . I don't . . .' he was trying to say.

'Forget those people, Puppo,' Haji Faroukh said, glancing sideways at Abu Nazir. 'They're not your parents. Get on with your work, now.'

When the chores were done, the four children walked silently back to the shelter and flopped down on the sand.

'Show me your elbows, Puppo,' Iqbal said suddenly.

Puppo stuck his arms out. Iqbal took hold of them and twisted them round, looking closely.

'There! Look! A scar! What happened, Puppo? How did you get this?'

'She said he burned it on a teapot,' said Amal.

'Did you?' demanded Iqbal. 'It must have hurt a lot. You can't have forgotten that.'

Puppo shook his head.

'Don't you remember anything? Didn't you recognize her at all?'

'My ma had long hair,' Puppo said, squeezing his

eyes shut. 'I don't know anything else. She tickled me with it.'

'Yeah, but was that her, the woman who came?' Iqbal asked impatiently.

Puppo put his hands over his ears and began one of his meaningless chants.

'Leave him alone,' Amal said. 'He doesn't remember. That's it. You don't remember stuff from when you were a baby.'

They all stared at Puppo, nonplussed.

'She said about a spot too. On his shoulder,' Rashid said.

They wrenched Puppo's shirt up, exposing his back. Puppo opened his eyes, unclamped his ears and tried to shake them off.

'It's all right, Puppo. Don't worry,' Rashid said kindly. 'We just want to look.'

Puppo looked at him, his eyes trusting, and put his thumb in his mouth.

Amal and Iqbal were leaning forward, examining Puppo's back.

'Look there. A spot! She was right,' said Amal, dropping the shirt.

Iqbal sat back on his heels and looked dispassionately at Puppo.

'They were your ma and pio then, those two. Pity you didn't recognize them, Puppo. They might have taken you home.'

'I don't know home,' said Puppo, taking his thumb

out of his mouth with a plop. 'Do they make you ride camel races there?'

'No!' said Rashid, putting his arm round Puppo's shoulders. 'You go and live in a house in Pakistan, and you don't ever have to ride a camel again. They look after you. It's nice.'

'Can you come, Yasser? I don't want to go without you.'

Rashid remembered how he'd asked Bilal to take Iqbal, when he'd thought that Bilal was going to rescue him. He was older now, and wiser.

'I can't, Puppo, but I'll see you later, when I get home to Pakistan too. If they come again, your ma and pio, you've got to say you know them. You've got let them take you.'

'There was a cat,' Puppo said suddenly. 'It sat on the wall.'

'Where? What wall?'

'I don't know.

'You know what, Puppo,' Iqbal said, 'you were really lucky, your parents coming to find you like that. Pity they had to leave you here.'

His remark hung heavily in the air.

'Where's the football?' he said at last. 'Aren't you lot coming to play?'

During the scorching months of summer, when Rashid had first come to Dubai, no cloud had ever crossed the sky. Now, during the slightly cooler months of winter, the sky was occasionally masked with cloud and, even more rarely, showers of rain swept in from the sea.

After an evening of rare and refreshing rain, the boys were deeply asleep in their hut. It was shortly after midnight, and there were still four hours to go before they would have to get up and take the camels out for exercise. Rashid was so used to being woken out of a deep sleep, that when a man crept into the sleeping shed and shook him, he sat up unprotestingly and reached out automatically for his sweater.

'Not you. I want Ejaz – Puppo,' the man whispered. 'I've come for Puppo.'

His head muzzy, Rashid struggled to understand.

'I'm Puppo's father. I've come to get him. Isn't he in with you?'

'Here. Beside me,' Rashid said thickly.

'Shh! Please don't make a noise. I can't see, it's so dark in here. Can you wake him for me?'

Rashid woke up properly, with a jolt, and understood in an instant.

'You really are his father, aren't you?' he whispered. 'You came with his ma that time. To the race course.'

'Yes.'

Rashid turned over and shook Puppo, who was curled up beside him. Puppo, still asleep, sat up uncomplainingly, fumbling for his sweater.

'Puppo,' Rashid whispered. 'Wake up. It's your pio. He's come to take you.'

'Come, darling,' the man said, reaching down to feel for his son, then gathering him up into his arms.

Rashid could tell that Puppo was frightened. He was struggling to free himself, about to protest loudly.

'Puppo, listen,' Rashid said earnestly. 'This is your real, real pio. You've got to go with him. Don't make a noise, or – or – Haji Faroukh will come and beat you.'

Only a threat, he knew, would work. He was right. Puppo, though rigid in the man's arms, was still. The moon had been covered with cloud, but suddenly it came out, and in the shaft of light which shone in through the shed door, Rashid could see the glint of Puppo's huge round eyes.

'Come with me, Yasser,' he said in a loud whisper. 'I think he's your pio too.'

'No.' Rashid suddenly felt awful, knowing that he was sending Puppo away. 'He's yours, not mine. Go on. I'll see you one day. I promise.'

The man was already at the door of the shed, looking up at the sky, waiting for the silver-fringed bank of cloud to cover the moon again. As soon as the white light dimmed, he took off, running across the empty sand towards the uzba entrance.

It had happened so quickly that Rashid felt shocked, unable to take in that Puppo had gone, so suddenly, from one moment to the next. His feet were still tangled in his blanket. He shook them free and ran outside.

It had really happened. He hadn't dreamed it. He could hear, through the silence of the desert night, a woman's glad cry, and then the slam of car doors closing and the sound of an engine starting up.

The moon was out again, bathing the uzba in a cold, clear light. A movement from the far corner by the fence caught his eye. He turned and saw that Haji Faroukh was standing motionless in the doorway of his house, his hand on the latch.

He saw it happen! He saw them take Puppo away, Rashid thought. Why didn't he stop them?

Haji Faroukh, as if afraid of being seen, melted back from his doorway into the darkness.

It was cold out in the open. Rashid shivered and crept back into the shed. He lay down. The mattress next to him was still warm where Puppo had been sleeping. He gathered up Puppo's blanket and held it in his arms. A few minutes later, he was asleep again.

A tempest of fury swept across the uzba four hours later when Puppo's disappearance was discovered. The three remaining children, woken before four o'clock, as usual, for the camels' nightly exercise routine, blundered heavy-eyed and shivering into the darkness and stumbled across towards the camel pen. To Rashid, who was still more than half asleep, the spectacular events of the night had wavered out of reality into a kind of dream. He hardly heard Haji

Faroukh bark, 'Where's Puppo? Iqbal, go and wake him up. If he makes us wait, he knows what he'll get.'

Iqbal, rubbing his eyes and yawning, went back to the sleeping shed and returned a moment later.

'He's not there, Haji.'

'What do you mean, he's not there? He's rolled into a corner. Go and look again.'

Rashid was suddenly fully awake.

Puppo's gone, he thought, with a surge of excitement. And Haji Faroukh knows it. He's just pretending to look for him.

Iqbal came back.

'I really, really looked, Haji. He isn't there.' He was looking fearfully at the masoul, afraid of his anger.

'Salman!' Haji Faroukh roared suddenly, making the three boys jump. 'You lazy slob, where are you when you're needed?'

Salman staggered out of the kitchen, where he had been sleeping on a mat on the floor, his hair standing up all over his head in uncombed knots.

'Where's Puppo?' demanded Haji Faroukh.

'Puppo?' repeated Salman, stupid with sleep.

No one said anything for a moment.

'Search the uzba!' commanded Haji Faroukh. 'The little monkey's playing a trick on us. Look everywhere!'

Rashid couldn't hide his smile as he joined in the hunt.

'Listen, Iqbal,' he said softly, as they crawled under

a feeding trough in the old, empty camel pen by the back fence, making a diligent show of searching. 'Puppo's pio came last night. He took Puppo away. I saw him.'

'*What?*'

'Shh.' Rashid was proud of the sensation he had caused. 'Don't tell. I'll get into trouble if you say. Haji Faroukh knows though. I saw him. He was watching them go. He didn't stop them.'

They had stopped moving. Still on their hands and knees, they peered at each other through the darkness.

'What do you mean, he let them go? Why?'

'I don't know.'

'You mean Puppo's gone? He's really gone? He's not coming back?'

'I don't think so. They took him in a car. I heard it.'

He tried to read Iqbal's expression, but it was too dark to see.

'Don't say I told you, Iqbal. Don't say I saw them go.'

'Course I won't. What do you take me for?'

'Are you sorry Puppo's gone?'

'Who me? Why should I be?'

Iqbal spoke lightly, his tone careless, and Rashid sensed, without being able to put the thought into words, that the shell, which had formed long ago round Iqbal's lonely heart, was adding another layer of hardness.

'Come back here, you little devils!' Haji Faroukh was yelling from the camel pen. 'You're not looking! You're skiving off!'

Rashid and Iqbal scrambled backwards out from under the trough and ran back to him.

'Puppo or no Puppo, these camels must be exercised,' Haji Faroukh blustered. 'The little imp's run off somewhere. He can't be far away, and when he gets back here I'll see he knows all about it. Saddle up! Iqbal, you ride Lashmi and lead Duda and Nanga. Amal, you ride Soudani and lead . . .'

His instructions went on. Automatically, the boys obeyed, and the miserable routine clicked into place but Rashid could tell that the other two, and even Salman, were alive with excitement. He noticed, too, that Haji Faroukh was trying to avoid catching his eye.

Lucky you, Puppo, he thought as he went through the familiar motions, riding out after the others at the start of the long, cold, dreary hours of exercise. I wish I had a father who could come and find me.

16

Weeks had passed since Puppo's sudden disappearance. The fuss had gone on for days and Rashid had half expected to see Puppo come trotting back into the uzba, cowering in advance from the beating he would get. His parents had seemed too thin and poor, too ragged and weak, to carry off such a snatch successfully, winning against the formidable Haji Faroukh, and outwitting the combined might of Syed Ali and Abu Nazir.

But Puppo didn't come back, and as the days went by no one expected his return any longer.

The boys speculated on what had happened to him.

'I bet they caught him and they're all in prison,' Amal said gloomily.

'No.' Iqbal tapped a dog-eared playing card authoritavely against his chin. 'They'd only have put his ma and pio inside. They'd have sent Puppo back here if they'd caught him.'

'I think they got away. I think they've all gone

home,' Rashid said enviously. 'He'll be in Pakistan right now, just playing around and having lots to eat.'

'That's all you know,' Iqbal said roughly. 'Why do you think they sent him here if they had lots to eat? I'm sick of talking about Puppo, anyway. He was a silly baby, that's all. I'm glad he's gone.'

'You're not really,' Amal said softly, but though Iqbal turned on him angrily, he wouldn't say more, but lay down, resting his head on his crooked arm, and shut his eyes.

Rashid missed Puppo all the time. He'd been like Shari. He'd been *instead* of Shari, a little brother to protect, and impress, and boss around. In return, Puppo had given Rashid his dog-like devotion, and although this had sometimes been irritating, it had warmed Rashid too.

He loved me more than Shari did, he thought. He didn't answer back all the time, and fight me, like Shari did.

And yet, now that Puppo had gone, Rashid thought about Shari more and more, and worried about him. They had met again once or twice, on race days, but Shari, being younger and lighter, usually rode smaller camels in races where the jockeys were little more than toddlers, and feather-light. When they did meet, Shari had been confused and distressed, with a fresh crop of bruises and welts to show Rashid. This was so upsetting that Rashid was almost glad when he wasn't there, though his relief made him feel guilty too.

As the racing season progressed, Rashid's riding became more skilful, and his wins more frequent.

'The boy's got a flair for it,' he overheard Syed Ali say to Abu Nazir, as they stood admiring the dazzling new car that Rashid had just won for them in a race of fifty top-class camels.

Abu Nazir nodded.

'Have you decided yet about Abu Dhabi next week? Are you entering for it? I think Yasser's up to it.'

'After a win like this, I should think he's up for anything!' Syed Ali said, patting his new car with satisfaction. 'You'd better arrange the transport, cousin. Sort it out with Faroukh.'

In spite of the weariness that dogged him at the end of such a sweltering, gruelling day, Rashid felt a spurt of triumph and excitement. He was good, he knew. He was the best. He'd proved it.

'Where's Abu Dhabi?' he asked Salman. 'What's it like?'

'Abu Dhabi? Is not far. Is same as Dubai.' Salman flicked the questions away with a shake of his head.

'Did you get a tip? How much?' Amal asked when the three boys were resting together again.

'Two hundred dirhams. Syed Ali made me give it to Haji Faroukh to look after,' Rashid said, looking sideways at Iqbal. He had learned not to crow about his victories. Iqbal kept up a pretence of not caring, but he would snap irritably, and say hurtful things after one of Rashid's big wins.

The first Rashid knew about the expedition to Abu Dhabi was the arrival of an open-backed truck just after sunrise. It was a race day, so there had been no night-exercise session, and the boys had had a few blessed hours of extra sleep. They watched the truck as it reversed into the uzba and backed against the high flat end of a ramp near the entrance. The driver climbed out and let the back flap down, creating a walkway from the top of the ramp across to the truck.

Haji Faroukh hurried to meet him with a polite greeting.

'Off to Abu Dhabi today, aren't you?' Rashid heard the driver ask. 'How many camels?'

'Four,' answered Haji Faroukh, measuring with his eyes the space in the truck. 'There's room back here?'

'Easily. I've taken four often. Yours are quiet ones, I hope?'

'One's a bit restive. Khamri. But the boys will travel in the back with her and keep her quiet.'

Boys! One of them must be me! Rashid thought. Who's the other?

'Are your camels used to getting into a truck?' asked the driver. 'The nervous ones will only go on if they have another one they can follow.'

Haji Faroukh frowned magisterially.

'You think I don't know that? Twenty years I've been in this job.'

He shouted an order. Salman appeared, leading Hamlul on a tight rein, with Soudani following close behind. Hamlul strolled peacefully up the ramp and into the truck. Soudani fidgeted nervously, trampling sideways. Haji Faroukh ran to his head and brought him round, deftly avoiding a kick, coaxed him successfully into the truck, and bent his front leg at the knee, forcing him to kneel. Then he tied his back legs together, immobilizing him. Salman was already leading Hamlul back down again.

One of the hired hands was watching.

'Stupid beasts, camels,' Rashid heard him say contemptuously. 'Don't have the wit to do anything unless they can copy another one doing it first.'

Rashid watched as Hamlul led first Shahin, then Khamri on to the truck. It was these four he would have to ride today. Hamlul, his favourite, was easy enough, though hard to whip to a win. Shahin, nervous and unpredictable, was easily spooked. He hated riding her. Mujib had been riding Shahin, Amal had told him, when he'd fallen to his death. Rashid shuddered every time he looked at her. Soudani was all right, he supposed. And then there was Khamri. He'd got the measure of her now. As long as someone else saddled her and took her muzzle off, and as long as she was handled calmly into the starting pen, he knew he could ride her well. He'd ridden Khamri to

189

victory before and he could do it again whatever the competition.

Syed Ali had arrived and was watching as the tail board was raised.

'Ready to go?' he asked Haji Faroukh anxiously. 'You followed my instructions this morning? They've had nothing to eat or drink?'

Rashid could see, by the compression of Haji Faroukh's lips, that he was becoming irritated.

'Of course, sir. I know what to do.'

'Good man. Where's the boy?'

'Yasser!' Haji Faroukh called out. 'Get in the back with Salman and the camels!'

Salman had already climbed up and into the truck. He leaned down to give Rashid a hand up.

'You have the boy's whip, helmet, harness, radio?' fussed Syed Ali.

Haji Faroukh picked up the bundle he'd laid by the ramp.

'All here.'

'Good. I'll lead the way. Let's get going, for heaven's sake. The traffic will be building up already.'

Haji Faroukh didn't deign to answer. He had already climbed into the front passenger seat, and let out his feelings by shutting the door with a slam.

It was a couple of hours drive to the race course in Abu Dhabi and there was no shade in the back of the truck. Rashid had been allowed only half a chapatti and a cup of water for breakfast. He knew he could expect no more until the racing was over, late in the afternoon. He knew not to think about it. It would only make things worse.

The camels had settled down to the journey with surprising patience. Once kneeling, they had relaxed and began to chew the cud, their long-lashed eyes fixed on nothing.

'One day, when I am big masoul, I learn to drive truck like this one,' Salman announced out of the blue.

'I'm going to be a motor mechanic,' Rashid said. 'I like cars and stuff too.'

Salman shook his head.

'Mechanic no good. Masoul good job. Nice salary. Haji Faroukh, he got plenty money.'

Rashid thought about this. Haji Faroukh didn't seem rich to him.

'He send all his money to Pakistan,' Salman went on, 'to his wife and kids. Kids going to school. Nice clothes, house, everything. His wife, she came last year to visit. End of racing season, Haji go nice holiday to Pakistan.'

Rashid said nothing, digesting this new information. He couldn't imagine Haji Faroukh being married, or with children of his own.

'I bet he's kind to his kids,' he said at last. 'I bet he doesn't beat them with a plastic hose.'

Salman shrugged.

'Haji not bad. You see some of the others. Worse than him. Is not so easy, to be a masoul. You find that out, Yasser, when you a masoul yourself.'

'I told you. I'm not going to be a masoul. I'm going to be a mechanic, back home, in Pakistan.'

Salman snorted.

'You think you can choose? You here now, Yasser. Your life is here. Make the best of it. Like me.'

Rashid shivered in spite of the heat.

I'm not like you, he thought. I'm not going to get stuck here. I'm going home.

They had slowed down, held up by the increasing traffic. A long line of SUVs and camel trucks was heading for the race course. Its long white buildings lay along the flat horizon, shimmering in the haze.

Rashid shivered again, but from nerves this time. Today was really important. The races were big ones. There'd be hundreds of camels competing and dozens and dozens of jockeys, who he didn't know at all.

He didn't like the idea of a strange course. What if the starting barrier was a different kind here, and he misjudged the way it went up? What if the turns of the course were sharper, and the camels jostled too closely together as they ran round them? And who would he talk to in the breaks? The other boys might all have friends. They mightn't let him join in with them.

The truck entered an enclosure and backed up to

the unloading ramp. Haji Faroukh climbed out of the passenger seat and hurried round to the back.

'Any problems?'

'No, Haji,' Salman said, looking serious and responsible. 'Khamri even quiet all the way.'

Rashid wasn't listening. He was looking out across the huge mass of vehicles, picking out the hundreds of little boys who were standing in knots, talking to each other, or running to greet newcomers.

There might be someone I know, he told himself, but he couldn't see anyone.

'Get down from there, Yasser,' Haji Faroukh said.

Rashid climbed over the side of the truck and slid to the ground. He stood beside it, feeling shy. Then he saw Syed Ali walking towards him with Abu Nazir beside him.

'All well?'

Syed Ali ran an eye over the camels, then put a hand on Rashid's shoulder.

'I'm counting on you, young man. I'm up for the golden sword today, if we do well. There'll be a tip for you too, if you pull it off.' He turned to Haji Faroukh. 'You know how much last year's winner in yesterday's final was sold for? Four hundred thousand dollars! If Khamri wins the big one, that's the kind of money we're looking at.'

Haji Faroukh was up in the truck, bending over to untie the ropes that were binding the camels' legs, but he raised his head with a jerk.

'You'll sell Khamri if she wins?'

His expression was impossible to read.

'Yes, of course. If I get a good offer.'

Haji Faroukh didn't answer him, but shouted to Rashid, 'Fetch your helmet and your stuff from the front. The first race is starting soon.'

As the day wore on, Rashid realized that there was nothing special about this race course or race day. The desert all around was the same here as in Dubai – hot, empty and dry. The race course was as long, the barriers as hard, the sand as churned up. The camel owners wore the same clothes, drove the same kinds of cars, and talked the same talk on and on, comparing camel speeds and camel prices, camel diets and camel treatments, camel-training programmes and camel-racing rules. Several times, though, as he waited wearily in the enclosure for a race to start, he heard the word 'robot' again, and wondered idly what it meant.

He was glad that Hamlul was the first runner of the day. With her placid temper and easy stride, he had a chance to settle down and get to know the course. He brought her in at a respectable eighth place out of forty.

Soudani came next. No one expected too much of him. Young and inexperienced, he was unpredictable and easily distracted. He took a savage bite at another young male as the camels lined up at the start, nearly starting a rumpus. Salman had to dart in through the throng of nervous animals, risking a kick or worse, to jerk Soudani's head round and prevent a catastrophe. Unsettled, Rashid bodged the start of the race and, in spite of near hysterical curses from Abu Nazir, he finished badly, earning a savage tirade when the race was over, and a painful smack over the head.

Shahin's race, though, was the hardest. By the afternoon, the numbers of SUVs roaring round the track alongside the camels had multiplied to an army. Each one was crammed with spectators, and others clung to the outsides, standing on the tailboards and hanging on to the roofs. Horns blared, men yelled, radios crackled and the racket spooked Shahin, who veered sideways, almost crashing into the rails, then tried to turn and bolt back to the starting line. Only strenuous whipping brought her round and set her running in the right direction. To Rashid's surprise, she then put on a violent spurt, streaking forward down the straight, overtaking one camel after another. The messy start had lost her all hope of winning, but she had done well, and Syed Ali praised Rashid when at last he slid off her back, trembling and sweating from the fear and strain of it.

'She's shaping up,' he heard Syed Ali say to Abu Nazir. 'I didn't know she had it in her. Our number-one winner next season, if she goes on like this.'

By the last race of the day, Rashid's head felt as heavy as a stone, while his legs seemed to drag as he walked. He barely heard Syed Ali's excited instructions as he climbed wearily on to Khamri's back and rode her to the starting line.

The barrier seemed to swim in front of his eyes.

I don't care if I hit it, he thought. I don't care if it breaks my neck. What does it matter anyway if I die?

The starting gun sounded. The barrier shot up. He was under it, and off. He lifted his whip, and at that moment Khamri slipped and skidded in the sand, her back legs splaying outwards so that Rashid had to struggle to keep his balance and prevent himself from falling backwards over her tail. There was a scream behind him as another camel, out of control, skidded into Khamri's rear. Rashid, regaining control, looked round and saw the little jockey hurtle off into the air, hit another camel, then crash to the ground and lie still.

A tide of red anger rose up in Rashid's head, almost blinding him.

'I hate you! I hate you!' he shouted, beating Khamri's rump with demented strength.

Khamri, galvanized by the impact, set off and begin to run like the wind.

'I hate you, hate you, hate you! You stink, stink, stink!' screamed Rashid, marking every word with a blow from his whip.

Tears were streaming from his eyes. Hatred boiled in his heart. And yet, through his passionate rage, he knew that they were running as they'd never run before, that they were flying, leaving one camel after another in their wake, and that Khamri was winning, that he was going to win.

17

Rashid was half dead with exhaustion after the race. He swayed on Khamri's back, not caring if he fell. He didn't even have the energy to dismount, and had to be lifted down by Haji Faroukh, who held him for a moment in his arms. It was almost, Rashid thought with wonder, as if he was being hugged. For a breathtaking moment he remembered Pio's arms round him, and had a sudden urge to fling his own round Haji Faroukh's stout neck, and burst into tears, but Haji Faroukh had already set him down on his feet, and called to Salman to bring him water. With the bottle to his lips, Rashid sank down to sit on the ground, leaning his back against Hamlul's soft side as he placidly chewed the cud.

He knew nothing of the celebrations, the presentation of the golden sword or the fuss that everyone was making of Syed Ali, and he barely heard Khamri's groans as Haji Faroukh led her away. His head ached.

He felt dizzy. He was almost too hungry to bear the thought of eating.

'Here, Yasser. I bring for you.' Salman was squatting beside him, pushing a candy bar into his hand. 'No tell I give you sweets, all right?'

Rashid lifted the bar to his mouth and bit into it. The heavenly taste flooded through him, bringing him to life.

'Is there more water, Salman?' he croaked.

The second bottle made him feel even better.

'Are we going back now?' he said, seeing that the holding pen was already half empty, and that the few remaining masouls were making their camels rise, and leading them away.

'Soon,' said Salman, taking the crumpled wrapper of the candy bar away from him and shoving it deep into his pocket. 'You don't know what happen? The sheikh send a message. He want to buy Khamri. Maybe he take you too.'

'Me? What do you mean, take me?' Shocked, Rashid sat up with a jerk. 'You mean to his uzba? To stay there?'

Salman laughed at his horrified expression.

'Not to worry, Yasser. Syed Ali not let you go, I don't think. You very good for riding camels. Sheikh has too many jockeys already. He not need any more.'

Rashid subsided again against Hamlul's flank.

'Is that why Haji took Khamri away? To sell her? She's gone already?'

Salman nodded.

'If Syed Ali satisfy with the price.'

Yes! Rashid thought jubilantly. I'll never have to ride that monster again.

Haji Faroukh came back into the holding pen.

'That's it. It's over. Khamri's gone,' he said to Salman. 'Get the others up. Get them going. Let's get on home.'

He jerked Shahin's bridle to make her rise. Soudani and Hamlul rose too. Rashid automatically put out his hand to take Hamlul's leading rein, ready to walk her back to the loading ramp, but Haji Faroukh took it from him.

'Syed Ali wants you,' he said. 'In the car park. Go and find him.'

Rashid's heart leaped sickeningly.

'He's not – he hasn't – I'm not going to the Sheikh's uzba?' he stammered.

Haji Faroukh rolled his eyes.

'What put such a daft idea into your head?' He took off the little gold embroidered cap he always wore on race day, and ran his fingers over his thick black hair. 'I've had that camel since she was a calf. Trained her. Nursed her. Groomed her. Not a word of—' He broke off, aware that Salman and Rashid were staring at him open-mouthed, frowned and slapped his cap back on his head again.

'What are you still doing here?' he growled at Rashid. 'Do you want to make them wait forever?'

In the car park, Syed Ali and Abu Nazir were in the centre of a crowd of admirers, both of them smiling with delight. A long jeweller's case lay on the hood of Syed Ali's white SUV. The lid was open, and Rashid caught the yellow gleam of the golden sword, lying on a bed of scarlet velvet.

He hung back, feeling shy. Abu Nazir saw him.

'Get into the car,' he said, with a jerk of his head, and turned back to talk to the others.

Rashid slipped on to the back seat of the car and rested gingerly against the soft leather, afraid of dirtying it. The driver, slouching behind the steering wheel, didn't bother to turn round. He was leaning forward, fiddling with the knobs of the radio. He found the station he wanted, and sat back, listening to a stream of Arabic.

Rashid's stomach was curdling with fright.

Haji Faroukh was lying to me, he told himself. They *are* going to sell me. To the sheikh. Why else would they have called for me? I won't see Iqbal and Amal ever again. Uncle Bilal won't know where I am. I'll be miles away from Shari. The sheikh's masoul might be horrible, and beat everyone all the time, like Shari's does.

He was in a fever pitch of worry by the time the group of men outside had dispersed. Syed Ali snapped the catches of the sword case shut, and brought it round to the far side of the car, laying it reverently on the back seat beside Rashid. Then he climbed into the front, lowered the window and called out a farewell to Abu Nazir, who was getting into his own car. They both laughed. Syed Ali pulled his head in and nodded to his driver, who started the engine.

They're planning it, Rashid thought. They're going to take me to the sheikh now.

Syed Ali looked over his shoulder at Rashid.

'I was going to take you back to the uzba, Yasser,' he said casually, 'but you know what? I'll take you home with me instead. I told my son about my champion jockey. He wants to meet you.' He reached back and slapped a delighted hand down on Rashid's knee. 'I couldn't believe the speed you got out of Khamri in that last race. Amazing!'

'How much did the sheikh give for her, sir?' asked the driver.

'You'll never believe it. Half a million dirhams, on top of the golden sword!' He turned back to Rashid. 'You'll do the same with Shahin next season, I'm sure of it. That's another winner in the making, I can tell.'

Rashid understood enough to know that he was not, after all, being sold to the sheikh's uzba. He took in a deep breath of relief.

'Your house, sir? I go your house now?' he asked, in his halting Arabic.

'Yes! I told you! You can see Abdullah – my son, tonight. I'll get you back to the uzba tomorrow.'

The radio was still on. Syed Ali leaned forward to turn up the volume. Rashid recognized the excited voice of a race commentator. The driver and Syed Ali were listening hard now, and when the race was over, they began to discuss the result. Rashid didn't bother to listen to them. He looked unseeingly out of the window. The long straight road ran on and on through the desert, sand whirling over its black tarmac surface. Along the seafront, to the left, endless rows of high-rise apartment blocks pointed to the sky, like the fingers of raised hands.

A lifetime ago, when he'd first come to Dubai, when he'd been a different person, he'd been in a car like this, expecting to go to a grand house, and live there, and play with a rich man's son. Was it going to happen at last? Or was this going to turn out badly too, another trick, the start of an awful new life, worse even than being a camel jockey?

At last, they reached the outskirts of Dubai. The car pulled off the busy main road and began to work its way through the city streets. Rashid sat up with his nose pressed against the window, staring with awe at the bright shop fronts and stream of vehicles, the women in skimpy western clothes, the glass-fronted office blocks and porticoes of grand hotels.

Syed Ali's house was in a quieter area of town. The driver stopped outside a pair of high metal gates, which swung open at the sound of his horn. Rashid barely had time to take in the big white house, the pink stone terrace, the bright green lawn and the glossy-leaved palm trees ranged in a row along the high white garden wall, before a boy came hurtling down the marble steps.

'Aba!' he was shouting. 'Have you got it with you? Can I see the golden sword?'

A little girl in a pink frilly dress and shiny white shoes was running after him. Syed Ali jumped out of the car and swung her up into his arms.

'Yes! It's in the case. On the back seat. Bring it inside.'

The boy wrenched open the car door and saw Rashid. He took a step back. His father laughed at his surprise.

'That's Yasser, the jockey. Take him to the kitchen, Abdullah. Tell them to give him something to eat.'

Shyly, Rashid stepped down from the car. The two boys stared at each other for a moment, then Abdullah reached past Rashid and reverently picked up the sword case.

'Here, give it to me,' said Syed Ali, putting his daughter down. 'You might drop it.'

He went into the house with the children running after him. It was getting dark now, and from the open door light streamed out into the garden. It disappeared as the door swung shut.

Rashid didn't know what to do. He looked towards the driver, who had lifted the car's bonnet and was poking about inside the engine.

'Go on in,' the driver said. 'They won't eat you. Anyway, you can't go wrong today.'

Rashid walked slowly up the steps, his face hot with embarrassment. He put his hand out to pull the door handle, but as he did so someone pushed the door open, nearly knocking him over.

'What are you hanging about out there for?' demanded Abdullah, turning round and going back in. His heart in his mouth, Rashid followed him.

It was cool, almost cold, inside the house. A vast expanse of shiny white marble floor lay ahead. Rashid followed Abdullah down a short corridor, which opened out into a huge spacious room. To the left was a long white table with eight white chairs drawn up to it. To the right were cream coloured sofas and armchairs. Lamps on little tables cast circles of warm yellow light. In the middle of the room, a fountain played, the water splashing down on to coloured pebbles in a pool.

Paralysed with shyness, Rashid stood motionless, not knowing where to look or what to do.

A woman came out of a door at the far end of the room. Her carefully plucked eyebrows rose in surprise at the sight of Rashid.

'Who's this?' she said.

'It's Aba's jockey, Mama,' Abdullah said. 'Have you seen the golden sword? It's brilliant!'

The woman looked briefly at Rashid.

'He should be in the kitchen. He looks half starved.'

The little girl, who had been kneeling up to one of

the sofas, playing with a doll, suddenly wailed in frustration.

'Sweetie, what is it?' the woman said, and the little girl held up the tiny spangled dress that she had been unsuccessfully trying to force over the doll's head.

'You're not hungry are you, Yasser?' Abdullah said carelessly. 'I'm not. I've had my supper. Let's go and play.'

The kitchen door swung open and through it came a smell so delicious that Rashid almost thought he would faint. A man appeared, an apron stretched over his comfortable stomach. He beckoned to Rashid.

'I not – eat – today,' Rashid found the courage to say to Abdullah, leaving him to follow the irresistable summons of the cook.

The meal that was set in front of him on the kitchen table was the most sumptuous he had ever eaten. There were lamb meatballs in a rich tomato sauce, rice glistening with butter and studded with pine kernels, stuffed vine leaves, a stew of aubergines and beans and flaps of bread still warm from the oven. The cook laid a plate out with a spoon and fork.

'Are you from Pakistan?' He spoke in Punjabi, with the accent of home.

'Yes!' Rashid nodded, relieved. He had found an ally, then, in this strange place.

'Proper little champion, aren't you?' The man was spooning out the rice. 'The driver was telling me. Rode like a demon, he said.'

Rashid sat down and picked up the spoon. He scooped up a meatball and put it in his mouth, but he wasn't used to eating with cutlery and the sauce dribbled down his chin. The cook was watching.

'You don't have to use the spoon. Eat with your fingers.'

Rashid ate as fast as he could, cramming the food into his mouth as if he was afraid that it would be snatched away.

'Here, go easy. You're not in a race now. Make yourself sick, you will, if you gobble it all down like that.'

Rashid sat back at last, his eyes glazed with satisfaction. The cook handed him a glass of Pepsi. He drank deeply, gulping the unfamiliar sweet, bubbly liquid down and handed back the empty glass.

Then his smile wavered. He felt horribly ill. His stomach heaved as the gaseous drink met the unaccustomed richness of the food. Beads of sweat sprouted from his forehead and he gripped the edge of the table. Then, just when he was afraid that he was going to throw up the whole delicious meal, the wind burst up from his stomach and out of his mouth in a violent resounding belch.

Abdullah came to the kitchen door just in time to hear it.

'Does your mother let you do that?' he said, with a mixture of envy and contempt. 'Mine's furious when I do.'

Rashid, feeling much better, slid off his chair.

'Come on,' said Abdullah.

He went across to a door at the far end of the room behind the fountain. Rashid, following him, stood on the threshold, gazing in wonder. There was a bed in one corner, and a child-sized desk in another, with a little chair drawn up to it. On the desk was something that looked like a TV screen. A young woman with a dark African face was folding clothes and putting them away in the big cupboard that ran along the whole of one side of the room.

'Go away, Meseret,' said Abdullah. 'We're going to play.'

The woman went out silently.

'She from Sudan?' asked Rashid, thinking of Salman.

'Who? Her? I don't know. Ethiopia, I think. Do you know computer games?'

Rashid, not understanding, said nothing. Abdullah sat down at the desk and began to move a lever sticking up out of a pad. Pictures and writing appeared on the screen. Fascinated, Rashid stood behind him, watching. There seemed to be a fight going on. Monsters with green faces were running about. Now there was a boy with a gun. Red streaks of light were shooting out of the gun. They exploded when they hit a monster.

'Pah! Gotcha! Ye-es!' Abdullah was calling out, his whole body moving with the lever.

Absorbed in the game, he had forgotten Rashid, who stood watching for a while, then lost interest. He stepped back, and looked around the room.

There were camels everywhere. Cartoony pictures of camels with big eyes and silly smiles hung on the wall. A stuffed camel lay on the neatly made bed on top of a pile of other fluffy animals and teddy bears. A string of wooden model camels, linked by a brass chain, marched along the window sill.

Then Rashid saw that Meseret, the maid, had left one of the cupboard doors half open. There were shelves inside, spilling over with toys. Holding his breath, he tiptoed across the room, eased the door fully open and stood gazing at the marvels within.

There was a toy helicopter taking up one whole shelf, with a pilot in its cockpit. On the shelf below were some plastic guns, a couple of tanks and a box full of soldiers. Below them were roller skates, balls of different sizes and a round globe, mostly coloured blue, but with odd shapes in other colours patterning it.

But straight ahead, on a level with Rashid's eyes, was a jumble of toy vehicles, too many for the space, crammed in on top of each other. He could see buses, trucks, an ambulance, a police car, SUVs like Syed Ali's, hatchbacks, limos, sports cars, saloon cars, white cars, black cars, green, blue and yellow cars. And a red car.

Rashid looked over his shoulder.

'Ee!' Abdullah was saying. 'Pow!'

Rashid dared to put out a finger and touch the red car. It was a little saloon with four doors and grey seats inside. The painted metal was silky smooth. He leaned in to look more closely. The car had proper rubber tyres, like real ones, and the inside was perfectly modelled, with even a miniature steering wheel. Very slowly, holding his breath, he let his hand close round it, then eased it out of the cupboard. He held it, exploring it reverently, touching every part. When one of the little doors swung open under his probing fingers, he gasped with delight.

He wanted to try out the wheels and squatted down on the floor, put the car down gingerly and pushed it across the shiny marble. It ran with perfect, satisfying ease.

It was the most beautiful thing he had ever seen.

There was a final burst of noise from the computer screen and a scraping sound as Abdullah pushed his chair back.

'What are you doing? That old thing? That's nothing. I'll show you.'

He began to pull the cars off the cupboard shelf. They rained down to the floor around Rashid.

'Where is it? Meseret never puts things away properly. Oh, it's here.'

He brought out a car that was four times the size of the red one. It was black and had yellow numbers painted on the doors. A long stick-like thing poked up from the roof. Abdullah put it down on the floor and scrabbled again in the cupboard, emerging at last with a small square plastic block.

'Watch this.'

Under Rashid's astonished eyes, the car began to move by itself, careering across the floor. It hit a leg of the bed and bounced backwards, landing on its roof.

'Turn it over,' ordered Abdullah, pressing the buttons on the block.

Rashid put the little red car down carefully on the rug beside the bed, then set the black car on its wheels again. At once, it took off. He began to chase it, running back and forth across the room while Abdullah made it hurtle away from him in all directions, shouting with laughter. Rashid began squealing with excitement too. The car seemed to be alive. However hard he tried, Abdullah always managed to get it away.

At last it came to rest, wedged between a plastic stool and the wall. Rashid dived for it, slipped, fell on to his stomach and slid the last few metres across the shiny floor.

'I can do that,' said Abdullah, throwing the console aside. He lay down on his stomach and propelled himself across he floor, flailing his arms like seal flippers. He stopped when he reached Rashid and clambered to his feet, red in the face from the effort.

'Watch this,' he panted. 'I can get all the way to the door in one go.'

He took a few running steps then pushed himself into a slide. His feet, clad in socks, moved effortlessly over the polished marble. Impressed, Rashid tried to copy him, but his feet were bare and they stuck to the floor.

Abdullah slid over to the cupboard, pulled open a drawer and grabbed a pair of socks.

'Put these on. I want to race.'

Rashid felt shy again. Abdullah's socks looked new. They were made of thick, expensive cotton and were perfectly white. Someone might be angry if he put them on. The Ethiopian maid might see, or Abdullah's mother, or Syed Ali himself. They might think he'd done something wrong.

'Hurry up!' Abdullah said crossly. 'Put them on!'

Rashid sat down and put the socks on. He'd never worn socks before. They felt comfortable but odd, enclosing his thin hard-soled, calloused little feet in a strange softness.

Abdullah yanked him to his feet.

'Beat you to the window.'

Rashid, who had raced four camels that day, and had no desire to race again, cast a longing look at the scatter of cars on the floor.

'Come on!' Abdullah was shouting. He was sliding off already.

Rashid bit his lip and copied him reluctantly,

taking a couple of running steps, then letting himself go in a slide. Surprised by the ease and speed of it, he nearly lost his balance, but regained it with a wild thrashing of his arms and ended up at the window just behind Abdullah.

'To the wall!' shouted Abdullah.

This time they started off together, and Rashid, lighter and infinitely more agile than the heavy, unfit Abdullah, reached the cupboard first. Abdullah scowled at him.

'You cheated. To the door!'

Rashid saw the scowl.

I didn't cheat. You're just lazy, he thought.

But sliding was fun. He wanted to do it again. Laughing out loud, he shot from one side of the room to the other, beating Abdullah every time.

'To the bed!' shrieked Abdullah at last. Desperate to win, he set off before Rashid had a chance to start. The mat by the bed caught his foot and made him stumble. He fell with a thud, and yelped with pain.

'I landed on something. It dug right into me. It hurt.' He reached underneath his thigh and brought out the little red car. 'It's your fault. What did you leave it there for?'

Pettishly, he threw it across the room. It hit the wall and crashed to the ground. Rashid ran anxiously to pick it up. The doors had flown open. He shut them carefully and then saw that a crack now ran across the tiny windscreen.

'Broke,' he said.

He turned away, afraid that Abdullah would see in his face the fury he felt for the spoiling of the little car.

Abdullah had recovered from his fall. He lumbered to his feet. The door opened and Syed Ali looked in.

'Abdullah, come and say goodnight to your mother. Meseret's coming to put you to bed. Yasser, go to the kitchen.'

The little girl's voice, whining with tiredness, echoed from some distant room. Abdullah followed his father out of the room leaving Rashid alone. He put the car down while he peeled off Abdullah's socks and placed them carefully on the bed, then he picked the car up again.

His heart thumped.

'You're mine,' he whispered to the car. 'They promised me a car. You're going to be mine.'

He slid it into his pocket.

In the kitchen, the cook was slumped in a chair by the table, yawning. He got to his feet and nodded to Rashid to follow him.

The servants' quarters behind the house consisted of a row of small rooms running along the back wall of the property, beyond a strip of concrete and network of washing lines. They had no windows. The door of one was open and through it Rashid saw the driver, dressed now in a white vest and long cloth tied round his waist. He was sitting on his bed reading his Koran.

The cook pushed open the door of the next room and switched on the light, a shadeless bulb hanging from the ceiling. A bed took up most of the space in the tiny room. A few clothes hung from nails on the walls. The only other items were a battered kitchen chair and a suitcase pushed under the bed.

The cook had placed a pillow and a folded blanket on the mat beside the bed.

'You sleep there, all right?' he said, with a gigantic yawn, climbing on to the bed.

Rashid nodded. He too was overwhelmed by utter exhaustion. He lay down on the mat and pulled the blanket up over himself. His hand closed round the bulge that the car made in his pocket, and he shut his eyes and slept.

18

Rashid started awake as the loudspeaker on the minaret nearby crackled into life and the muezzin began to chant the dawn call to prayer. He sat bolt upright in a fit of panic. Where was he? Had he overslept? Had the others already gone out on the night exercise? If he'd slept in and stayed behind, Haji Faroukh would lose his temper and send Salman for the plastic hose.

Then he heard a cough and looked up to see the cook swing his legs over the edge of the bed. Rashid jumped up, scooping his blanket and pillow into a bundle, and moved back out of his way. The toy car shifted in his pocket and his heart leaped guiltily at the thought of what he had done.

The cook, who had been so friendly the night before, was sleepy and grumpy now.

'Never enough time to sleep,' he was muttering. 'Keeping me up till all hours, then expecting breakfast on the table first thing.'

He stumbled off to the toilet.

The household slowly stirred to life. Rashid sat on the string bed outside the back door, swinging his legs, waiting to be told what to do, while the cook busied himself in the kitchen, the driver took a cloth to polish the car to a new brilliance and from the grand rooms within came the wails of the little girl, loud complaints from Abdullah and the irritated voice of Syed Ali.

Rashid went to peep in through the kitchen door. The cook saw him and beckoned him inside, setting some bread, yoghurt and an egg down in front of him. Rashid could only nibble at this unusually lavish breakfast. His stomach was still protesting from the feast of the night before.

The door burst open as he sipped the hot tea the cook had given him, and Meseret came in, biting her lip and scowling.

'What now?' the cook said sympathetically.

'That little monster. Moaned to Madam, didn't he, that I hadn't put his toys away properly. He's got it in for me.'

The sound of an argument came from the other side of the kitchen door.

'It's not *fair*, Aba!' came Abdullah's raised voice. '*Why* can't I go to school in our own car? I don't like going with Ibrahim. He teases me all the time. And his driver's lousy. He stinks.'

Syed Ali's voice was too low for Rashid to hear. He

217

caught sight of Meseret, who was pulling down the corners of her mouth, waggling her head and making a silly face.

'It's not fair!' she said in a squeaky voice, imitating Abdullah. 'I don't like going to school with another spoilt, fat, rich little brat. I want to be a spoilt, fat, rich little brat all by myself.'

Rashid giggled. The cook, snorting with laughter, gave her the plastic beaker full of warmed milk that she'd come in for, and she went out, letting the door slam behind her.

'She's a one,' the cook said. 'Here, little champion, you'd better go out and wait by the car. Syed Ali will be off in a minute and he doesn't like to be kept waiting.'

Rashid slid off his chair and went out through the back door, running down the passageway at the side of the house to where the car stood on the driveway at the front, conscious at every step of the stolen toy banging against his thigh. The driver acknowledged him with a silent nod, then went back to his endless polishing.

Rashid leaned against the wall and waited. From the road outside the big double metal gates came the sound of a car drawing up, and then the beep of a horn. The watchman opened it a crack, spoke to someone outside and looked back to the house. The horn beeped again. Abdullah came reluctantly down the steps. His heavy schoolbag, dragging from his hand, bumped against his round thigh. He caught sight of Rashid and scowled.

'Lucky you,' he said, 'not going to school.'

Rashid straightened up and smiled uneasily, but Abdullah had forgotten him already. He was walking out past the watchman, who was holding the metal gate open for him.

Ten minutes passed, then Syed Ali emerged from the house. The driver snapped smartly to attention and opened the front passenger seat door.

'Into the back with you, young man,' Syed Ali said to Rashid.

The car rolled out through the open gates and turned into the road.

'Well,' said Syed Ali, looking over his shoulder at Rashid. 'You've had a wonderful time, haven't you?'

His mobile rang. He put it to his ear.

'Yes? Ah, Gaman Khan. Thanks for calling me back.'

Rashid started at the name, and felt goose pimples rise along his arms. He shivered, in spite of the heat of the morning.

'That's right, I need a replacement,' Syed Ali was saying. 'A little one, to ride the smallest camels. Four or five years old.'

The voice crackled at the other end.

'I know there are difficulties.' Syed Ali's usually calm voice betrayed impatience. 'Look, it's urgent. The season's in full swing. Good. I'll wait to hear from you.'

He folded his phone away. Rashid, who had

listened with all his might, was trying to make sense of what he'd heard.

'I suppose you miss your family sometimes, Yasser?' Syed Ali said after a while.

'Yes, sir.' Rashid guessed at the desired answer.

'You should look on your work here as an opportunity.' Without grasping the meaning of Syed Ali's words, Rashid was astonished to detect in his voice an almost apologetic note, as if he was trying to justify himself. 'You're making good money, you know. It's all going back to your family. You're being paid every week here more than you could possibly earn in a month at home. You have sisters?'

Rashid didn't answer.

'Sisters, Yasser. You have a sister?'

'Yes. One sister.'

'And she has to have a dowry, of course. You'll be providing that for her. Brothers?'

'One, sir.'

'Younger or older than you?'

Rashid grasped the back of the driver's seat in front of him, trying to work out what the question meant.

'Your brother, what age is he?' Syed Ali asked patiently.

'He is little, sir. Four. Maybe five years old now.'

'Ah.' Syed Ali's voice warmed with interest. 'He is at home, with your mother and father?'

'He is here. In Dubai. At an uzba.'

'Really? Which one? Who owns it?'

'Bedu name, sir? I not know. But masoul, he very bad. Name is Mr Boota. He—'

Rashid stopped, afraid that he would make Syed Ali angry.

Syed Ali spoke to the driver, whose reply Rashid didn't hear. They talked on together. Rashid sat back and looked out of the window, trying to remember everything he could about Syed Ali's magnificent house. Surreptitiously, he slipped his hand into his pocket and touched the car. He was hearing again the splash of the fountain, tasting the meatballs he'd had for supper, and the drink full of bubbles, watching once more the fight of the monsters on the computer screen, and the car that ran by itself, reliving the sensation of the slippery marble floor as he slid across it in Abdullah's cotton socks. He'd tell Iqbal and Amal everything, and watch their eyes grow wide with satisfying envy. He might even let them hold the car and play with it. They'd love him for that.

They reached the uzba at last. Rashid tumbled out of the back seat and ran round to the shelter. No one was there.

Still out exercising, he thought, disappointed. He had thought they'd be home by now.

He walked back slowly to the entrance. Syed Ali was talking to Haji Faroukh, who was nodding, his expression hard to read.

From outside came the familiar grunting complaint of a camel, and in through the gap in the palm-frond fence strutted the string of Syed Ali's precious racers, with Salman, Iqbal and Amal riding three of them, leading the rest by the bridle. Rashid ran after them into the camel pen.

'I won the golden sword in Abu Dhabi,' he burst out before they'd even dismounted. 'Syed Ali took me to his house. I stayed there all night. It's so amazing, you wouldn't believe. Abdullah, he's Syed Ali's son. He's got this car that goes by itself. A toy one. He's stupid. We slid on the floors. He gave me this.'

He pulled the toy car from his pocket and held it up to show them. Iqbal took it and turned it over, examining it.

'It's broken,' he said carelessly, pointing to the windscreen, and handed it back.

Amal didn't even look at it.

'You didn't hear then, about Shari?'

'What about him? It doesn't matter about the broken bit. The wheels turn and everything. It's lovely, don't you think so, Iqbal?'

'Shari was at the race here yesterday,' Iqbal said. 'He was really sick. Then he fell off his camel and it trod on his arm. He's hurt bad.'

A cold hand clutched at Rashid's heart.

'What do you mean? Shari? He's not dead?'

'No, not dead.' Salman came up. 'But that masoul not take him the hospital. Should take him. He just put in car and drive back to uzba. Sorry to tell you,

Rashid. Your brother, he very sick. Iqbal see his face. No open his eyes at all.'

For the rest of the day, Rashid felt jangled and restless. His mind was still full of the glories of Syed Ali's house, but nobody wanted to hear about them. Iqbal and Amal wouldn't listen, and Salman said only, 'I know that place. I go there one time with Haji.'

The news about Shari took some time to sink in, but as the morning turned into afternoon, the image of Shari lying injured, sick, perhaps even dying, with no one near to help him, grew and grew inside his head like a big black cloud swelling before a storm.

Zero five zero seven seven . . . he began chanting to himself, as he helped the others lay out fodder for the camels on the feeding racks. Zero five zero seven seven . . .

He stopped, his mouth falling open as he realized what he was doing. He was reciting Uncle Bilal's phone number. Uncle Bilal. He had to tell his uncle what had happened. Uncle Bilal was a grown-up. He would know what to do.

One of the hired men, who was supervising the boys, saw that he had stopped working.

'Get on with it, you little slacker,' he called out.

Rashid saw Iqbal grin, and flushed. Iqbal was pleased he was being told off, he could tell. He began to work again, but his mind was racing. How could he call Uncle Bilal? Where would he find a phone?

There was only one on the uzba. It belonged to Haji Faroukh. It lived in his pocket and was never out of his sight.

The boys were released at last and drifted back to the shelter. Iqbal had laid his arm over Amal's shoulders, and they were walking ahead together, leaving Rashid to trail behind them. Once, he would have minded desperately, but he hardly noticed today. He walked with his eyes on the ground, his brow furrowed, his mind working round and round the problem of the phone.

When they reached the shelter, and had dropped down on the sand, Iqbal said nastily, 'What's got into you then? Think you're too good for us now, do you?'

Rashid, surprising himself as much as the other two, burst into violent sobs.

'Shari!' he managed to get out. 'What if he's dying? What if he's dead already? I've got to call my uncle. I want Uncle Bilal.'

Iqbal's manner changed. He leaned forward and gently shook Rashid's arm. Amal shuffled closer on the other side. They waited till Rashid's loud crying had begun to subside into hiccups.

'Haji's got a mobile,' Amal said at last.

'I know,' Rashid cried despairingly, 'but it's always in his pocket!'

'Not always,' said Iqbal. 'Not when he takes his bath. Not when he's asleep.'

Rashid's hiccups stopped at once. He stared at Iqbal, his cheeks growing pale with fright.

'I wouldn't dare,' he whispered. 'I couldn't.'

'Yes, you could.' Iqbal was nodding at him vigorously, a spark of mischief in his eyes. 'For Shari. You've got to. Soldiers do stuff like that all the time.'

For a long moment, the three boys sat staring at each other, then they scrambled to their feet all at the same time, went out of the shelter and stood looking out across the uzba.

It was early afternoon, the quietest and hottest part of the day. The two hired men had gone into the village. Salman's feet could be seen jutting out of the kitchen door, where he was sleeping on a mat.

Moving as one, the three tiptoed across the sand towards Haji Faroukh's little house, drawn by the regular rhythm of snores that emanated from it.

'He's asleep. You can get it now,' whispered Iqbal.

'No I can't. It'll still be in his pocket.'

'Bet it's not. Bet he's taken it out. Go and look.'

'I can't go in there!' Rashid's voice rose to a high-pitched squeak. 'What if he wakes up? He'll kill me!'

Iqbal gave him a shove.

'Go on. You've got to.'

Rashid crept across the hot sand towards the dark mouth of Haji Faroukh's open door. The snores were building to a crescendo. Rashid reached the doorway and peered inside, one trembling hand touching the door post.

Haji Faroukh was lying on his back on his string bed. His mouth was wide open and his large belly was rising and falling like huge bellows under his blue kameez. And there, on the ground beside the bed, its shiny grey metal reflecting the sunshine outside, was the mobile phone.

Rashid's heart bounded. He wanted to turn and run back to the safety of the shelter, but he could feel Iqbal's eyes on his back.

You've got to, Iqbal had said. *For Shari.*

Rashid shut his eyes, took a deep breath, opened them again, darted forward, grabbed the phone and ran outside. Just as he joined the others, Haji Faroukh's snores reached their peak with one last shuddering whistle. Then there was a long, terrifying silence.

'He's woken up. He'll see it's gone,' whispered Rashid.

'No he hasn't. Listen. He's starting again.'

Iqbal was already dashing back to the shelter.

Rashid and Amal followed. In the dim light of the room, their heads crowded together, the three boys stared down at the mobile in Rashid's hand.

'Go on then. Phone him,' urged Iqbal.

Rashid, concentrating furiously, pressed the precious numbers down one by one, then held the phone to his ear. He waited for a long time, expecting to hear Uncle Bilal's voice, but there was only silence. He had been so sure that the magic numbers would work, that they would summon his uncle at once, from wherever he might be, that he was crushed with disappointment.

'He didn't answer. He's not there,' he told the others, who were watching with eager expectation.

'Here, let me listen,' said Iqbal.

He bent his head sideways over the phone.

'There should be a light on in it,' Amal said. 'There is when Haji phones.'

Iqbal took the phone from his ear and they all examined it again.

'You have to press something to make it work,' Amal said.

'Press what?' Iqbal asked, glaring at him.

Amal took a step backwards.

'I don't know.'

Iqbal began to push all the buttons on the phone, one after another. Suddenly, it started to ring. He cried out and dropped it, shaking his hand, as if the phone had been red hot and had burned him.

Rashid's hair was standing on end.

'What do we do now?'

'Take it back, quick, before he wakes up,' Amal said.

Rashid picked up the phone and hared back to Haji Faroukh's house. The masoul was still asleep, his snores loud and regular once again, but the sound coming out of the phone, which had started out as a quiet tinkling, was growing louder and more shrill. It was impossible to believe that something so small could make such a terrible noise.

Panic seized Rashid. Blindly, he dashed through Haji Faroukh's open door. He didn't notice that the snores had stopped. He didn't see that the masoul had woken and was bending over to search for his phone on the ground. He was poised to throw it down and dash out again when Haji Faroukh looked up, and Rashid found himself staring straight into his face.

Rashid froze, the trilling phone still in his hand. With one glance, Haji Faroukh took in the appalling sight of the boy invading his sanctum, the phone in the boy's hand and the guilt on the boy's face. A roar gathering in his throat, he jumped to his feet, snatched the phone from Rashid's limp fingers with his right hand and grasped Rashid's arm in a vicious grip with his left.

He held the phone to his ear.

'*Han-ji?*' he barked. 'Oh, sir, it's you. Yes, sir. I'll expect his call. Thank you, sir.'

He thrust the phone into his pocket and Rashid saw with horror that the blind rage that the boys so dreaded had descended on him. There was a familiar redness round the masoul's eyes, and his full lips were drawn back into a snarl.

'Please, Haji, no, please,' stammered Rashid. 'Uncle Bilal. It was to call Uncle Bilal. I need him, Haji, for Shari.'

Haji Faroukh, still holding him, was groping under his bed for the length of plastic hose.

'Thief!' he was shouting. 'Imp of Satan! Thief!'

Drops of spittle flew from his mouth.

As he felt for the hose, his grip slackened and Rashid twisted his arm free. In an instant he was out of Haji Faroukh's house, haring away across the sand. He bolted round the corner towards the kitchen. Salman, who had woken up, was sitting, still bemused with sleep, scratching his head and yawning. Rashid ran into the kitchen and hid behind him.

'Salman, help me! Haji's angry. I took his phone. To call my uncle. To save Shari!'

'What?' Salman rose shakily to his feet. 'What you talking, Yasser? You take Haji phone? Are you crazy boy, or what?'

'For Shari! To call Uncle Bilal! So he can come and look after him!' Rashid explained desperately. 'Tell Haji, Salman, please!'

Haji Faroukh, the hose in his hand, had already stalked up to the kitchen door. Iqbal and Amal were shadowing him as closely as they dared.

'Haji, it was my fault,' Iqbal was saying bravely. 'I told him to, for his brother. Shari's injured, Haji.'

Haji Faroukh lifted the hose and swiped at him, and Rashid, peeping out from behind Salman, saw him fell Iqbal with a blow.

'Come out here, you!' roared the masoul. 'How dare you run away from me! Thief! I'll show you!'

'No! Please! No!' shrieked Rashid, but Salman had already been swept aside and Haji Faroukh's fingers had closed once more round Rashid's thin arm. He was dragging him out of the kitchen.

Rashid looked up at his face and saw that the masoul was deaf now and blind to everything but the rage that consumed him. He gave up trying to explain. He bent down, covering his head with his free arm to protect it from the beating to come.

But as Haji Faroukh raised the hose for the first vicious cut, his phone ran again. He hesitated, swore, flung Rashid away from him, wrenched the phone out of his pocket and answered it curtly.

His expression changed. He walked away from the boys, listening intently.

'Gaman Khan?' they heard him say. 'Yes, I'll expect you. Tomorrow. Yes.'

Blinded by panic, with the single idea in his head that he had to flee from the masoul's wrath, Rashid was out of the uzba entrance and racing along the outside of the palm-frond fence before he knew what he was doing.

He'll kill me! He'll kill me!

The words banged in his head like a drum beat.

He was up on the road and halfway to the cluster of buildings near the mosque before lack of breath made him slow down. He bent over, clutching at the stitch in his side.

I'll just go on running. I'll keep running on, he thought. I'll never go back.

He started walking again, his feet taking him automaticaly in the familiar direction of mosque. The shopkeeper was outside his door, fiddling with the awning that shaded his window. He nodded at Rashid, who slowed down, his resolve weakening at the sight of this familiar person.

'Hello, young man. Where are you off to? Your masoul sent you on an errand?'

Rashid stared at him, the enormity of what he had done dawning on him. How could he possibly run away? Where could he go? What would he eat? How could he hide from the grown-ups who would come after him?

'Here, are you all right? You're Haji Faroukh's boy, aren't you? You're the one who wins all the races.'

Rashid didn't take in the man's words but the kindness in his voice overwhelmed him. He felt sobs rise in his chest and knuckled tears out of his eyes.

'Done something you shouldn't?' the shopkeeper said shrewdly. 'Scared of a beating? You'll only make things worse, hanging about round here.'

'My brother,' Rashid managed to say. 'He sick. I want call—'

A woman's voice called out from inside the shop. The man lost interest in Rashid and shouted back at her. He turned to go back inside.

'Please!' Rashid gasped out. 'Please, my uncle, he—'

The door of the shop was swinging shut behind the man. Rashid darted after him.

'He going to die!' he yelled desperately.

'Who'll die?'

The shopkeeper's wife had come out.

'My brother. He too sick and fall off camel and masoul no get doctor, and my uncle, he got a phone, and I try call him but no good.'

He was gabbling too fast, and he saw she could only just follow his halting Arabic.

'Your brother is sick? You want to call your uncle?' she said, puzzled.

'Yes! Yes!'

She darted a look back into the shop.

'You know his number? Your uncle's number?'

'Yes!' He reeled the numbers off.

'Wait.' She took a pen from her pocket. 'Say it again.'

He repeated the numbers slowly, watching as she wrote them down on the back of her hand.

The sound of a car braking sent her darting back into the shop. Rashid swung round. His knees turned to water as he saw Haji Faroukh climb out of the car and rush at him. It was too late to run away.

Haji Faroukh took his arm in a painful grip, marched him back to the car and threw him into the back seat. A short ride later, they were back in the uzba, and Rashid tumbled out on to the sand.

'Don't – you – ever – ever – ever – go into my house again!' Haji Faroukh roared, taking hold of Rashid's shirt and shaking him like a wet cloth.

Rashid waited, his eyes screwed shut, for the blows to fall, but instead he was hurled aside. Looking up, he saw Haji Faroukh stalk off, and realized that the peak of his rage had already inexplicably passed.

19

Iqbal, his earlier jealousy and hostility forgotten, was silently sympathetic to Rashid for the rest of the day. He even relented over the little car, letting Rashid see how much he liked it and wanted to play with it. Amal was kind too, quietly helping Rashid to lift the heavy buckets as they watered the camels. Rashid barely noticed.

She won't call Uncle Bilal. I know she won't, he kept thinking. Anyway, did I say the numbers right?

When at last the work of the uzba was done, he lay down on the mattress beside the empty place where Puppo had always curled up, his mind filled with dread. What if Shari had died already, and been buried in a hole in the sand? He might even now be no more than a shadow, a wisp of memory like Mujib, existing only as a name, which would haunt other little boys from the shadows of his uzba.

He tossed and turned for a long time, while outside the heat of the desert day gave way to the cold of

234

night. He tried to sleep but his eyes wouldn't close. The three-quarter moon had risen and a ghostly beam shone in under the door. It seemed to call him, to draw him outside.

He reached for his sweater, got up and opened the door. Amal turned and muttered in his sleep, and then was quiet again.

Rashid had never been outside at night on his own before. He hadn't known how quiet and still it would be.

No one else is awake, he thought. And it's light enough. I could find my way to Shari, if I had to, and come back quickly, and no one would know.

He didn't have to make a decision. His feet began to move of their own accord. He was already beyond the camel pen and passing the kitchen. The moonlight glinted on a plastic bottle lying by the kitchen step. It was the kind that Salman took to the races, to give the boys drinks at the end of the day. Rashid picked it up. It was still full of water. He'd take it in case Shari needed a drink.

The water made him think of food. Meagre though the diet was at Syed Ali's uzba, the boys belonging to Shari's owner were notoriously starved. Rashid hesitated. There was no chance of taking anything from the kitchen. The door was shut and padlocked. But that day the camels had been given a special ration of dates and honey. The boys hadn't been allowed near it, of course, but Rashid had seen the buckets in which the mixture had been carried out by one of the hired men. They were lazy, sometimes, about fetching them all in. A bucket might still be out there, in the camel pen, with a little food left inside it.

He stole into the pen. The camels were kneeling, at rest. Their heads swivelled curiously towards him, their long-lashed eyes following his movements. But none of them made a noise.

A bucket *was* there, under the feeding rack. Rashid felt inside it. A little of the sticky mixture was still left at the bottom. He tasted it. Yes, it was honey and dates all right. Sweet and delicious. Shari would like it, he knew.

But first he had to find a way to carry it. The bucket was big and the handle clanked noisily. He needed something smaller.

A light breeze, riffling through the palm-frond fence of the camel pen, sent something else fluttering. Rashid grabbed at it. He knew without looking what it was. Old plastic bags often blew into the fence and got stuck there. This one would do perfectly.

He scooped the mess of dates and honey into the bag and licked his fingers, feeling proud of his cleverness. The next bit, though, was going to be harder.

With the bottle of water in one hand and the plastic bag in the other, he was starting back to the entrance of the pen when his foot caught the side of the bucket. It rolled away, the handle clattering loudly, and landed against Shahin's back leg. She gave a startled groan and began to rise to her feet. Rashid jumped with fright, then bolted. He was out of the pen, outside the uzba and racing off down the lane before he knew what he was doing.

It was a long time since he'd visited Shari's uzba with Uncle Bilal, but every Friday since then, on the way to the mosque, he'd looked down the path they'd taken that day and remembered the way to it. The path was straight, he was sure, with no turnings. He only had to run down it past all the nearest uzbas, then go on till he reached Shari's place, the most ramshackle and tumbledown, out on its own beyond the others.

He was running without thinking about it, his bare feet making no sound in the soft sand.

Why was the world so different at night? Why did the fences seem higher, the road longer, the shadows so deep and threatening? The wind whined through the metal struts of the water towers and strips of chain-link fencing. Something scuttled across the sandy track in front of him. A scorpion. He took a flying leap and was over it, running on.

In less than twenty minutes he was at the entrance to Shari's uzba. He skidded to a halt, panting for breath. He hadn't wanted to think about this part. To steal food from his own camels and come here through the night had been frightening, but it was nowhere near as hard as creeping into a strange uzba, which was ruled by a monster of cruelty, not knowing where, in the huddle of buildings ahead, his brother might be.

He watched and listened, gathering his courage. There was no sound except for the familiar snufflings and grunts of the camels resting in their pen. No lights shone from the huts. The humans must all be asleep.

Rashid took a deep breath and, grasping the bottle and plastic bag even more firmly, he darted towards the water tower in the centre of the uzba, which cast a dark shade. He could hide there and take a better look around.

He could see four or five buildings. One was obviously the owner's guest house, though it was nowhere near as smart as Syed Ali's. The one next to it must be the kitchen. Then there was a camel-food store.

He needed to get closer. Creeping out of the shadow, he found another patch of shade beside what looked like a toilet. Now he could see, behind the guest house, a low, shapeless tent. Its roof sagged and even in the dim moonlight he could see that drifts of sand had collected in the folds.

Shari had said something about a tent, the first time they'd met at a race. He was inside it, Rashid felt certain, sleeping in there. The other boy, Imran, would be in there too.

He crossed the open ground quickly and knelt beside the tent flap, listening. A snuffling, whimpering sound came from within, as if from a little animal in pain.

'Shari!' Rashid whispered. 'Are you there?'

He lifted the corner of the flap cautiously and peered into the pitch darkness. Raising the flap higher to let the moonlight shine in, he saw the shape of a little body lying flat under a thin blanket. A pair of eyes glinted in the darkness.

'Shari! Is that you?'

There was no answer, only a shuddering gasp.

'It's me, Shari. Rashid.'

He crawled right into the tent and peered around, trying to make out where Imran was, but saw with surprise that no one else was there. Shari was alone.

'Imran,' Shari mumbled. 'Want water. Get me water.'

'It's not Imran. It's me, Rashid.'

'Not Rashid. Imran, Yass—'

He began mumbling, sounding confused.

'Water,' he said more clearly. 'Imran, water.'

'Stop going on about Imran,' Rashid said impatiently. 'It's me.'

The blanket rustled as Shari moved his head.

'Is the goat there?' Shari's voice sounded weak, high and funny, and something bubbled in his throat as he talked.

'What goat?'

'It hits me with its horns.'

'Are you crazy? That was at home. We're not at home now.'

239

Shari said nothing. His breathing was fast and noisy.

'I didn't fall off because I was stupid,' he croaked after a pause. 'The boss said I was. But I wasn't, Rashid. My head was hurting and I couldn't see properly.' He paused to cough. 'I was tired all over. I could only see black. I woke up on the ground. My arm hurts. I can't move it.'

His voice was cracking with dryness and with every breath the air whistled in his chest.

'If you want water,' said Rashid, 'I've got some.'

'Good.' The voice was no more than a thread. 'You should have come before. I feel all hot and horrible inside. Why didn't you come before?'

'How could I? You know I can't just come like that. My masoul'll go mad if he finds I'm not there.' He unscrewed the cap from the bottle. 'Sit up.'

There was a feeble movement under the blanket.

'I can't. I told you. I can't move.'

'All right. I'll lift your head.'

He held Shari's head up and tilted the bottle awkwardly to Shari's lips. The little boy's skin was burning hot. He took a couple of mouthfuls, then his head fell back as if the effort tired him.

'Don't you want any more?'

For answer, Shari's shivering, claw-like hand fastened round Rashid's arm. Rashid held the bottle up again. Shari took another mouthful but the water went

240

down the wrong way. He spluttered, dribbles running down his chin, and cried out with pain.

'Shh! Your masoul might hear. Where's the other boy? Imran?'

'Boss takes him away at night. He has to sleep in boss's bed. Imran won't talk about it. He just cries.'

He had recovered from his choking fit and drew more strongly on the water.

'I got you something to eat too,' Rashid said proudly.

'I'm not hungry.' Shari had fallen back again.

'Yes you are. You only think you're not because you haven't eaten. I know that feeling. You'll like this stuff, Shari. It's dates and honey. What the camels get. It's lovely.'

He reached into the plastic bag, scooped up some of the sticky mess and put it to Shari's lips. Shari licked feebly at his fingers.

'There's lots more. I got it for you. Look, here's a whole date.'

He fed the date between Shari's parted lips, hugging himself with pride. He was being a hero, rescuing Shari. He could imagine what the food and water would be doing to him. He knew the feeling of strength flowing back into bones and muscles after a long time without food and water.

He'd expected Shari to feel better at once, to reach for the bag and greedily feed himself, but it wasn't working out right. Shari was actually spitting out the date.

'What are you doing that for?' Rashid hissed at him, annoyed. 'It's a date! It's lovely!'

Shari pushed his hand away.

'Want water.'

Desperate for the bottle, he managed to raise his head a little on his own. Disappointed, Rashid helped him drink.

'Your mouth's all sticky,' he said. 'I'll clean you up. You don't want them to know.'

He took the corner of the blanket, dribbled a little water on to it, and wiped Shari's face.

'I'm going to die, aren't I?' Shari said suddenly. 'Boss says I am. I heard him. He said he wouldn't bother with a doctor because I'm no good at riding camels. I'm not worth it.'

The long speech had tired him out and he gasped for breath.

Rashid said nothing.

'I'm cold,' Shari whispered at last. 'Why did you take the blanket off?'

'You're not cold. You're boiling hot.' Rashid could feel the heat radiating off him.

'Not hot! Freezing.'

'All right then.'

Rashid tucked the blanket round him, but Shari didn't stop shivering.

'Do you want me to warm you up?' Rashid said, puzzled.

'Yes.'

Rashid lay down on the mat and put his arm round Shari. Shari gasped with pain.

'Not like that. You hit my arm. It hurts. Everything hurts, all over.'

Rashid didn't know what to do. He took his arm away, but lay down close, touching Shari all down the side. Shari's dirty, uncombed hair tickled his chin.

'I don't think you're going to die,' he said. 'People don't usually. Not just like that.'

But he thought of Pio, and knew he was wrong.

'When you die, does it hurt?' Shari asked, his voice bubbling again.

'How should I know? I've never done it, have I?' Rashid felt so bad that by mistake he sounded angry. 'Anyway, I don't think so.'

'You go somewhere afterwards, don't you?'

'Yes, to Paradise. The imam said about it, at the mosque. It's nice there.'

'The mosque's nice, or Paradise?'

'Paradise, silly.'

'Nicer than Pakistan?'

'I thought you'd forgotten Pakistan.'

'Not the goat. And Imran hasn't forgotten. He tells me about it sometimes.'

Another cough was gathering in his chest. It came out in a weak burst, leaving Shari breathless.

'I told you, you're not going to die, so you don't have to think about Paradise,' Rashid said firmly. 'Anyway, you can't die because I've got something to show you. I'll bring it next time I come. I might even let you play with it. It's a toy car. A red one. It's lovely.'

'Mm.'

The sound was no more than a faint pulse from Shari's chest. It sounded as if his life was ebbing away. Rashid was seized with terror.

'Hey! Don't! Stop it!'

'Don't what?' Shari sounded reassuringly irritated. 'I was going to sleep.'

Rashid let out a long shaky breath.

'Go on then. Go to sleep. I've got to get back now.'

'Don't, Rashid. Stay with me. A bit longer, anyway. Please, Rashid, don't go. I can't be here by myself any more.'

The thin voice, so small and pleading and weak, made Rashid feel horribly frightened and helpless.

'All right, Shari. I'll stay.'

Only for a minute, he told himself. Just till I'm sure he's gone to sleep.

Shari turned his head towards him. Rashid pulled the blanket over both of them and, without meaning to, fell asleep himself.

Shari's next coughing fit woke Rashid a short time later. Alarmed, he started up, not knowing where he was, then as he remembered, he was seized with panic. How long had he been asleep? Would the others be out on the night exercise already? Would Haji Faroukh be raging up and down, brandishing the plastic hose?

'Shari!' he whispered. 'I've got to go. I'll come back again tonight. You'll be all right. Here, I'll leave the dates for you.'

He wasn't sure if Shari had heard. He was muttering something, his head rolling from side to side.

'You'll be all right,' Rashid whispered again uncertainly, and then he was wriggling out of the tent and streaking out of the uzba, racing back down the lanes, himself no more than a moving shadow in the paling light of the moon.

The uzba was still quiet, the kitchen door shut, the camels settled. The boys' shed, too, was as profoundly still as when he had left it a couple of hours ago.

He crept inside and lay down.

It seemed as if only five minutes had passed before Iqbal shook him awake. It was time already for the night exercise. Automatically, Rashid followed the others outside and, dazed with sleep, stumbled to the camel pen, saddled Duda and mounted.

All through the dreary hours of exercise, as the black sky turned first grey, then pink, then took on the hard, hot blue of day, Rashid fretted, shivering with fear as much as with cold.

I'm going to tell Haji Faroukh that I went to see Shari, he kept telling himself. Even if he gets into a rage and beats me, I'll do it. I'll ask him to get Shari out of there. Or at least let me go back and get him some more water. And I'll make him call a doctor.

Several times, as he swayed aloft on Duda's humped back, he broke into silent tears, letting them run down his cheeks and rubbing his wet nose on the sleeve of his sweater. Then, instead of being sad, he would start to feel angry; angry with Ma for selling him, and Pio for dying, and Uncle Bilal for not rescuing them, angry with Dubai, and camels, and masouls, and even with Shari for getting sick, and most of all with himself, for not being able to help him and make him better.

By the time the string of camels turned in at last through the uzba entrance, his face was streaked with tears and dust, but his mouth was set in a straight line of determination.

A strange car, a big white SUV, had just driven into the uzba and was pulling up in front of the guest house. Rashid's heart sank. If Syed Ali had visitors, Haji Faroukh would be much too busy to listen to him. The whole day might pass before he could catch him alone. He wanted to do it now. He couldn't bear to wait.

The other camels were already inside the pen.

From his vantage point high on Duda's back, Rashid could see over the fencing. Haji Faroukh was coming forward to talk to the two men who were getting out of the SUV. Rashid gasped as he recognized them. One of them was Bilal. The other was his old enemy, the man who had stolen him from home. Gaman Khan.

Rashid let out a shout, and was half sliding, half falling off Duda's back before she had even come to a halt.

'Hey! Yasser! You crazy?' Salman yelled at him. 'Come back here!'

But Rashid was running across the sand towards the knot of men, and didn't even hear him.

'Uncle Bilal!' he was shouting. 'Shari's ill! You've got to help him! His masoul says he's going to die!'

He reached the men and skidded to a halt, staring at his uncle. Bilal looked different. In the last months he seemed to have grown. Hard work on a building site had made his shoulders broader and put heavy muscles on his arms. He was no longer a slim youth with a light fuzz on his chin and upper lip. He had a man's strong black stubble, and he was standing up to Gaman Khan as if he didn't fear him at all. He was actually shouting, his face red with rage.

'What kind of a man are you? Shari's no more than a baby! After all you promised! You've seen what that masoul's done to him. It's disgusting! A disgrace!'

It worked! Rashid thought triumphantly. That woman must have phoned.

'Have you been to see Shari then, Uncle Bilal?' he asked. 'Are you going to look after him now?'

No one seemed to hear him. Gaman Khan, looking uneasily at Haji Faroukh, said something soothing and spread out his hands.

'Wait till they hear about this at home!' Bilal raged on. 'No one will ever do business with you again!'

Haji Faroukh was staring from him to Gaman Khan and back again.

'What is all this?' he said. 'Who is this? Gaman Sahib, is this man causing you trouble?'

'No, no!' Gaman Khan tried to put a comradely arm round Bilal's shoulders, but Bilal shook him off. 'This is my friend, Bilal. His nephew's here, in your uzba.'

Haji Faroukh's eyes narrowed as he recognized Bilal, then he smiled warily.

'I remember. Yasser's uncle. Your nephew's doing very well. No need to worry about him. He's just won the golden sword in Abu Dhabi. Earned some good tips too. Is that what you've come for? His money? I have it safe for him here. He's a good boy. No trouble.'

Bilal was shaking his head angrily.

'Not Yasser! Shari!' He stabbed an accusing finger at Gaman Khan. 'Starved, neglected – his fever's so high he's delirious!'

Rashid had crept up to stand beside Bilal, but a sound from inside the car caught his attention. The back window of the SUV was so high that he had to stand on tiptoe to see inside.

Shari lay on the back seat, his grubby blanket slipping off him. His eyes were half shut and his lips cracked with dryness. In the full light of day Rashid could see how desperately ill he was. He grabbed the door handle, wrenched it open and climbed inside.

'Shari! It's me!'

Shari seemed barely conscious. His breath was coming in short gasps.

Rashid backed out of the car.

'Uncle Bilal! He's going to die! Uncle Bilal!'

He was sobbing hysterically.

The adults broke off and crowded round to look in through the windows of the car.

'The ambulance is coming,' Gaman Khan said defensively. 'I called them half an hour ago. Look, Bilal, I'm doing what I can. Whatever you say, I'm not a monster. How was I to know what that man would do to him? Look at Yasser. He's flourishing, isn't he? I thought Shari would be fine too.'

The other boys, with Salman and the hired men, had now finished seeing to the camels and were crowding round the car. Gaman Khan was biting his lip and looking uneasily from side to side.

Rashid was back inside the car, kneeling down by the seat.

'Shari! Stop looking like that! Open your eyes!' he was crying.

He didn't hear the sound of another vehicle arrive, and was indignant when a pair of strong hands plucked him out of the car and his place was taken by two men in white jackets. But then he saw them lift Shari out of the SUV, and carry him tenderly across to the ambulance, and he watched, almost faint with relief, as one of them listened to Shari's chest through a stethoscope, and the other calmly set up a drip and worked over Shari's arm.

'Seriously dehydrated. Never seen anything like it. And, look, the little chap's arm's broken. A bad fracture too,' he heard one of the ambulance men say with disgust.

'Ready?' said the other. He turned to the watching crowd. 'Who's accompanying him?'

Rashid looked up beseechingly at Haji Faroukh, but Bilal was already saying, 'I am. I'm his uncle,' and was stepping into the ambulance.

'Is he going to die then, or not?' Rashid shouted, as the ambulance doors closed, but no one answered, and a moment later the big white vehicle had disappeared and the purr of its engine was fading away down the lane.

Gaman Khan had recovered his composure and was shaking his head sorrowfully.

'That Bilal!' he said, with a sidelong glance at Haji Faroukh. 'So ignorant. You do what you can for these people. I admit the child's masoul seems to have gone too far. A really cruel taskmaster. I won't supply him again. But if these kids had stayed in Pakistan, they'd have starved to death by now. I tell you, Haji—'

But Rashid could see that one of Haji Faroukh's rages was descending on him. Iqbal and Amal had already backed cautiously away. He retreated quietly too.

'I'm sick of it!' Haji Faroukh roared. 'I've had enough of all this! Children injured, children killed! You think it gives me pleasure to see them thrown off and trampled by stampeding camels? You think I enjoy seeing them stick thin and hungry all the time?'

'Come now, Haji,' Gaman Khan said calmly. 'You benefit from the system as much as any of us. I'm sure you've got a nice little pile of savings stashed away. It does most of the boys no lasting harm. We're doing them a favour – you know we are. They'll go home soon enough, when they get too big for all this, and their families will have prospered on their earnings. As for young Shari, he's a tough kid. The trouble I had with him, bringing him over here, you've no idea. Now he's getting proper treatment he'll be better in no time. But we have some business to do. Syed Ali tells me you need a replacement jockey. A young one.'

Haji Faroukh's anger had blown itself out already. He seemed to the eyes of the fascinated boys to deflate like a slowly puncturing tyre.

'A young one,' he said flatly. 'Yes, I suppose we do.

Come into the guest house, Gaman Sahib.' He raised his voice. 'Salman! Coffee! Hurry up! You boys –' he assumed for the children's benefit an expression of ferocity that sent them falling over each other as they retreated even further – 'eat your breakfast, then start cleaning this place up. It's a disgrace.'

20

It was Haji Faroukh who told Rashid that Shari was getting better.

'You've got Syed Ali to thank,' he said, nodding impressively. 'He's even paying the hospital bills.'

Rashid, light-headed with relief, hadn't known how to show his feelings. When Haji Faroukh had turned round, he scampered crazily about, then stood on his head, and fell over on his back, choked with laughter.

'Is he still in hospital, Haji?' he asked later, when he'd had time to think about it. 'When can I see him? When's he going back to his uzba?'

'He's not going back to that place at all.' Haji Faroukh scowled over Rashid's shoulder as if something in the distance was angering him, but he said no more, and Rashid didn't dare ask again.

Salman brought more momentous news. He had been serving coffee in the guest house to Syed Ali and Gaman Khan, who had returned for yet another visit.

'Your little brother,' he told Rashid. 'He coming here. New jockey for us. Take place of Puppo.'

Rashid gaped at him.

'Shari? Here?'

Salman nodded.

'I hear them talk. Your trafficker, he say no good any more bring new boys from Pakistan. Police careful. Too many arrest at the border. Question, question all the time.'

'But Shari can't work here, Salman. He's useless at riding camels. He'll only fall off again.'

'Need only training, I hear Abu Nazir say. Then maybe he turn out like you. Champion brother, after all.'

'But he's too sick! And his arm's broken!'

'Better soon, after a few week. Arm good again. He can ride little camel, new, young camel. Syed Ali, he buying new camel now.'

This news, once he'd digested it, made Rashid feel grown-up and important. He was not only the acknowledged star jockey of the uzba, the favourite of Syed Ali, the winner of the golden sword. Soon he would also be a big brother again, with a little ally and follower all of his own to protect and lead.

But he knew, in his heart of hearts, that it wasn't only someone to boss around that he wanted. He needed Shari's friendship too. It was always complicated now with Iqbal. The boy he'd so admired was often surly and sometimes, Rashid thought to himself daringly, mean and unfair. Once he'd acknowledged the weakness in his hero, he no longer yearned for his approval. When Iqbal said something ill-natured, Rashid could turn away with a shrug, instead of wanting to burst into tears. Sometimes he even answered with an insult of his own.

It was Amal, oddly, who kept the peace between them. Withdrawn though he was, he became so distressed when an argument broke out between the other two that they learned to back away from each other. In any case, they were too busy and too tired to spend their energy on real fights. In their precious hours of freedom they would lose their bad feelings in a bout of football, or make up long, complicated games involving the few remaining marbles and surviving playing cards, with the little toy car in pride of place.

It was three weeks before Shari came at last, brought in a taxi in the heat of the early afternoon by Bilal. He slid off the back seat on to the sand, looking around shyly, but when he saw the large, ponderous figure of Haji Faroukh approach, he gasped with fright and hid behind Bilal, clutching at his uncle's trousers.

Rashid, coming out as usual to see who had arrived, shouted 'Shari!' and dashed forward. Shari peeped out and saw him, and his face split open into a smile.

He was no longer the broken waif of a few weeks earlier. His trimmed hair was clean and glossy and his face, though still stark and thin, had filled out a little. In the place of his dirty rags he wore a blue top with a picture of Superman on the front, and some clean tracksuit trousers. The shadows under his eyes, though still large, were no longer the purple pools they had been. A plaster cast covered one arm from the fingers to the elbow.

'Hello, Rashid,' Shari said, but his smile had faded and his voice was only a whisper. His eyes were still fixed on Haji Faroukh, and when the masoul turned to look at him, he put up his hands to cover his head and cowered back behind Bilal, as if he was expecting a blow.

Haji Faroukh cleared his throat.

'There's no need for that, young man. You do what you're told and you won't suffer here. Rashid, take your brother and show him where he'll sleep. He doesn't need to help out today. Still very peaky, I must say. And there's not much he can do till that arm's out of plaster. Just make sure he stays out of mischief, that's all.'

Shari stuck closely to Rashid's side, hanging on to his sleeve. Rashid could feel him trembling.

'Is boss coming today, to take me back?' he asked.

Rashid stared down at him.

256

'Your old boss? Didn't they tell you? He's gone to prison, for being cruel to you.'

'Did Imran go too?'

'I don't know. No, I don't think so. He didn't do anything wrong, did he? I don't know about Imran.'

'No, but when am I going back?'

'You're not going back, Shari. Get that into your head. You're going to stay here with me. I thought Uncle Bilal would have told you.'

'I didn't believe him.'

'Don't you believe me?'

'No.'

Rashid stopped walking and bent down so that his face was on a level with Shari's.

'Look at me, Shari. I'm telling you. It's the truth. You're never going back there again. Forget about it. That masoul, your boss, he's gone. You're here now. Here! With me and Iqbal and Amal and Salman. Now do you believe me?'

Shari's huge eyes stared solemnly back at him.

'I'm telling you the truth!' Rashid said, exasperated. 'Listen, back then, in your tent, I said you weren't going to die, didn't I?'

Shari nodded.

'And you didn't die, did you?'

Shari shook his head.

'Well then. You can believe me.'

'You said you had a red car,' Shari said with sudden

shrewdness. 'You said you were going to let me play with it.'

The look in his eye, funny and knowing, was suddenly so like the old Shari that Rashid burst out laughing.

'You little –' he began, but Shari had seen Salman approaching. Instantly, fear turned him back into a petrified little animal again, and he darted behind Rashid.

'It's only Salman. He's our friend. You don't have to be scared of *him*,' Rashid said, and Shari, impressed by his lordly confidence, peeped out, daring to take another look, then hastily retreated, scared all over again at the sight of Salman's blind, milky eye.

For the first few days after he had arrived, Shari stuck to Rashid like a shadow. He watched Iqbal and Amal curiously, but shrank into himself if they spoke to him.

Iqbal treated him with the magnificent condescension that had so impressed Rashid when he had first arrived at the uzba. It had the same effect on Shari, and from the safety of Rashid's side, he gazed in awe and admiration at the older boy.

By the end of the week, he had grown used to the other children and even to Salman, but if Rashid was out of sight for more than a few minutes, his mouth would turn down at the corners and he would wait anxiously, staring around wide-eyed until Rashid returned.

Rashid had been afraid that Shari would embarrass him by putting on his old screaming tantrums, but he soon saw that there was no danger of it. Now, when Shari was upset, he cried silently, seeming to expect to be punished for it. He would crawl away and hide under the water tower, or creep inside the sleeping shed, even though it was stuffy and almost unbearably hot during the day. He would curl up there, furiously sucking his thumb.

The nights, though, were another matter. Shari would shout and cry in his sleep, thrashing about in the grip of nightmares. At first the others woke and were annoyed with him, but after a while they learned to sleep through the noise, tired out as they were. Several times, Shari wet himself in the night. Rashid scolded him for it.

'It wasn't me! I didn't! it was Amal!' Shari would say, panting with fright.

'Amal? Don't be daft. Look, you're all wet down the front,' Rashid would shout at him. But it was useless. Shari did it again and again. The shelter began to smell, and when Haji Faroukh passed by and caught a sniff of it, the mattress that Rashid and Shari had shared was taken out and a mat laid down, which could be taken up and washed.

Everyone was being kind to him. Not only was he allowed to stay in bed while the others went out on night exercise, he was even given extra food, although he had no appetite for it.

'Nice bit of chicken for you, Shari,' Salman would say, putting a whole drumstick into his bowl, and Rashid, looking up, would be amazed to see Haji Faroukh nod with grave approval as he stood and watched the boys from the entrance to the guest house. It was all the more infuriating to see Shari take no more than a couple of bites of the succulent flesh, and drop the still meaty bone back in his bowl, while the others looked on with frustrated envy.

Even Syed Ali seemed to take a special interest in Shari. He tried to coax him out from behind Rashid, and laughed when Shari wouldn't respond.

'I can't understand you, cousin,' Abu Nazir said to him one morning, as they walked across to the pen to inspect Soudani, whose left hind foot was worryingly swollen. 'You paid the kid's hospital bills and now you're letting Faroukh spoil him here. We're not running a children's charity, or hadn't you noticed?'

'Where's your heart, cousin?' Syed Ali said, shaking his head. 'The boy nearly died. Anyway, think about it. If he's anything like his brother, we'll have another champion jockey.'

'We won't have any jockeys at all if the new rules go through,' Abu Nazir responded.

It was a Friday, and Rashid was waiting nearby for the others to get ready for prayers at the mosque.

What are they talking about? he thought, puzzling over the men's conversation. No jockeys?

'All this talk of robot jockeys! They'll never work,' Abu Nazir continued bitterly. 'Without the boys, the sport will die.'

Robots again, Rashid thought, losing interest.

The others appeared, ready to set off. As they walked out through the entrance, Shari clung so closely to Rashid's side that he was in danger of tripping them both up.

'Knock it off, Shari,' Rashid grumbled at him. 'Walk on your own. What are you so scared of, anyway? We're only going to the mosque.' Shari didn't answer, and only increased his grip on Rashid's hand.

'He's worried about that boss of his,' Amal said, with one of his flashes of insight. 'Thinks he's going to meet him out here.'

'You don't have to worry about *him*, Shari,' Iqbal said grandly. 'There are five of us and only one of him.'

He puffed out his chest and tried to make himself look taller.

'That man in prison,' Salman said. 'Anyway, bad man like him never go to mosque. Never pray to God.'

They walked on in silence. Salman's words had made Rashid feel solemn. An odd sense of duty was weighing on him. He ought, he knew, to be teaching

Shari his religious duties, but he didn't know what to say.

'You have to be quiet in the mosque and sit still,' he began, remembering Puppo's restless wrigglings. 'And you have to copy what we do. Wash yourself, and kneel down and stand up like us.'

He knew that something important was missing, but didn't know what it was.

Salman helped him out.

'In the mosque good thing is to pray to God. You know what God do for you?'

Shari, looking worried, shook his head.

'Why you not die,' Salman asked earnestly, 'when you so ill with fever?'

'I was going to, but then Rashid came and told me I mustn't, and gave me water to drink,' Shari said, and Rashid's heart glowed with a rush of pride.

'No, is because your fate not to die. Is because God decide you better stay alive,' Salman said earnestly, kicking off his sandals and leading the way into the mosque, fortunately unaware that Shari's mouth had set in a mulish line and that he was silently shaking his head.

Rashid need not have told Shari to be quiet and still. It was his usual condition now. He seemed, fortunately, to have accepted that his masoul would not appear, and sat gazing around at the arched white walls, the smooth marble floor, and the pigeons circling in the open sky above, then over his shoulder at the rows of kneeling men. His mouth hung open, until Rashid, fearing that he looked silly, told him sharply to shut it.

At the end of the prayers, the masouls and farm workers usually dispersed rapidly back to their uzbas, their small jockeys in tow, but today they lingered, talking together in small groups. Salman hovered on the edge of one of these, and when at last he summoned the boys for the return walk to the uzba, he was holding a piece of paper in his hand.

'What's that?' asked Iqbal.

Salman stopped in the middle of the road, directly opposite the auto-repair shop, and frowned down at the leaflet.

'About camel jockey boy,' he said uncertainly. 'A date here. Thirty-first of May.'

Rashid's attention had wandered to the wheel-less truck propped up on bricks in the forecourt of the auto-repair shop. The man he'd often watched there before was lying on his back, easing himself beneath the truck, inspecting the underside of the chassis. Rashid itched to go in under there too, and have a good look at it.

Salman folded the leaflet and tucked it into his pocket.

'Not important,' he said, striding ahead.

It was clear to the boys though, when, later in the day, they watched Salman hand the leaflet to Haji

Faroukh, and saw the shock on his face, that the message it contained was indeed momentous.

'By the end of May! In three months' time!' they heard him say. 'Trials of robots to start and all of them out by then! So they really do mean it, after all.'

21

Shari mended slowly. He clung closely to Rashid at first, but as his confidence returned, he began to trot around after Iqbal, and Iqbal, pleased to be hero-worshipped once more, treated him with off-hand generosity.

Rashid watched, and was annoyed. Although he had shaken Shari off irritably, he was jealous when his brother's loyalty was so obviously transferred. He was too proud, though, to try and lure him back.

It was anger and hatred that had driven Rashid to ride Khamri to victory, but it was pride that drove him on in races now. The endless weeks of the racing season were studded with major events, and Syed Ali, delighted with his star jockey, was working him hard. There were other journeys to other cities of the Gulf. Rashid no longer travelled out to the race course in the truck with Salman and the camels. He rode with Syed Ali and Abu Nazir in the car. Once, Abdullah came too.

Rashid sat sullenly beside Abdullah on that long journey.

It wasn't really stealing, he told himself. He didn't want the car anyway. He broke it. He breaks everything. He's just stupid.

That day, he was riding Hamlul in the first race. No one expected Hamlul to win, but Rashid brought him in at a respectable fourth place out of the field of twenty-five. Shahin, though, was Syed Ali's great new hope, his star entry for the afternoon race, and Rashid was twitching with nerves in the holding pen as the moment approached.

'Win this for me and you'll get a double tip,' Syed Ali said, as Rashid mounted Shahin, and Salman rattled her chain to make her rise.

'Lose it, and you'll see what *I* give you,' growled Abu Nazir.

Abdullah said nothing, only craned his neck to look up at Rashid, perched high on the camel's back. Rashid saw, with a jolt of triumph, that there was admiration in his eyes. He tilted his helmet forward and flourished his whip with expert professionalism. Syed Ali reached up to give Rashid's knee a final encouraging pat, and Rashid grinned at the sight of Abdullah biting his lip with envy.

Abdullah's face was in his mind's eye as Shahin pranced to the starting line.

I'll show you. I'll show you, you stupid rich kid, he shouted in his head as he whipped Shahin with such

266

passionate energy that she came in first by a full length, winning yet another brand-new, sparkling white Land Cruiser for Syed Ali.

The very next morning, when the boys had just returned from the night exercise, Syed Ali's car arrived, swinging in through the uzba's entrance in a spatter of sand, and stopping with a jerk. Syed Ali, though dressed immaculately as usual, was looking almost rumpled, the ropes of his headdress awry. He hurried towards the guest house with Abu Nazir talking excitedly beside him.

'Faroukh!' Syed Ali shouted. 'Come here!'

Haji Faroukh had been forking fodder from the store into fresh containers, but he stopped at once and ran to the guest house, brushing hay off his hands, his sandals slapping on the sand.

'Bring coffee! Tea!' he called to Salman on the way past the kitchen.

Salman hastily dumped the boys' breakfasts into their bowls. As they ate, they could hear the sounds of a furious argument in the guest house. Shari, unnerved by the angry voices, shuffled closer to Rashid. Iqbal and Amal, who could understand Arabic better than Rashid, ignored the adult talk at first, but after a few moments their attention was caught. They exchanged looks and, having scraped up the last smear of the yoghurt they had been given, stood up and slipped quietly towards the guest house, listening hard. Rashid followed them, with Shari at his heels.

'What is it? What are they saying?' Rashid whispered to Iqbal.

'Shh! I can't hear if you talk. It's about us!'

Over the past months, without quite knowing how, Rashid's Arabic had become much better. Though he couldn't say much, he could understand most of what he heard. He needed all his new skill, though, to follow the argument that was raging in the guest house.

'Are you crazy?' Syed Ali was shouting with unusual vehemence. 'What do you mean, take them to the police station? We can't just dump them there! Have you forgotten that we acquired them illegally? What do you think I'm going to say if the police start asking questions?'

'They won't!' Abu Nazir answered. 'All the camel owners are in the same boat. They just want to get rid of the kids quietly without a scandal. The less fuss the better. Anyway, you don't need to show your face. Get Faroukh to take them and leave them there. Who's to know they were yours or how you got hold of them?'

'But what'll happen to the boys then, sir?' Haji Faroukh put in.

'They'll be fine,' Abu Nazir said impatiently. 'All of a sudden everyone seems to think they're little princes. Special hostels set up, a package of compen- sation – they're even being given bicycles, I'm told.'

The four listeners outside drew in a collective breath of excitement.

'I don't like it,' Syed Ali was saying. 'We can't treat them like discarded rubbish. Especially Yasser. He's done so well for us. Besides, Abdullah's fond of him.'

Abu Nazir tutted with exasperation.

'What do you propose then? You'll hire a private jet and fly him back to Pakistan like a film star?'

'Fly him home . . .'

Though Rashid, listening avidly, couldn't see Syed Ali's face, he could hear the thoughtfulness in his voice. He gripped Amal's shoulder, holding it so tight that Amal frowned and shook him off.

'Don't be ridiculous, Ali!' It was Abu Nazir again. 'How can you fly a boy home alone? How old is Yasser? Seven? Eight? If you wanted to arouse suspicion, I couldn't think of a better way of going about it.'

'Not alone, but with Gaman Khan. He brought the children here. Let him take them back.'

Haji Faroukh coughed.

'Gaman Khan has been arrested. They rounded up a whole group of traffickers at the airport in Lahore last week.'

'The uncle then! What's his name?'

'Bilal,' answered Haji Faroukh.

'Bilal! We'll get this Bilal to come and take them back. All four boys can go back with him together. The cost will be negligible. A few flights to Karachi, or wherever, and we're off the hook. Problem solved. Call him today, Faroukh. We must get on with it at once.'

'Excuse me, sir,' Haji Faroukh said, 'but the uncle will only be able to take Yasser and Shari. The authorities are very tight, now, on proving family relationships. He'd never get through with the other two.'

Silence fell inside the guest house. Outside, Shari, made nervous by the loud voices and the air of tension, was holding on tight to Rashid again. Rashid, not daring to believe what he'd heard, was clasping him round the shoulders. They had drawn apart from Iqbal and Amal, who were inching forward, listening with shocked intensity.

'Iqbal, now, what are we to do with him?' Syed Ali was saying. 'He's been with us so long I can't remember how we got hold of him. It wasn't through Gaman Khan, was it, Faroukh?'

'No, sir. The man who brought Iqbal was caught last year smuggling children through Iran, along with Iqbal's father, who was trafficking children too. The boy's real name is Javid, I think. Anyway, the whole gang's in prison now.'

Iqbal flinched, as if he'd been slapped. Amal and Rashid turned shocked faces towards him.

'Iqbal's father was trafficking? I didn't know. Are we in touch with the mother?' Syed Ali was saying.

'Only when we send on the money we're paying for

270

him. She's spending it all on lawyers to try and get her husband freed. She never enquires about Iqbal. She doesn't seem particularly concerned.'

A strange little noise came from Iqbal's throat. He thumped a furious fist against the wall of the guest house and dashed off, disappearing round the corner towards the shelter.

Haji Faroukh appeared at the guest-house door. The three other boys didn't wait to see if the redness of rage was in his eyes. They had already bolted.

Iqbal was standing waiting for them at the shelter. His arms were crossed over his chest and his head was thrown back defiantly.

'It's not true, any of it,' he said. 'My – my father's never trafficked anyone. Someone else was doing it and they blamed him. Anyone who says different, I'll punch them.'

Rashid nodded, but he had barely taken in what Iqbal was saying.

'Did I hear right?' he asked. 'Are they going to get Uncle Bilal to take me and Shari home?'

Iqbal stared angrily back at him.

'Yes! Little prince, that's what you are. They said so. Nice Uncle Bilal's going to come with a private jet and take you home to Pakistan. And what about me and Amal?'

Amal had retreated to the far corner of the shelter. He was standing with his face to the frond wall, stripping out the brittle brown leaves.

271

'Where's your family then, Amal?' Rashid asked. Questions seemed to be all right now. Things were coming out at last.

Amal said nothing, but went on pulling at the wall, leaf by dry leaf.

'He doesn't know,' Iqbal said. 'You were stolen, Amal, weren't you? You told me once. In Karachi.'

'I was with a lady,' Amal mumbled so quietly that the others had to lean forward to hear. 'I think she was my ma. We were in the street. There were lots of people. I couldn't see her. I started crying. Then a man picked me up and took me away. And there was a long journey. And I came here. I don't know any more.'

'They can't send you back then, can they?' Iqbal said practically. 'They wouldn't know who to send you to.'

Amal turned round. His face was pale and he was blinking rapidly.

'Why don't you ever leave me alone, Iqbal? Just shut up, and leave me alone!'

He went outside.

'Are you really paying for your father's lawyers, Iqbal?' Rashid said after a silence.

Iqbal looked at him suspiciously, but seeing only respect in Rashid's face, the hardness went from his eyes and he swung his arms, recovering a little of his usual swagger.

'Yes, I am. And it's not true that my ma doesn't care

about me. She's too busy, that's all. She can't write, anyway. And I haven't seen any letters from your ma, either.'

Rashid was shaking his head in wonder.

'I can't believe it! We're going home! Don't you understand, Shari? We're going back to Pakistan!'

Shari butted against him with his head.

'I don't want to go anywhere else. Boss might find me if I leave here. They might take me away from you again.'

Rashid rolled his eyes.

'Leave off about your stupid boss. I keep telling you. He's in prison.' He shot an apologetic look at Iqbal as he said the word, and turned back to Shari. 'Can't you get it into your head? We're going home!'

As usual, the boys woke automatically some time before four in the morning and stumbled out shivering into the black night. Silent, yawning and rubbing their eyes, they stumbled to the camel pen, ready for the long misery of the night exercise.

The camels were kneeling quietly, but began their usual grunting and moaning as they sensed the little jockeys' presence.

'Where's Salman?' croaked Rashid.

No one answered.

Iqbal led the way to the store and they began to load up with saddle cloths and muzzles. A beam of light cut across the sand as Haji Faroukh's door creaked open.

'You're not going out tonight,' he called across to them. 'Go back to bed.'

The boys blinked at him, bemused, as the masoul's door shut and his light was extinguished. Then Iqbal let out a whoop, and Rashid danced a little jig, and they ran back to the shed, where Shari was still fast asleep, rolled in his blanket like a caterpillar in a cocoon.

Rashid lay down beside him, but he couldn't go back to sleep. Wide awake, he stared up into the darkness.

Home, he thought.

When he'd first come to Dubai, a year ago, he'd missed home all the time. Now, only a few pictures remained: the little house with its dun-coloured walls, the neem tree with its long pointed leaves, a black bird that flew about and cawed. And hadn't there been a string bed outside in the courtyard? And a goat, the one that Shari went on about all the time?

I'm going home, he whispered experimentally.

But the words meant nothing. The pictures, too, were unreal. They floated like dreams, bright as bubbles, exploding at a touch.

He tried to remember his mother, but her face refused to appear.

What if she doesn't remember me, either? he thought. What if she doesn't want me and Shari any more? She sold us before. Perhaps she'll sell us again. Or perhaps she's dead, like Pio, and we don't belong to anyone. Or she might have gone to the brick factories, and we'll have to go there too.

He tried to imagine a woman coming towards him, her long scarf streaming out behind her as she ran, her arms open to embrace him.

'Yasser!' she'd cry. 'My little Yasser!'

No, that was wrong. He was Rashid. His name was Rashid. That's what she'd call him. Rashid.

Iqbal was awake. Rashid could hear his breath rasping unevenly.

'I'm scared, Iqbal. Are you?' he asked.

There was silence.

He's asleep, thought Rashid. He didn't hear me.

Then Iqbal whispered, 'Yes.'

Rashid's heart thumped. Iqbal had never confessed to fear before. If Iqbal was afraid, who would give him courage?

'I can't remember my ma,' he said.

'I can't remember mine.'

Shari moaned and stirred in his sleep.

'Are there camels in Pakistan?' Iqbal asked. 'You were there last. You ought to know.'

Rashid hesitated. He thought he had once seen a great beast harnessed to a cart, padding superciliously along the edge of a road. 'Yes, but only to pull things. I don't think they ride them there.'

'Good.' Iqbal's voice was savage. 'I don't want to ride a camel again, ever, ever, ever.'

Rashid said nothing. He was surprised by a pang of regret. Would he feel happy if he never rode a camel again? Would he miss the rocking rhythm of the hump underneath him, the thrill of the race surging through him, the wild excitement, the joy of winning, the envious eyes of the other jockeys?

'Abu Nazir said we'd get bicycles,' he said at last.

'I don't believe it.' Amal's voice came out of the dark. 'They never tell us the truth.'

An awful sorrow welled up in Rashid's heart.

'We won't be together any more! You're my brothers! What'll I do when you're not there?'

'You've got Shari.' Amal's voice was bitter. 'And you're going home.'

'Come too! Come with us!' Rashid rolled on to his stomach and propped himself up on his elbows. 'My ma wouldn't mind. You could live with us.'

'She would mind. She's not my ma. There's no one who'll want me.'

The faint greyness of dawn was seeping into the shed through the crack beneath the door. Salman was getting up. Faintly, from the village, came the chant of the muezzin, calling the faithful to prayer. The uzba day was beginning, with its duties, its meagre food, the unpredictable moods of its masters, and the relentless grind of work. It would be hot and hard as

276

usual. But it would be familiar. And there would be football when the sun began to sink.

The world beyond the palm-frond fences loomed terrifyingly.

'I want to stay here, with you!' cried Rashid.

But he knew even as he spoke that he didn't mean it.

Unsure what to do on this strange day, the boys congregated by the kitchen door, where Salman doled out to them an unusually generous breakfast.

'You want more, Iqbal?' he said, holding out another flap of bread. 'Maybe last time breakfast in uzba. You going today, maybe.'

No one was surprised when Iqbal turned the offer down. None of them wanted to eat much. Their stomachs were churning with excitement and dread.

'What are you going to do, Salman?' asked Rashid. 'Are you going home to Sudan?'

Salman shrugged.

'I tell you before, no home. I stay in Dubai. Be a big masoul, like Haji.'

He had been squatting beside them, but now he stood up and Rashid noticed for the first time that he had grown, and that a little black down was clinging to his upper lip.

'I like you, Salman,' he said, a rush of tears pricking his eyelids.

He jumped to his feet. Automatically, Shari stood up too. Rashid pushed him away.

'Leave me alone!'

He ran off blindly, and found himself in the camel pen.

The camels were standing at the food racks, lipping over the piles of green stuff. Rashid breathed in their pungent, earthy smell. Why hadn't he noticed it properly before? Shahin was the nearest to him. Her huge, heavy-lashed eye caught sight of him and she turned her head to stare, a green shred dangling from her mouth. She began to shake her head irritably, lifting her long upper lip. Rashid stepped back. She looked as if she might lunge at him with her powerful yellow teeth. Next to her, Hamlul was restless too, shifting his weight from one horned back foot to the other. A kick from Hamlul would be no joke.

He might never have to ride them again. He might never mount them in the dead of night, and sit hunched on their backs, cold and tired, through the miserable hours of exercise. He might never again have to carry their piles of food and buckets of water. He might never stand waiting in a holding pen before the start of a race, parched with thirst, his stomach clenched with fright, or endure the terror of the race's start, or the wild thrill of the dash to the finishing line. He wouldn't have to fear the camels any more. He wouldn't have to master them.

'I hate you, anyway!' he shouted, and ran out of the pen.

He hadn't heard a car arrive. It was Abu Nazir's, and he was standing beside it, tapping one hand on the white roof impatiently.

'Hurry up!' he was shouting. 'I haven't got all day!'

Iqbal and Amal emerged from the sleeping shed. Each carried a little bag. Salman, watching from the kitchen door, was working a tea towel over and over in his hands. Haji Faroukh took the boys' free hands in his, and walked them down to the car, one on each side of him.

'No!' Rashid shouted. 'Don't go! Not yet!'

But Iqbal and Amal were already being chivvied into the back of the car. The doors slammed shut. Through the glass, Rashid saw Amal's face, pale and set, his head rocking back and forth. Iqbal's face had crumpled and his mouth was open in a round O of anguish. He put both hands against the glass of the window, and Rashid heard him howl.

He was no longer the dauntless hero, the brave one, the leader. He was sobbing out his pain and fright, like the little boy he was.

'Iqbal! Where are you going? Where will I find you again? Amal!' yelled Rashid.

But the car was moving already, bouncing across the rutted sand, gaining speed as it disappeared out through the palm-frond fence.

'You'll meet up with them again in Pakistan,' Haji

Faroukh said with gruff sympathy. But Rashid knew he was lying.

He stood weeping uncontrollably on the very spot where Iqbal had come to him and comforted him on his first day in Dubai.

Bilal came as Rashid's storm of tears subsided. He arrived in a taxi, stepping out of it with a flourish. Haji Faroukh greeted him with a warmth that he'd never shown to him before, and even invited him into the guest house.

'I can't stop,' Bilal said regretfully, conscious of the honour. 'I have to get the boys to the airport.'

'The airport?' gasped Rashid, shocked out of his despair. 'We're going now?'

'Yes. Where are your things?' Bilal was grandly jingling some money in his pocket. 'Where's Shari?'

Rashid looked around, realizing with surprise that he hadn't seen Shari for a while.

'Find him quickly,' Bilal said. 'We've got to get going.'

Shari was hiding in the sleeping shed.

'Go away!' he shouted at Rashid. 'I'm not going anywhere! You can't make me!'

'Shari, you little fool, it's Uncle Bilal. He's going to take us home. To Pakistan. To Ma.'

He found it hard to believe his own words.

'The goat will be there,' he added cunningly.

'Is Iqbal coming? Where did they take him?' said Shari.

'I don't know. Come on. Where are the clothes Haji gave you?'

A few minutes later they had bundled everything into a bulging plastic bag.

The little red car had been lying under Rashid's sweater. Rashid picked it up, and was about to put it into his pocket when something turned inside him.

'Go to Uncle Bilal,' he told Shari. 'I'm coming.'

He darted out of the shelter and ran to the open space at the back of the uzba where he had played football so often with the others.

He hesitated for a moment, then lifted his arm and hurled the car away from him. It sailed up and over the palm-frond fence, and disappeared.

He watched it go, imagining it landing on the ground out there, lying motionless, to be buried soon in drifting sand.

'Good,' he said out loud. 'Good.'

He had been holding the car so tightly that it had left marks on his hand.

He ran back to the shelter, picked up the bag of clothes and walked slowly to where Uncle Bilal was still talking with Haji Faroukh.

'I'm telling you,' he heard Bilal say indignantly as he approached, 'Gaman Khan is the biggest crook in the business. He's stolen half the boys' money. My sister got much less for them than she should have done. She's managed though. She's opened a little shop. That man cheated me too. At least I'm free of him now he's locked up. What I earn, I'll keep.'

Haji Faroukh was no longer listening. He astonished Rashid by kneeling down on the sand, lowering himself with the awkwardness of a heavy man. Putting an arm round Rashid and Shari he pulled them into an embrace.

'Don't think too badly of me,' he said gruffly. 'It was your fate to be born poor and to work here to help your mother. God go with you, and give you both a long life.'

He rose with difficulty to his feet.

'I'll miss them, God help me,' he said to Bilal. 'They're good boys. I don't know how we'll go on now. There are such changes round here. Robots and all – I don't know.'

He saw Salman come, and called out, 'Have you got it, Salman?'

'Yes, Haji.'

Salman came up and handed him an envelope. Haji Faroukh put it into Rashid's hands.

'Here are the tips you earned for the races you won. I've kept them for you. You'll thank me now for not letting you fritter it all away on marbles and the like.'

The taxi driver tooted his horn.

'Where did they take Iqbal? And Amal? Will they

be all right?' Rashid asked breathlessly, as Bilal pulled him away.

But Haji Faroukh didn't seem to hear. He had bent down and picked up Shari, and he was carrying him to the taxi.

'Goodbye, Yasser,' said Salman, and Rashid, turning to him, saw that his good eye was wet with tears. Rashid flung his arms round Salman's waist and clung to him, but Bilal tugged him away.

There were no long bus rides on the journey home, no nights in filthy rooms, no tense and angry adults. There was only the brilliance of the airport at Dubai, and a plane so flooded with light that it seemed to Rashid as if it must be flying straight into the sun. And when it landed, there was the traffic, and noise, and hubbub of Pakistan, with everyone speaking Punjabi, and over it all the smell of spicy food.

They came to the village in the same way that they'd left it, in a rickshaw, whose little engine stuttered with a loud tic-tic as it bumped down pot-holed roads.

Familiar landmarks began to appear: the quiet courtyard of the mosque, glimpsed through open gates; the little shop on the corner with the same old pile of bricks tumbled outside it. Rashid's hands, clasped tightly together, were sticky with nervous sweat.

Now they were turning down the lane, and the

rickshaw was stopping outside the rough boards of the old door, and the door was opening, and a woman was rushing out of it, her arms wide, wide open.

'Rashid!' she was calling out. 'Shari!'

He knew her voice. He remembered it at once, and the sight and smell and feel of her. He tumbled off the rickshaw into her arms, and knew he had come home.

CRUSADE

By ELIZABETH LAIRD

When Adam's mother dies unconfessed, he pledges to save her soul with dust from the Holy Land. Employed as a dog-boy for the local knight, Adam grabs the chance to join the Crusade to reclaim Jerusalem. Soon determination to strike down the wicked enemy burns within him.

Salim is leading an uneventful life in the port of Acre until news arrives of an imminent Crusader attack. To keep Salim safe, his father buys him an apprenticeship with an esteemed doctor. But Salim's employment leads him to the heart of the mighty Sultan Saladin's camp – and into battle against the barbaric invaders . . .

TWO BOYS FROM DIFFERENT WORLDS COME FACE TO FACE ON THE ADVENTURE OF THEIR LIVES.

'An expertly researched, vividly told tale . . .'
Publishing News

'A fast-paced adventure story' *Scotland on Sunday*

Elizabeth Laird

John was half crazed with panic and grief.
The rocking sea beneath him and the vast bulk of
the ship louring over him seemed to have surged out
of a nightmare. He knew though that they were real.
He knew they had claimed him in one terrifying snatch,
and that everything familiar, everything he knew,
had been torn away from him.

Falsely accused of murder, twelve-year-old John Barr and his
father run for their lives through the dark and winding streets
of Edinburgh. At the harbour they are forced to join the navy
and posted on different warships.

On board the mighty HMS *Fearless*, a chance discovery
thrusts John into a shadowy world of secrets and spies. His
adventure has only just begun . . .

'Exciting action, alarming plot twists
and breathtaking near escapes' – *Books for Keeps*

ELIZABETH LAIRD

A LITTLE PIECE OF GROUND

Outside the home of the Aboudi family in the Palestinian city of Ramallah, an Israeli tank blocks the street. Armed troops have kept the inhabitants trapped indoors for two weeks: twelve-year-old Karim, unable to play football with his friends or escape from his unbearable teenage brother, is going crazy.

When the curfew ends, Karim and his mates make an exciting find – a piece of waste ground that's great for a new football pitch. It even has its own special hideout. But their secret den becomes a terrifying death trap when the soldiers return . . .

An exciting story about the experiences of an ordinary boy living through one of the most difficult and tragic conflicts of our time

RED SKY
IN MORNING
THE

By ELIZABETH LAIRD

Highly commended for the Carnegie Medal

A novel of exceptional emotional power

Anna's life is turned upside down when her brother is born. The doctor says Ben is profoundly disabled and will never live a normal life. But Anna loves him with all her heart. To her, Ben is perfect. So why can't she find the words to tell her friends that he's different?

'A wonderfully moving story' *TES*

A selected list of titles available from
Macmillan Children's Books

The prices shown below are correct at the time of going to press. However, Macmillan Publishers reserves the right to show new retail prices on covers, which may differ from those previously advertised.

Elizabeth Laird

A Little Piece of Ground	978-0-330-43743-1	£5.99
Jake's Tower	978-0-330-39803-9	£4.99
Kiss the Dust	978-0-230-01431-2	£5.99
Paradise End	978-0-330-39999-9	£4.99
The Garbage King	978-0-330-14502-6	£5.99
Secrets of the Fearless	978-0-330-43466-9	£5.99
Red Sky in the Morning	978-0-330-44290-9	£4.99
Oranges in No Man's Land	978-0-330-44558-0	£4.99
Crusade	978-0-330-45699-9	£5.99

All Pan Macmillan titles can be ordered from our website, www.panmacmillan.com, or from your local bookshop and are also available by post from:

Bookpost, PO Box 29, Douglas, Isle of Man IM99 1BQ
Credit cards accepted. For details:
Telephone: 01624 677237
Fax: 01624 670923
Email: bookshop@enterprise.net
www.bookpost.co.uk

Free postage and packing in the United Kingdom